The Firebird Inheritance

Steven Turner-Bone

Published by Turner-Bone Editions.
© Copyright Steven Charles Southcoat
All rights reserved

No part of this book may be reproduced in any form or by any electronic or mechanical means including information storage and retrieval systems, without permission in writing from the author. The only exception is by a reviewer, who may quote short extracts in a review.

This book is a work of fiction. Names, characters, places, and incidents either are products of the author's imagination or are used fictitiously. Any resemblance to actual persons, living or dead, events or locales is entirely coincidental.

Also by Steven Turner-Bone

Friends and Enemies

The Enemy Within

Farewell to a friend

In need of a Friend

The Firebird Inheritance

Also

Under the name S C Southcoat

Invitation to a Murder

The Five-Pound Murders

ISBN: 9780993548789

Printed by Book Printing UK
Remus House, Coltsfoot Drive, Peterborough, PE2 9BF

Acknowledgements

To people I owe much and without whom, I could not have written this book.

My wife Sue: for her help, understanding and patience, and putting up with me while creating this work.

And

Not least, Albert Henry Stopford, 1860 – 1939, the story of whom gave me the inspiration to write this book.

Also

Many thanks to Heather and John Keenan, owners of the Kirkton Inn and Hotel, for allowing me to use their hotel name in the plot of my story.

Dedicated to my Granddaughter
Alexandra Southcoat

Author's Note

Many people know that Tsar Nicholas II and his immediate family were brutally killed at Ekateringburg on the 17th July 1918. However, fewer people realise that the Tsar had two sisters and three brothers. The Tsar's mother and sisters escaped to the west along with other nobles of the Russian court. Today, it is one of the descendents of the Tsar's sisters who is the legitimate heir to the Russian Empire.

This book tells the story of one such person. Names, dates and places have been changed to protect the innocent. The question must be, is this story wholly made up or could it be true?

Alexander	George	Xenia	**Tsar Nicholas II**	Olga	Michael
1869-1870	1870-1899	1875-1960	1868-1918	1882-1960	1878-1918

Chapter One	1
Chapter Two	23
Chapter Three	41
Chapter Four	57
Chapter Five	76
Chapter Six	95
Chapter Seven	116
Chapter Eight	136
Chapter Nine	150
Chapter Ten	169
Chapter Eleven	189
Chapter Twelve	210
Chapter Thirteen	229
Chapter Fourteen	248
Chapter Fifteen	268
Chapter Sixteen	289
Chapter Seventeen	306
Chapter Eighteen	323
Chapter Nineteen	330

Chapter One

'Jason! Jason, wake up.' Celia shook her husband out of his nightmare. He awoke, shivering and covered in sweat, his hands entangled in the sheets. He stared at her face in horror until the image of a German fighter plane diving at him out of the sun faded away. Slowly at first, his breathing eased as he refocused on the woman he loved and the familiar surroundings of their bedroom. Celia held out a glass of water to him as Jason spun his legs around and off the bed. Sitting on the edge of the bed, he rested his head in his hands.

'Was it the same dream as before?' asked Celia.

Jason gulped down the water. 'More or less.' He stripped off his wet night clothes and took a shower before putting on dry pyjamas. Celia, in the meantime, stripped the bed and replaced the damp sheets.

'Feeling better?' she asked.

'Yes, thank you.'

As always, after his nightmare, he went over to a picture hanging on the wall and stared at it for a few moments, breathing deeply. It was a painting of a Firebird from an Old

Russian folktale. Memories of Nurse Xeina, the one who told him the folktale of the Firebird flooded back. Night after night she had sat by his bed in the Military Hospital telling him Russian folk tales.

Jason Parva, the second son of a wealthy East Yorkshire family, had been invalided out of the Royal Air Force just before the end of the Great War and returned home a war hero. The Yorkshireman had been shot down while on a mission in France, found by allied soldiers and had almost been given up for dead because of his horrific injuries. He'd spent many weeks in terrible pain during his time in hospital, waiting for his bones and wounds to heal. With his life in the balance, whilst he fought off one infection after another, he made a slow recovery back to health. Through all those weeks in the hospital, his one desire had been to fly again. But it was that Russian nurse who had saved his life.

    He turned away from the picture, making his way across to the window. Looking out across their farm, he inhaled deeply before slowly letting out his breath. The nightmare had left him exhausted, and his nerves still tingled as though he was still in the cockpit of his plane. Dawn was breaking. It was always around dawn when he had the nightmare. It had been the time his squadron took off to begin their missions over enemy lines. His heart thudded against his ribs as adrenaline raced through his veins, but it was easing now. He was awake. Reliving the war years was all over, for now. The view from the window, so different from anything he had seen in Europe, helped ease the tension. Celia came up behind him, put her arms around his waist, and rested her head between his shoulder blades.

'Did I ever tell you I love you?' she said reassuringly.

'Maybe - once or twice.' Jason turned to face his wife and kissed her upturned face, then lifted her off her feet and carried her back to the bed.

Later, after lovemaking, they held each other close as they lay on the bed.

'What was flying like during the war?' She knew he had been shot down while photographing the German trenches but, instead of answering her, he stood up and went to the bathroom to wash his face. Celia watched him through the open door, the silver scars on his torso glistening with wetness, and she wondered how he had survived such a horrific crash. He rarely spoke about it. All he would say was these things happen in war.

With the bed freshly made, they lay on top of it, in silence, Jason, lost, deep in thought. Celia snuggled up close, her arm over his chest, her fingers tracing the line of his chin. He hadn't answered her question. She felt hurt being left out and excluded from a part of him he wouldn't talk about. He'd told her about returning home after the war, battered and torn, with a chest full of medals and a mind trapped in the mud and the wreckage of his plane crash.

She also knew it had been impossible for him to settle back to his old life in Nafferton, so he had left home, England and Europe, to come to Africa and start a new life. With all that he had suffered during the war, Celia couldn't understand his unrelenting love of flying after such a terrible plane crash. It hurt her to admit it, but flying was in his blood. It must be. Flying still thrilled him. His own aeroplane was out there now in the field behind the house, calling to him, waiting for him to take the controls and bring it to life as they danced through the sky together. She had learned to accept the place flying played in his life and even enjoy the flights they took over the bush to watch the animals and take in the views of the mountains. From time to time, they would fly out to the coast and spend a few days lazing by the sea. On days such as those he never had the nightmares; it was only on the farm, after working hard rebuilding a broken bit of machinery or after dealing with a dispute between the farmhands, that's when the nightmares came to claim him.

He'd bought the farm after his medical discharge from the RAF, and an unsuccessful return to family life in England. Back in England, with reminders of the War to end all Wars still making headlines in the newspapers, with his parents dead and no job to relieve him of his boredom, being at home in Nafferton had become more than he could endure. So, after reading about the success of other farmers in East Africa, Jason borrowed some money from his brother, a surgeon at the Hull Royal Infirmary, and bought a coffee plantation in Kenya.

After five years in Kenya, the Parva plantation covered five thousand acres of prime hillside, growing Arabica coffee. The different lifestyle, the wide-open spaces, the friendly people, and the warm climate, all now gave him the chance to put the war behind him. Kenya had given him a new future and a career away from a devastated Europe still in political turmoil. There were only two things he'd brought with him from those bygone days. One was a framed painting of the fabled Russian Firebird. The second was his love for flying. He had fallen in love with flying during his very first flying lesson.

As a youth, he'd learnt blacksmithing and basic mechanics working part-time in Nafferton's local smithy. He had seen photographs of the aeroplanes and their daredevil pilots in the newspaper. So when he was old enough, he had applied to join the Royal Flying Corps. He'd started as a mechanic, but after being given his first flight in an aeroplane he had shown a natural aptitude for flying and had trained to become a Pilot Officer. As one after the other of his fellow officers were shot down over France or were killed while trying to land badly damaged aircraft, Jason had learned the odds were stacked against him. But despite this, on those flying days when no one was shooting at him, he'd felt peace and contentment. The vast expanse through which he flew gave him such feelings of freedom and belief in himself, a confidence like nothing else he had ever experienced. So, soon after arriving in Kenya, he bought a two-seater biplane to enable him to get to any part of his plantation within minutes and, more importantly, enjoy the freedom of the African skies. In this, his war-time crash hadn't made any difference to his love of flying.

On arriving in Kenya, he'd bought the first farm he'd been offered, which turned out to be more run down and dilapidated than advertised, but he'd used his mechanical skills to rebuild it. After being introduced to the local ex-pats club, it hadn't been long before word got around about the new young bachelor farmer, and he soon caught the eye of the ladies. After a whirlwind romance, Jason married Celia, another ex-pat and daughter of a tea planter. Together, with the help of local workers, they rebuilt the run-down farm and re-energised the coffee plantation. It had become so profitable that Jason had repaid his brother's loan after the first two harvests. But for Jason, now thousands of miles from Europe, the war was never further away than in his next nightmare.

Celia knew she shouldn't push Jason for answers about his war experiences, but sometimes the need to ask questions got the better of her. More often than not, he would go silent and walk away. But, one day, she knew he would tell her more, but not until he was ready. Little by little she had learned the names of his lost friends and gleaned an insight into his life as a wartime pilot and the daily dangers he'd faced. She just couldn't understand why he still loved to fly. Jason dressed and, after a quick kiss, left Celia while she prepared herself for the day ahead.

Breakfast was served, as usual, by Pili, their cook and housekeeper, on the veranda. Celia always had toast, marmalade, and coffee, whereas Jason insisted on a traditional English breakfast with tea and toast. Pili could never understand this English obsession with a fried breakfast. He preferred his favourite: Nduma, boiled arrowroot, made the way his mother had taught him, the way all Kenyan mothers made it for their families.

Up here in the farmland hills, the climate was warm, sometimes hot, but without the searing heat that beat down on the plains. It not only made it more pleasant for the Europeans who farmed here, the fertile volcanic soil and the temperate climate were ideal for growing tea and coffee.

Pili brought a fresh pot of tea and then began to clear away the breakfast plates, when a noise from the far side of the yard attracted their attention. Looking out from the veranda, they saw four elephants enter the farm. Stunned for a moment, they sat and stared at the animals in disbelief. His farmhands ran around shouting as the elephants made their way toward the barn where the hay for the horses was stored.

'Pili, quickly, get my gun,' demanded Jason.

'You can't go down there. You might get killed,' Celia yelled at him.

'I have to; we've worked too hard to make a go of this farm to see it flattened by elephants.'

Snatching his rifle from Pili, he ran into the yard, stopped about thirty yards in front of the elephants and fired two rapid shots over their heads. The elephants halted, flailing their trunks from side to side, opening their ears wide in a stance of fear and threat. Jason loaded another bullet into the chamber and waited. The elephants stamped their feet but seemed reluctant to charge. They were young males and hadn't yet gained the confidence of age. Jason opened his arms wide and took two great stamping steps forward. The lead elephant backed off slightly. Then, from behind Jason, Celia and Pili ran toward the elephants banging on the bottom of saucepans with metal spoons. The elephants had seen and heard enough. They turned and bolted back toward the bush, but not before demolishing a fence that ran around the stable.

Jason chased after Celia. 'What the hell do you think you were doing? If those animals had charged, they could have killed us.'

In reply, Celia simply banged the bottom of her saucepan a couple of times in Jason's direction to torment him.

'Well, they didn't, did they?' She gave him a quick kiss on the lips and ran back to the bungalow, shouting and banging on the bottom of the saucepan as she went. Jason wandered back to the veranda, infuriated with his wife for putting herself in danger, but admiring her pluck and courage for standing beside him when help was needed. He leaned his rifle up against the veranda rail and sat down to finish his morning tea. He loved this country. The farm was a success and Celia; how lucky had he been that day at the club when he met her?

'Don't forget we are going to the dance tonight,' she reminded him.

'Do we have to? You know Roger Davenport will be there!'

Yes, I know, and so will his wife. Margery and I have been friends forever. Roger will behave himself whilst she has her eye on him.'

'Um, maybe, but he'll still expect to dance with you every chance he gets.'

'Is that a touch of jealousy I hear?'

'Certainly not. I trust you implicitly. It's Roger, the weasel I don't trust.'

'Well, I have to have someone to dance with when you go off talking about coffee prices and yearly yields with the rest of the growers.'

Jason put down his tea. 'Come here.' He put his arms around Celia's waist and looked into her eyes.

'Truth be told, I am jealous of every man that looks at you. You are my heart and soul, my reason for living, and every breath I take. I love you so much it hurts. So if I want to be jealous of Roger or any other man that demands too much of your attention, I jolly well will be.' Celia kissed him on the lips.

'I know that, silly. That's why Roger, or anyone else I dance with for that matter, will be wasting their time flirting with me. I chose you, remember? I saw something special in you that night at that first coffee growers dance, and I decided, right there and then, that you were going to be mine. So now we each know we can go to the dance tonight, and enjoy ourselves.'

Jason's thoughts went back to that night at the club soon after arriving in Kenya. Being the new boy, he'd sat at a table with a couple of other farmers to ask their advice about making repairs to farm machinery before his first harvest was due. Celia had spotted him as she danced with another young man. Their eyes had met briefly as she glided around the dance floor. After that moment, whenever Jason glanced up from his conversation, he would spot her staring at him. It wasn't long before she plucked up the courage to come over and, without a word, she had taken him by the hand and led him to the dance floor. They danced and talked until after midnight. After that night, they had met more and more frequently until after three months, Jason had asked her to marry him. It had been one of the best decisions he had ever made.

By the time Celia and Jason arrived at the plantation club, the party was already in full swing. As they entered, they were met by a waiter carrying a tray full of drinks. A quartet of musicians played popular dance music in what had been the club's dining room. The bar and lounge were full of guests in evening attire, and it wasn't long before the couple were separated. Celia was taken aside to hear the latest gossip from her lady friends; Jason by their husbands, who were already engrossed in business conversation and speculation over crop prices. The world's growing demand for coffee was proving very profitable.

Jason was in the middle of explaining how he had been improving his coffee toasting ovens when Celia grabbed him by the arm, demanding it was time to dance. Once on the dance floor, she explained her urgency.

'I'm sorry to drag you away from your friends, but I couldn't stand listening to Lucy Watkins any longer. She just announced to everyone that she is pregnant, and now, all they want to talk about is having babies. What's worse, they were pestering me for news on when we were planning to start a family. I couldn't stand it. It's as though because one of them has a child on the way, they all want one. I tried to tell them that it's a lot of responsibility bringing up a baby out here in the bush, but I was just ignored.'

'Don't you want children?' asked Jason.

'Yes, of course, I do...but when the time is right. What about you?'

'Yes, I agree, when we are ready.' Celia rested her head on Jason's shoulder as they gently swayed to the rhythm of the music. The tune changed to a foxtrot, breaking the intimate, romantic mood brought on by the previous melody, so they wandered out to the veranda. The sultry warm evening air had cooled; the scent of the roses and jasmine from the garden filled the air. The sky was black and full of stars, crickets chirped and the occasional roar of a lion carried on the breeze from far away. They stood at the veranda rail and watched couples walking hand in hand through the garden.

'Shall we go home?' asked Jason. However, before Celia got the chance to answer, Roger Davenport came over to claim a dance from her. Roger's father followed him out and began asking Jason about the improvements to the coffee toaster he'd talked about earlier.

'Come and join our little group,' demanded sir Hubert Davenport. Jason watched helplessly as Celia was whisked away by Roger. Sir Hubert and his party always had a table reserved for them at the club, and Jason was placed at its centre to explain to sir Hubert's friends all about his latest innovation. Everything was going well. Jason had their full attention until Celia returned looking very cross. She pulled up a chair and sat down close to Jason. He looked at her, concerned at what might have happened. She reassured him by resting a hand on his arm. She smiled and nodded for him to continue with his explanation. A moment later, Roger arrived, wearing a bright red handprint across his cheek. He glared at Celia as he sank into his chair and slammed a large gin and tonic down on the table. His father ignored him, but everyone else around the table couldn't help noticing that something had happened between the newcomers. Jason gave Celia a searching look. She smiled back at him sheepishly, saying, 'later.'

Roger took a large drink before putting his hand to the side of his glowing face.

'You have a feisty little cat there, Parva. Are you up to taming her?' snarled Roger.

Jason instantly got to his feet, his fists clenched at his side.

'Take it from me, *you* are not up to the job,' he hissed at Roger.

Sir Hubert intervened. 'Apologise to the lady this instant and go home before you disgrace yourself further.'

Roger mumbled his apology, and sat down again. His father stared at him a moment before offering his own apology to Celia and Jason.

Jason turned to Celia. 'I think it is time we were leaving.' As Celia got up to leave, Roger couldn't help himself. He had to make one more jibe.

'That's right, fly away like two little lovebirds. Until next time Celia; we have unfinished business.' It was more than Jason could stand. Drunk or not, Roger needed teaching a lesson. Jason's punch landed squarely on Roger's nose, the cracking cartilage heard clearly above the sound of the music.

As Roger and his chair crashed to the floor, Roger's drink followed him, landing in his crotch. With blood all over his face and a stain growing in his trousers, making it look as though he had wet himself, he looked a mess. His drunkenness didn't help as he flapped about like an overturned tortoise trying to get to his feet. sir Hubert beckoned over two servants to remove his son before he could make an even bigger fool of himself.

'I'm sorry, Celia, Jason. I've done a poor job of bringing up the boy after his mother died. Maybe a good thrashing or two, when he was younger, would have done him some good. We can finish our conversation some other time. It seems we also have to leave.'

As Jason and Celia drove home, Celia explained about Roger's wandering hands while they had been on the dance floor. Jason drove on without saying a word. Not until they were going up the steps to their own veranda did he stop and turn to Celia.

'I warned you about…' began Jason.

'That was a cracking right-hander you gave Roger. You'll have to teach me how to do it one day,' interjected Celia.

The tension of the evening broke as they both burst out laughing. Pili appeared in the doorway, holding it open for them as they entered. Celia led Jason directly to the bedroom.

'I'll show you what a she-cat can do,' she said as she closed the door.

The following morning Jason was reluctant to get out of bed, but Celia insisted, reminding him he still had to finish working on the toasting oven. Breakfast was over and whilst sitting together on the veranda finishing their tea and coffee, two young boys came running up to the house, calling for Jason. It was Pili who intercepted the boys at the bottom of the veranda steps to listen to what they had to say. Celia had taught Jason Swahili, but the boys used a dialect he found hard to follow, though he picked up the urgency in the two boys' voices, and the concerned look on Pili's face seem to confirm something was amiss.

'Sir, the boys say that elephants have left the forest and are in amongst the crops ripping up the coffee bushes in the fields to the south.' Jason finished his tea in two swallows and grabbed his bush hat.

'Pili, thank the boys for me, and give them a Fry's chocolate bar each. I know they love those. Celia, I need you to come with me. Get the map of the plantation and have the boys show you where they saw the elephants; I'll get the plane ready?'

With Pili's help using the map, the boys showed Celia where they had seen the elephants. Jason ran around the house to his aeroplane. By the time Celia had joined him, Jason had the plane ticking over. Celia showed Jason the location of the elephants on the map.

'When we get there; mark on the map where the elephants left the forest and where all the damaged areas are, then mark the direction the elephants are heading. If we can't turn the elephants back to the forest with the plane, we'll have to truck out a load of men and scare the elephants off the plantation the old-fashioned way.'

Jason helped Celia into the front observer seat of the aeroplane before climbing in the rear pilot's seat to take the controls. After a quick burst of speed along the ground, the aircraft rose smoothly and steadily into the air.

Celia had never been a big fan of flying, but she had to admit it was thrilling to watch the ground flash by below them. Seeing their farm from the air, the plantation, the forests and the animals, all from a vantage point that very few other people had been lucky enough to experience, was exhilarating.

Heading south, it wasn't long before they saw the forests far ahead of them. Farmland gave way to coffee bushes of ripening coffee berries. The path that the elephants had made through the plants was clear to see from the air. They had left a broad scar of trampled vegetation as they meandered through the crops. Jason soon found the elephants, a small group of six, probably young males, expelled from the main herd by the matriarchal leader. They would wander through the bush until old enough to breed and find a new herd to join. In a few weeks, they would pass through this area of Kenya on their migration, but for now, Jason had few options if he wanted to save the majority of the coffee crop. With a gentle push on the stick, he turned the aircraft to the right, and back towards the elephants. He eased the stick forward. The aeroplane went into a shallow dive before levelling out and passing just in front of the lead elephant. He hoped it would be enough to turn the herd back towards the forest and out of his crop. On the first pass, all Jason managed to do was startle the elephants, bringing them to a halt. He pulled the plane up and banked it to the left. He could see the elephants over his shoulder. They were tossing their heads from side to side and raising their trunks in alarm at the mechanical monster from the sky. The elephants turned to face the danger from the sky, bellowing as the plane flew away.

On his second pass, he wanted to come upon them from their rear, wanting to drive them back in the direction they had come. Pulling back on the stick, he took the aircraft up higher this time, turning the aeroplane in a steep bank to come full circle as quickly as possible. He lined the plane up on the elephants. An engine screaming dive followed by passing low over the elephants backs was enough to get them moving.

'One more pass should do it,' Jason hollered into the speaking tube which linked the twin cockpits of the aeroplane. During the next pass, he flew lower and lower, waggling the aircraft's wings as he did so. Flashing low once again over the backs of the startled beasts, Jason pulled back on the control stick, making the aeroplane climb rapidly. With a flick of the controls, the aircraft dropped its right wing and turned back to line up for another pass. He pulled out of the turn, levelled the plane's wings, and then put the aeroplane into a dive towards the elephants.

'This should do it,' he called to Celia. As he approached, he could see the elephants were already heading back towards the forest. Flying at full throttle and as low as he dared, he passed over the backs of the animals, giving them a final scare and hurrying them on their way. He left it as late as possible before pulling back on the stick; the biplane responded instantly to his touch, and it climbed above the forest.

Suddenly, his view from the cockpit was filled with white, as hundreds of startled birds took to the air from the tree canopy below them, flying up right in front of the biplane. The view through his goggles became smeared with blood as more and more birds were caught in the propeller of the aeroplane. Through the speaking tube, Jason heard a scream from Celia just as a large bird crashed into the windscreen in front of her, tearing it away and covering Celia in broken Perspex and shredded bird bits. The accumulating bird strikes were affecting the aeroplane's engine, blocking the engine's air intake, causing the engine to splutter. Another large bird skidded along the fuselage, hitting Jason full in the face, and then all went black.

Jason heard voices a split second before his body screamed in pain and he blacked out again. The next time he awoke, the sun was shining full on his face. He couldn't open his eyes; they seemed to be sealed shut. He tried to reach up and touch his face, but his arms wouldn't move. The pain in his head intensified, and the blackness returned.

The next time he awoke, it was darker and also, thankfully, less painful. This time, he could open his eyes. A dim light shone above him in an otherwise dark expanse, but he still couldn't move. He tried, but with each attempt, he only felt a searing pain. He lay quietly, trying to remember what had happened, and why he was the way he was. It took a few minutes before he was able to recall what had happened and order the thoughts in his head. The elephants! The plane! The birds! 'CELIA!' He turned his head from side to side; he was in bed, a hospital bed. Had it all been a dream? Was he still in a hospital in France? A black woman in a nurse's uniform pulled open the mosquito netting that hung around his bed.

'Good Morning, Mr Parva, we had just about given up on you. I will inform the doctor you are awake.' With those parting words, she closed the netting and was gone. After what seemed like an eternity, she returned with a white man who introduced himself as Doctor Schafer. Jason tried to speak, but couldn't. Doctor Schafer soon explained why.

'Do you remember the plane crash?' Jason nodded. 'You are lucky to be alive.' All Jason could do to respond was make a grunting sound.

'You cannot speak, Mr Parva; your jaw is wired shut. It is just one of the many injuries you sustained in the crash. You have two broken legs, two broken arms, a broken jaw, as well as three broken ribs and a punctured lung. You are going to be with us for some time, I think.'

'Umm,' Jason made the sound again.

'I will come back later, Mr Parva. We can talk again then.'

They kept Jason heavily sedated for two weeks, after which his medication was reduced sufficiently enough for him to hold a pencil and scribble the questions to which he needed to know the answers. There was one word on the paper, 'Celia?' The nurse looked at the paper for a moment, then took it away. Doctor Schafer returned and got straight to the point in answering Jason's question.

'Mr Parva, prepare yourself for some bad news. I'm sorry to tell you that your wife died in the crash.' Jason's scream was trapped inside his wired jaw. The pain brought tears to his eyes. The doctor nodded at the nurse, who gave Jason a morphine injection. Within a few seconds, the noise and pain stopped, and Jason was lost to the world about him.

After many weeks in the hospital and now sitting in a wheelchair ready to leave, Jason said goodbye to Doctor Schafer and Nurse Mwangi, thanking them for all they had done for him.

'Remember, Mr Parva, you need to go back to England to recuperate. The climate here is not good for you. Find a good hospital in case of complications while you are recovering.'

Pili took charge of Jason's wheelchair, pushing him along the hospital path towards his waiting car. His bones were mended, his wounds healed, though his scars were still bright and vivid. However, it was his heart that was still broken. Pili fussed around Jason like an old mother hen as he settled him in the back of the car. Jason sat impassively, thinking about the plantation, farm and Celia. He'd made a decision while still in the hospital, with Dr Schafer giving him a good reason to do so. The car drove out of the hospital grounds.

'Pili, wait, I want to go into town. Take me to a hotel; I don't want to go home just yet.' Pili half turned in his seat to look at Jason, before slowing the car and making a U-turn.

'Are you sure, sir, I mean, who will look after you in the hotel?' asked the trusty servant.

'I will be fine. Thank you, Pili. I just need a little more time before I go back to the farm.'

'The farm needs you, sir, it cannot run itself; there is much work to be done.'

Yes, Pili, I know. However, the farm has managed without me for the past couple of months; it will hang on a few days more.'

The car stopped outside the Sarova Sydney Hotel. After booking a room, Jason sent Pili back to the farm to fetch him some more clothes and other necessities for a prolonged stay away from home. By the time Pili returned some hours later, Jason had written him a letter of authority, stating that Pili was now the manager of the farm and plantation. He asked Pili to send him regular updates on the plantation's progress. Pili was delighted and promised to be the most diligent of managers and increase the profits tenfold by the time his boss returned.

That first night in the hotel, Jason had one of his nightmares, only this time when he crashed in France he was surrounded by elephants and white birds covered in blood. Celia walked out of the forest and waved to him as he lay in the wreckage of his downed biplane. He awoke confused and in pain. He fumbled on the bedside table for the painkillers the doctor had given him. He swallowed two with half a glass of water before collapsing back onto the bed. He lay there a moment, gathering his thoughts before turning and dropping his feet to the floor. A brief look at his watch told him it was four a.m. He stripped off his shorts and went for a shower, letting the lukewarm water massage his skin. He cried for the first time since he was a boy. He sat on the floor of the shower as the water slowly increased in temperature and until it and the painkillers allowed his muscles to relax. After he was finished, he spent the next two hours writing letters. One was to Mrs Dendridge, the housekeeper at the family home in England, warning her that he was about to return. The second was to his solicitor in Nairobi advising him of Pili's new status as Plantation Manager and that the farm was to be sold with ten per cent of the sale price given to Pili. The third was to the Bank of Nairobi informing them of his plans to sell the farm and to transfer his account back to his bank in England. The last one was the hardest to write. It was to Celia's family, informing them he was returning to England and that he would like to call on them and explain his plans.

After breakfast, Jason booked passage on the first ship back to England. With the boat ticket safely in his pocket, he had one duty left to perform. He could not leave Kenya without visiting Celia's grave at the small church, just down the road from their farm. He had to say goodbye, ask for forgiveness and make his peace with her before he left for good.

The churchyard was quiet, just as Jason hoped it would be, with just a gardener picking weeds and watering flowers planted by loved ones of the now departed. He felt ashamed at having to ask the man where Celia was buried. The man pointed to the left of the church. Jason spotted the newly erected wooden cross. The grave was neat and tidy, covered in small white stones and with fresh flowers laid at the base of the cross. He wondered who would have placed them there, then thought of Pili and smiled. Placing his own flowers on top of the white stones, a tear dripped from his nose onto their petals.

'I'm sorry, Celia, please forgive me.' He leaned heavily on his walking stick as his body began to shake, tears flowing freely to drop into the dust.

No one came to bother him, and after repeatedly saying he was sorry and that he loved her and that one day he hoped to return, he turned away and slowly made his way back to Pili, waiting by the car.

'You can take me to the railway station now please, Pili; I have a boat to meet in Mombasa.' With just enough time for Jason to get one last look at the little church, the car rounded a corner and was gone.

Chapter Two

Dendridge, the gardener and odd-job man, was at Nafferton train station ready to welcome Jason home when he got off the train.

'ʼow do, sir. Welcome ʼome. My sincere condolences on your loss, sir. I'll just get y'ur bags, and I'll be back in a tick.'

Dendridge was well into his fifties and built of sinew and muscle. His untidy grey hair kept in place by a battered flat cap. He walked up the platform to where the luggage was being unloaded from the train and got a porter to collect all Jason's trunks together. Nafferton railway station was at the edge of the village about a half-mile from the Parva family home and, while Jason waited by the car, he looked out across the fields. Along Wansford Road, the farmland was just as flat and open as he had remembered it to be. Rich East Yorkshire soil, ideal for farming, but prone to flooding during bouts of prolonged wet weather. It was some of the best farming land in the entire country. On Station Road, opposite the ticket office, the coal merchant was busy loading his lorry with sacks of anthracite. Behind the coal merchant were the remains of the marshalling yard and railway warehouses.

Dendridge interrupted Jason's daydreaming, 'The missus 'as got the house ready for your homecoming, sir.' Jason nodded at him in acknowledgement.

'Thank you, Dendridge.'

Dendridge loaded the two smaller trunks onto the luggage rack of the Morris Cowley, and then opened the door for Jason to get in the back seat, placing the remaining suitcases on the floor next to the door.

'I'll come back for the big trunk later if that's all right, sir'. Without waiting for an answer, Dendridge opened the driver's door and hopped in for the short drive to Parva Manor.

Mrs Dendridge, the housekeeper, was waiting for Jason at the front door as the car made its way up the drive. As Jason got out of the car, she got her first sight of his walking stick and, with no deference to formality, rushed forward and put her arms around him.

'Oh sir, it's good to have you home again. I never thought I'd live to see the day what with you going to Africa of all places.' Suddenly remembering her place, she released Jason and stepped back. Regaining her composure, she led him into the house.

'My deepest sympathy for the loss of Mrs Parva, sir, Mr Dendridge and me was right worried when we heard the news about the plane crash. But, now you're home, I can look after you like I used to do when you were a lad. Oh, I do miss those days when the family was all together. I've aired your room, and supper will be ready at six o'clock. It's only something simple until I get to know what you like, but I dare say it's not changed much since you were a nipper. Come along to the drawing room, and I'll go make a pot of tea. I've made you some of your favourite ginger cake to go with it.'

Mrs Dendridge scurried out of the drawing room, leaving Jason alone to look around the room and reacquaint himself with his childhood home.

He searched the walls, staring at the family portraits. The history of his family was all here, going back through the many generations to the first Jason Parva, who had bought some land to farm and then gradually increased the size of the farm until the family owned most of the land in the district. His eyes fell on the large portrait hanging over the fireplace. There was just a single name printed in a cartouche on the frame 'Susannah.' He wondered who she was. As a child, he had asked his parents, but they had said they didn't know. They had only told him that the picture was old and had to stay there. Going over to the window, he looked out on All Saints'' church beyond the garden wall. It felt strange being home after so many years away. Different: but the same. Memories of his childhood flashed before him, birthdays, Christmas's, family, friends; so many of them were now gone.

There was a knock on the door. Mrs Dendridge entered. 'I've brought your tea and cake, sir.'

'Thank you, Mrs Dendridge. Tell me, do you know who Susannah was?'

'No sir, all I know is that portrait has hung on that wall for years and years. Apparently, it's in the deeds, sir. The portrait cannot be removed from the wall, no matter what. Legend says that the first Mr Parva put it there, but who the woman is has long been forgotten. All I can say is, he must have loved her a great deal else why fix it in the deeds that she must always stay. A beautiful lady, don't you think, sir?'

Jason took another look at the portrait. She was a fine lady with auburn hair and milk-white skin. Her dress looked seventeenth-century in style. As Mrs Dendridge put the tea tray down, there was a knock on the front door.

'Excuse me, sir. I shall just go and see who it is.' Jason poured himself a cup of tea and wandered back to the portrait of Susannah. *Now I'm home, I must find out who you are.*

There was a tap on the door, and the housekeeper returned. 'Reverend Blackhouse has called to see you, sir. Shall I show him in?'

'Yes, please do, and bring a cup for the reverend, Mrs Dendridge.' The servant showed the minister into the drawing room, then went to bring more crockery.

'Good day to you, Reverend. Please take a seat and tell me what I can do for you?'

'Oh, nothing really. I am just making a courtesy call. Word soon went around the village that you were returning, and I thought I would call and express my condolences for the loss of Mrs Parva, and ask if there is anything that you needed.' Mrs Dendridge momentarily interrupted them with another cup and saucer, and more slices of ginger cake.

'Thank you, Mrs Dendridge.' 'No, Vicar, there is nothing I require right now, except a little time to recuperate and heal. My doctor in Kenya recommended I return to England in case any complications arose from my injuries after the aeroplane crash. Kenya is a country that is still lacking some of the more advanced hospitals found in Europe, but I believe it will become one of the great modern African nations someday.'

'Yes, yes, quite so, quite so.' The reverend helped himself to a second slice of cake before continuing.

'I was just wondering if you will be in church on Sunday. It would provide me with an opportunity to introduce you to some of the newer members of the congregation and village.'

'I will consider it. I hadn't thought that far ahead yet; I only arrived home a short time ago.'

'Oh yes, of course. How rude of me, I'm sorry. I saw the car arrive and hurried around to see you. I will leave you to settle in. I forget myself now and then. I get a thought in my head and have to do it there and then. It is easy to forget other people have lives outside the church.' Reverend Blackhouse finished his tea and got up to leave.

'Oh, there is one other thing I wanted to ask you about. Thursday evening is bell ringing practice. I do hope you will come along. We are short-handed these days, and you took to it so well when you were younger. I'm sure you would soon pick it up again.'

'Very well, Reverend. I will see you on Thursday evening. I may not be able to play for a full hour, but change ringing is one of the English customs I have missed during my time in Africa.'

At seven o'clock on Thursday evening, Jason entered All Saint's' Church to find Philip Garton, the Tower Captain and the rest of the church's bell ringers waiting to meet him. After reacquainting himself with some old friends and an introduction to the newer members of the band, they ascended the steps to the ringing room. The bell ropes were lowered from the ceiling on the bell-rope spider, and the regular bell ringers rang up their bells, setting them for the evening practice. Jason took a seat. His turn would come later. Once everyone was ready, Dorothy, on the smallest bell (the treble) called out, 'Look too- Trebles going-Trebles gone.' With a steady pull on the sally, the first bell swung into action, followed in turn by the following five bell-ringers. They started with rounds (each bell ringing in turn, the most familiar peal of bells from a church tower.) After a few rounds, the tower captain called the changes (the order in which the bells are rung.) The memories of years of practice as a boy came flooding back. Apart from a few minor errors, the band played well. After fifteen minutes, the tower captain called 'rounds, and shortly after that, 'stand'. Each bell stopped ringing, and the band took a break for a five-minute chat.

'Your turn now, Jason,' said the tower captain.

Jason stepped forward to take one of the ropes.

'It's been a long time since I was here last,' Jason said to Philip.

'Don't worry, lad. It's like riding a bike, you never forget how. You just need to build up your confidence again, and I'll be here to take over if it goes wrong.'

After a few practice rings under the captain's supervision, Jason got his touch, rhythm, and timing back.

'Do you feel up to joining in?' asked Philip.

'Yes, I'd like to try.' The other bell ringers took up their positions on the remaining five bell ropes.

'We'll keep it simple, just a few rounds of call changes. I'll stay here to keep an eye on you. Just give me the word if you want me to take over.'

Jason acknowledged Philip's instructions just as Dorothy called, 'Look too…'

After an hour's practice, the bell ringers retired to The Bell public house just across the road from the church.

'I suppose the first round is on me, as I'm the new boy,' said Jason. There were no dissenters, and by the time they were on their second round of beer, Philip was telling stories of Jason as a young lad. How Philip had spotted Jason playing in the churchyard on practice evenings, listening to the bells ringing on a Sunday and at weddings, and then invited him in to learn the art of bell ringing.

Later that evening, when Jason was walking home after closing time, he was glad that the vicar had talked him into going to the bell ringing practice. It had given him a feeling of peace, fulfilment and home.

Mrs Dendridge was still up and waiting for him as he arrived home. She greeted him as he walked through the door, 'did you have a nice time, sir?'

'Yes, thank you, Mrs Dendridge. There was no need for you to wait up for me, but it was kind of you to do so.'

'There is a fire in the library if you're not ready for bed yet. Would you like a cup of tea or maybe something a little stronger before you turn in?'

'No, thank you. I think I've had quite enough to drink for tonight. I'd forgotten how strong Yorkshire beer can be.'

'Very well, I'll have your breakfast ready at eight o'clock. Good night.' Once Mrs Dendridge had retired for the evening, Jason went through to the library and settled into a leather wing-backed chair in front of the fire. The room smelled of polished wood and leather-bound books. A single standard lamp stood tall in the corner of the room, giving off a soft warm glow through its maroon shade. Staring into the flames, he felt comfortable and relaxed. He smiled to himself. He'd enjoyed the evening reacquainting himself with bell ringing and the convivial company of the vicar and the other bell ringers in the pub afterwards.

A breeze caught his cheek which grew into a buffering against his face. A roar filled his ears, and as he looked around, he was surrounded by blue sky and two other aircraft. He looked down to muddy scarred terrain four thousand feet below, then he turned his head quickly left and right, searching for the Hun in the sun he knew would be out there waiting for him. He didn't see or hear the first attack; it was only when his starboard wing-man's aircraft burst into flames that he caught sight of the enemy. One of the stricken plane's wings folded and broke away. The aircraft immediately banked and spiralled towards the earth, trailing flames and thick black smoke. His own aircraft vibrated as a row of holes appeared in the fuselage just in front of him. He instinctively turned the aeroplane to port. There was no longer any chance of him completing his mission of photographing the enemy trenches. He momentarily got a glance at two German aircraft chasing his remaining patrol partner as his own aeroplane increased speed rapidly and dived towards the ground. A quick look over his shoulder told him what he had suspected; two Fokker triplanes were on his tail. The closer one was trying to get below him, to shoot upwards at what would be a larger target. The second aircraft was higher than the first. Jason recognised the trap. If he tried to climb, the higher aircraft would have him in its sights. He turned to starboard. He hadn't seen the third German aircraft at all. He just felt his own plane shudder violently and the spray of hot engine oil coming over the windscreen into the cockpit.

Jason awoke to the sound of his own voice shouting, 'No!' He looked around the room, confused at first. He'd expected Celia to be by his side speaking soft words of comfort, a glass of water in her hand, but he was alone, with a heart beating as though it was fighting to escape from his chest. Once he'd stopped trembling, he rose from the chair and went to the sideboard and poured himself half a glass of single malt, draining the glass in two swallows. The hot fiery liquid made his head swim. Putting down the glass, he removed a handkerchief from his pocket and wiped his mouth. Having regained his composure, he crossed to the fireplace, put the mesh guard in front of the fire and turned out the light.

The following morning, Jason took a stroll through his home village on the edge of the Yorkshire Wolds. Curious to reacquaint himself with the changes that must have occurred over the years he'd been away. The path from his home ran downhill to a crossroads. Ahead of him was Coppergate, the horse-wash and the mere. His first stop was the village horse-wash where, as a child, he liked to play on hot summer days. It was still the same; fish swam in the shallow spring-fed freshwater which bubbled up through the ground. Out on the mere, an island covered with trees and bushes, provided a safe haven for the ducks and swans to roost at night.

A small farm nestled up to the mere's eastern side, the village crowded around the other sides. From the crossroad in the centre of the village ran Middle Street, Westgate and then Priestgate. Middle Street continued up to meet High Street at the Methodist Chapel. Opposite the mere and horse-wash, the ground rose sharply; and on top of a rise stood All Saints'' Church. There had been a church on the site since before the doomsday book was written.

Jason turned away from the mere and made his way along Middle Street, where the general store and the blacksmiths were already busy. Jason stopped to look at the blacksmiths working at their forges. To one side there was a car with a dented front wheel arch and one of the blacksmiths was beating at it with a hammer to bring it back to shape. *'That's progress,'* thought Jason. Moving further along Middle Street, he came across the barber, the bakers, the newsagent, the coal merchant and the market gardener. They were still there, just as he remembered them. So was The King's Head public house. Inside, he could see the landlord preparing for opening time. Opposite The King's Head was the fish and chip shop. It had been many years since he'd had fish and chips. *Umm, I'll have to get Mrs Dendridge to buy some for supper one evening.*

'Is that you, Jason Parva?' the voice took him by surprise. He spun around to see who'd called his name. A tall man, about his own age, was marching towards him.

'Aye, I thought it were you. Come home, have you? All that African sun and native girls got too much for you?'

Jason blinked at the face that looked familiar, but one he couldn't put a name to.

'What's up, cat got your tongue?' said the familiar face.

Just in the nick of time, he recognised the man.

'Jimmy Walker, hello Old Chap. I almost didn't recognise you. It's been a long time since we were at school together.' Jason shook his old schoolmate by the hand.

'You coming for a pint?' asked Jimmy.

'It's not opening time yet,' countered Jason.

'Oh, don't you worry about that; we'll go in Ned's back room. I'll introduce you to the rest of the lads.' After a little further encouragement, Jimmy led Jason around the back of the pub.

'How did that happen?' asked Jimmy.

'What?' asked Jason.

'Your buggered leg. During the war was it?' persisted Jimmy.

'No, it was in Kenya,' replied Jason.

'That's in Africa, is it?' asked Jimmy, as he pushed the rear door to the pub open and entered without giving Jason time to answer.

Jason wondered if he was doing the right thing. Not only going into the pub out of hours, but trying to rekindle lost acquaintances from his youth. In a small room, six men sat around a table, chatting. When they spotted Jason, they all fell silent and stared at the stranger.

'Now then, lads, you remember Jason Parva from up at Parva Manor, the silly bugger who got himself shot down during the war,' Jimmy announced to the gathering.

'Aye, we remember,' said one. And, as if it had been choreographed, six-pint pots were emptied and slammed down on the table.

Jason looked at the expectant faces. 'My round I think, Gentlemen.' As though he had been summoned by telepathy, the landlord opened the door.

'That'll be eight pints of your best, Ned,' requested Jimmy, before he sat down with his mates, leaving Jason facing the landlord.

'That comes to six shillings and eightpence, sir,' Ned held his hand out for the money with a wry smile on his face.

Jason fished the coins from his pocket and dropped them into Ned's palm before joining the men at the table.

'Now then, Jason, tell us all about your adventures in Africa,' said Jimmy. A murmur of encouragement rippled around the table.

'Well, there's not a lot to tell, really. After the war, I went out there to do a bit of farming. All was going well until I had a bit of a bash in the plane I was flying. My wife was killed, and so I decided I'd come back home.' His companions stared at him in amazement, each with a roll-up cigarette hanging from the corner of his mouth.

'We heard about the plane crash and your wife. Sorry mate, that was really bad luck,' said Jimmy. A Few murmurs of agreement came from the rest of his pals before their mood changed back.

'Would that be the kind of farming we do here, then?' asked one.

'I've got a couple of dozen porkers on me land down Nethergate, something like that you mean?' asked another.

'No, not really,' said Jason, sombrely. 'I had a five thousand acre coffee plantation with my farm.'

'Bugger me. The lad must be gentry to own that much land,' chipped in the pig owner. Just then, Ned returned with a tray of beer. No sooner had the glasses been placed on the table than they were emptied, all except Jason, who had only managed a couple of swallows.

'Another round, Ned. Jason's got a lot to talk about,' said Jimmy. Ned held his hand out to Jason, and once again he furnished the coins.

Jason had had enough. This was not what he'd come home for.

'How do you manage that much land? You must have had an army of workers out there,' questioned another member of the six.

Jason stood up, 'I'm sorry, Gentlemen, I really must go. I have an appointment with the doctor,' he tapped his injured leg with his walking stick. 'Enjoy your drinks. It was nice meeting you all.'

'Aye, right you are. We'll look forward to seeing you again soon.' Came the chorus of disappointed voices.

Once again on Middle Street, Jason felt the bitter-sweetness of being home with people who didn't or couldn't understand how he had changed.

His aching leg reminded him of his need to register with the doctor so he could get the painkillers he needed. He'd thought about getting the doctor to visit him at home, but had decided that reacquainting himself with the village would do him more good. Doctor Schafer had given him enough medication to cover his journey home, but he would need more. The slow cruise had certainly allowed him the time he needed to recover from the worst of his injuries, but he couldn't imagine enduring the pain without some help. However, it was a relief to know that he only needed the tablets when he overdid it, and the pain became too much for him to sleep or rest comfortably. He crossed the street to number nineteen Middle Street, found the doctor's surgery, and knocked on the door.

After a thorough examination, the doctor declared Jason fit, so long as he rested and gave his wounds time to heal properly. Moderate exercise was recommended along with a light, but balanced diet, with only moderate amounts of alcohol, and definitely no smoking. He wrote Jason a prescription for more morphine tablets before sending him on his way with the advice to come back if he didn't continue to improve.

With his main objective for the day done, Jason went to explore more of the village he hadn't seen for over ten years. Calling in at the florists, he bought a large bunch of flowers. With hindsight, what he needed to do now should have been his first priority after arriving home, and now his nagging conscience made him feel guilty. It was time to visit his parent's grave. It had been five weeks since he had visited Celia's grave and now he had to visit the resting place of his parents. The thought filled him with dread. They had died in the nineteen-eighteen flu pandemic while he had been in the hospital, recovering after being shot down. He felt guilty about not making their graveside his first visit now he was home. At his parents' resting place at All Saints'' Church, he laid the flowers on their grave and said a short prayer. Standing over their grave brought on feelings of sadness and bitterness. He'd seen too many graves and said too many farewells to friends and loved ones during and after the war. As he looked down at their gravestone, he made a vow. These feelings of pain and loss each time he lost someone he loved were too much to endure, too higher a price to pay for brief moments of happiness in between. From now on, he would live alone.

By the time he'd finished paying his respects, the day had turned cloudy and chilly, so Jason went home. The portrait of Susannah stared down at him from above the fireplace. Tomorrow he would call on his brother and ask him if he knew anything about the portrait, and who Susannah was. Mrs Dendridge brought him a plate of sandwiches, cake, and a pot of tea.

'Thank you, Mrs Dendridge.'

'It's good to have you home again, sir. It's just a pity, Mrs Parva... well, you know what I mean. If there is anything else you need, just ring the bell.'

The following morning, after Jason had made a telephone call to his brother, Mr Dendridge drove him to Cottingham, where his brother James had bought a house and now lived with his family. He'd wanted a house closer to Hull and the hospital where he worked as a surgeon. He often had to work late into the night and a house in Cottingham was far more convenient at the end of a busy day than travelling all the way out to Nafferton to go home. James was his elder brother by two years. Jason wondered if becoming a doctor had helped him improve his arrogant, big brother attitude or whether he was just as aloof as he had always been. He owed his brother this visit if only to inform his elder sibling how successful he had been in Kenya, but no doubt his brother would counter his success with a boast of his own.

James welcomed him warmly, introducing him to his wife Sophia and their daughter Francis. They spent a pleasant morning talking over old times, Jason's time in Africa and James' time at the Royal Infirmary. Jason noted the change in James and put his brother's new amiability down to being married and to having a charming wife and daughter. He asked James about the portrait of Susannah at home. His brother informed him that he had done some research on documents found in the attic after their parents had died. He'd discovered that Susannah was their ten times great-grandmother and had been married to a Jason Parva in Oxford in Sixteen Forty-three, a full thirty years before the house had been built in Nafferton. Sophia asked Jason to stay for lunch, but he declined, saying he would call again soon, and that Dendridge was waiting to drive him home. When his leg was stronger and he could drive himself, he promised to stay the whole day.

By mid-afternoon, Jason found he was tired and needed a nap. The pace of life in the village was somewhat slower than he was used to and but for his injuries, he would have been looking for some activity to occupy his time.

The following morning, while he was eating breakfast, Mrs Dendridge brought him three letters left by the postman. He recognised the first one; it was from his solicitors in Nairobi. It informed him that they had sold the plantation and farm, and dispersed the monies as he had wished. Jason was pleased to see that the plantation and farm had sold for a good profit and that he was quite a wealthy man in his own right now. The second letter was from Pili, thanking Jason for the money he had been given and that he was going to buy himself a herd of cattle, marry, and have many children.

The postmark on the third letter showed it had been sent from Paris, and the address on the envelope was written in a hand he didn't recognise. Inside the envelope, he found a single sheet of paper on which was written one line.

Train leaves London for Oban 06:15 Monday 20th April. Firebird.

Jason stared at the letter. The memories of Firebird made him run hot and cold. Memories of pain, hospital and death flashed through his mind as though they had happened yesterday. He turned the paper over and over, frantically looking for anything else that may have been written on it or he might have missed. Then he examined the envelope inside and out for any further clues. He found nothing. He knew who had sent the letter. The question was, why? With one final look at the last word written on the paper, he folded the note and placed it inside his jacket pocket. He guessed it was a cry for help. He had three days to wait until he had to be in London and catch that train to Oban. His boredom and tiredness evaporated as he stood up and made for the door. Nothing but his own death was going to stop him from being on that train.

'Mrs Dendridge!'

Chapter Three

As soon as Mrs Dendridge had finished packing Jason's suitcases, Mr Dendridge took it down to the car. The odd-job man drove Jason to the railway station to catch a train to Hull. Jason's plan was to be in London one full day before the scheduled departure of the train mentioned in the note.

After arriving at King's Cross Railway Station, Jason took a taxi to the Metropole Hotel. His leg ached a little, and he was tired after the early start and long journey. After checking in at the hotel, and a light supper, Jason retired to his room to rest and read the newspaper. But, unable to settle because of tomorrow's unusual and secretive rendezvous with the nurse he hadn't seen for over ten years, he made a phone call to the hotel concierge, asking him to buy a ticket for the theatre. He hoped the distraction would allow him to relax and not constantly think of why, after all this time, the woman wanted to see him so secretively.

The show he went to see was The Cat and The Fiddle, with Francis Lederer and Peggy Wood, at the Palace Theatre. The musical proved a useful distraction, and, after returning to his hotel, Jason had a nightcap at the bar before going to bed and sleeping soundly until his early morning call at 5am.

The train for Oban was already waiting on the platform when he arrived at Euston Station. The highly polished maroon and cream first-class carriages looked smart, sporting their individual names written in gilt paint. A steward stood at each carriage door waiting to greet passengers and organise porters to deal with their luggage. Parting couples and families lingered on the platform, saying last minutes farewells, and exchanging hugs and kisses. All these people made Jason suddenly feel very lonely. The platform was full of people waiting to board the train. He searched their faces, looking for his nurse. He waited as long as he dare on the damp cold platform that morning at the end of April. Finally, Jason stepped off the platform and into the carriage. A porter whisked his luggage away to his sleeper while he settled in the saloon carriage, hoping to find Firebird.

The plush carriage with its deep pile carpet, polished wood-panelled walls, and leather armchairs was the height of luxury. The saloon carriage was sectioned into three parts, separated by walls of frosted glass in the latest geometric art déco designs. Jason slumped into one of the voluptuous leather armchairs. Tea, coffee and crumpets were being served by stewards in white starched jackets. Cold from standing on the station platform, and despite having eaten an early breakfast at the hotel an hour before, Jason asked for tea and crumpets. In Jason's third, at the rear of the saloon carriage, there were more armchairs and sofas, each discretely distanced from its neighbour by a small table. The middle third of the carriage was taken up by the bar made from polished mahogany decorated with various coloured fruit wood in geometric designs. Mirrors and glass shelves, with chrome fittings, lined the back of the bar. In front of the bar, was a row of tall chrome and leather padded stools. This was the smallest third of the carriage. Jason assumed the last third of the carriage was a mirror image of the one in which he was now seated. More people arrived.

On a sofa opposite him, sat a young woman. She was slim and elegant, attired in a red and white flowered dress. Her face, expertly made up with the latest style of cosmetics, was framed below a perfectly cut bobbed hairstyle. She had the look and style of a woman who turned heads when she entered a room. Next to her sat a young girl of about ten years of age, also immaculately dressed. The young girl sipped pink lemonade through a glass straw from a tumbler made of cut crystal. At first, Jason assumed her to be the daughter of the woman at her side, but changed his mind as the woman looked a little young to be the mother of a child of the girl's age. He glanced at the woman's hands. She had perfectly manicured nails, but her fingers were unadorned, not a ring on either hand. In fact, the only jewellery he could see was a pair of simple but tasteful gold earrings. The young girl had to be a niece or a younger sister. The woman glanced across the carriage at Jason and noticed him staring at her. He nodded to her politely and smiled but, before he could introduce himself, she looked away. Jason, hurt by the slight, then remembered his walking stick and how it made him look older than his actual age, though he would be only thirty-two at his next birthday.

A man in a dark suit entering the carriage distracted him from the woman opposite, and while one steward took the man's bags, another led him to the bar. Ignoring the woman opposite for a moment, Jason studied the man as he took a seat and ordered a drink. He couldn't help but disapprove of drinking so early in the morning, though a shot of brandy to ward off the chill could be classed as medicinal. Losing interest in the newcomer, Jason removed a copy of National Geographic from the magazine rack next to his chair. He needed something to distract him from the vision on the sofa in front of him. Finding a story about a previously unknown tribe of natives from South America, he became absorbed in the article. The men from the tribe had come out of the forest and walked into one of the logging camps when the workmen had come close to their village. When the natives saw the giant steam shovels clacking and hissing as they devoured the trees, the natives had thrown themselves in front of the logging machines, believing them to be gods that ate the forests. By the time Jason had finished reading the article, the woman and child were gone, disappearing without a sound to distract him. He glanced up and down the carriage, but they were nowhere in sight.

Two more people entered the carriage, a man and a woman. From the colour of their grey hair, he guessed they were both in their sixties. They were well dressed, a businessman and his wife going on holiday to the Highlands, he suspected. Jason ordered more tea and settled back to read the next article in the magazine. It turned out to be one about a new species of reptile discovered in Africa. The memory of the plane crash flashed before him, followed by the image of Celia's face. He skipped the article and put the magazine down. The entrance of two more passengers, gave him something new to focus on. They were a couple in their early thirties, all smiles and giggles, newlyweds he supposed or maybe lovers escaping London for a private getaway in the Highlands of Scotland. They occupied the sofa left vacant by the goddess and the child. He was disappointed he hadn't noted her departure. The couple were sitting so close to each other that it would have taken a crowbar to separate them. They sat entwined around each other, just long enough for the steward to return and inform them that their overnight compartment was ready. They left the carriage with the woman nibbling on the man's ear as he held her tightly around her waist.

Jason called the waiter over and asked for another crumpet. 'Who are the newlyweds?' he asked the steward, mildly interested in the couple.

'The Viscount of Holderness and his new bride, sir,' said the steward, raising his eyebrows and giving a sniff of dissatisfaction, showing his disapproval of their behaviour in the carriage. Jason settled back in his comfy chair to enjoy his tea and crumpets.

The train juddered ever so slightly as it began to leave the station. Then, slowly at first, the train pulled away smoothly without causing so much as a ripple in Jason's teacup. The train gathered speed quickly. Jason could hear the faint sound of the engine chuffing powerfully up ahead. Through the windows, the view of the station gave way to one of houses and streets before the train entered a tunnel. When it emerged again, there were still more houses, but this time smaller ones, with larger gardens. The houses and streets got fewer until the train broke out into the countryside. Then the train seemed to pick up more speed, as though it was enjoying its freedom from suburbia. The steward returned asking if Jason would like to reserve a table for lunch, which would be served at twelve noon. Jason told him he would, and that he was now retiring to his own compartment to rest.

The train pulled steadily as Jason lay on his bed. With the gentle sway of the carriage and the repetitive, but faint clackety-clack sound of the wheels as they crossed the joints in the rails, his eyelids became heavy. An hour's sleep would refresh him so, setting his travelling alarm clock for nine o'clock, he allowed himself to be rocked to sleep by the motion of the train.

His dreams took him back to the war. The gentle rocking of the carriage, simulating the motion of flight, the clickety-clack of the carriage wheels, the sound of distant machine guns closing in on his aeroplane. He saw his little aeroplane dodging and weaving as the German plane closed on him relentlessly. Regardless of how expertly he manoeuvred his own plane to avoid it, the German biplane stayed with him, bullets ripping through his fuselage and wings. No matter what he did, no matter how hard he tried, he couldn't shake off the devil on his tail. A burst of machine-gun fire blasted in his ear, the sound changing to one of a tiny bell ringing close by. The vision of the German biplane evaporated, and the ceiling light in his railway compartment came into view. Jason rose, wishing he'd never gone to sleep. However, the heat of the water and the scented soap helped to wash away his tension. As he dressed, the reassuring comfort of putting on a civilian shirt and tie was the reminder that those days of fear, stress and tiredness were behind him and that he had survived.

Now ready to find the author of his cryptic letter, Jason returned to the saloon carriage, hoping that his nurse would look for him in the same place. But she wasn't there, and neither was his mysterious young goddess. But the newlyweds were back, only this time, they occupied opposite ends of the sofa and were ignoring each other. He was about to strike up a conversation with the man, but he was interrupted when three strangers entered the carriage. Jason assumed they had boarded the train into a different carriage. From the accent of the one who ordered their coffee, he guessed they were Eastern European. Jason had heard many foreign languages spoken during the war. However, the strangers looked out of place in the elegant surroundings of the first-class carriage.

Their cheaply made, ill-fitting suits, and rough mannerisms, a contradiction to their superior surroundings. This bunch, Jason felt, he could impose upon for some company, so he went across and introduced himself.

'Good day, Gentlemen. Enjoying the journey? My name is Jason Parva.'

There was a sudden exchange of words in their native language before one of the trio, in a thick accent, said. 'Sorry. We are on holiday from Sweden, and our English is not good. Please excuse us.'

They moved to the other end of the carriage, keeping away from everyone else. Jason watched them walk away, suspicious of what the man had said to him. He'd been to Sweden with his parents before the war. That was not Swedish, he had heard them speaking to one another. Disappointed by their rebuff, he returned to his seat to study the newlyweds. They were still not speaking, but at least they had shuffled a little closer together. The man was reading the newspaper, and she a magazine. As the man held up the newspaper in front of him to read the sport on the back page, Jason could to read the headline on the front of the newspaper 'French businessman shot on the streets of Paris.' With no one to talk to and, with there still being a couple of hours before he could have a pre-lunch drink, he went to look for the nurse who had sent him the cryptic note.

A diagram on the wall of the carriage showed the order in which the carriages were attached to the engine. The saloon carriage in which he had been sitting was in the centre of the eight carriages. The next carriage forward was the dining car, with three sleeping cars ahead of it. To the rear, there were three sleeping cars and, last of all, the luggage and guards' van. Having decided to look through the rear carriages first, he was still in his seat when the little girl he had seen earlier entered the carriage, this time escorted by a man. Judging by the way she held his hand and her relaxed manner, this was no doubt her father. They moved down the carriage before taking an armchair each. The man called a steward over and ordered pink lemonade for the girl and coffee for himself.

Where was the young woman? He wondered.

Jason suddenly realised he'd learnt something. The man and girl had come from one of the carriages to the front of the train, so there was every chance the young woman who he had seen with the child must also have a sleeper in one of the forward carriages. Maybe she was the sister of the girl and the daughter of the man. He waited to see if she would turn up. He was disappointed when the next person to enter the carriage was a short, slim, middle-aged man in a black tie and dress suit. '*Somewhat overdressed for this time of day*,' thought Jason. It wasn't until he heard the soft sound of a piano being played that he understood who the middle-aged man was. Had Jason ventured down the other end of the saloon carriage, he would have spotted the piano. The gentleman piano player was good. His first tune was Clair de Lune, by Debussy. Jason settled back to enjoy the music as the gentle melody filled the carriage.

He noticed how many passengers stopped talking to listen to the music. Even the little girl was captivated by the tune.

The pianist followed his first tune with Chopin's Nocturne in E-Flat Major. It was some of the most magical pieces of piano playing Jason had ever heard, and in his opinion, was worthy of Covent Garden Opera House. Just as the pianist finished the Chopin piece, the three foreign gentlemen returned to Jason's end of the carriage. They found a corner and realigned the chairs so they faced inward towards each other. Jason took their action to be 'do not disturb' sign. Still, they had piqued his interest; he definitely wanted to know more about them.

The elderly couple returned, arm in arm, and took seats near the three foreigners. They ordered tea and crumpets and settled to read the newspapers. Soon after, a short, lean, well-dressed man entered the carriage. His suit was loose fitting but well cut. He sported a thin black moustache and slicked back hair, which was growing a little thin on top. He paused at the entrance, adjusted his jacket, and then, with a smile, a nod and a good morning to everyone as he passed, he walked down the centre of the carriage to the far end.

This seemed to cause a little ripple of comment from all those present. The piano player changed what he was playing to tunes Jason was unfamiliar with, so he recovered the magazine he'd been reading earlier from the table at his elbow, and opened it to look for another article. Before he found anything that took his fancy, another man entered the carriage. He, too, paused at the entrance to adjust his attire, then saunter casually to a seat in the corner. A steward rushed over.

'Good morning, Mr Ventura, not a very pleasant day today, I'm afraid. May I fetch you some coffee?'

Jason stared at Mr Ventura for a moment. He'd seen the face somewhere before. Mr Ventura smiled back as he noticed Jason's attention. It was then that Jason recognised him. Robert Ventura, the actor. He'd seen his photograph in the magazines that Celia would read. Jason gave him a nod of recognition and smiled back before returning to his magazine and thumbing through the pages. He found an article on the decline of British Industry, the Great Strike of 1926, another on the Stock Market Crash of 1929, and another on the pros and cons of every woman over the age of twenty-one being able to vote. The last article he came to was on a chap by the name of Gandhi and his march to the sea in India. Jason had heard of Mohandas Gandhi when he was in Kenya and started to read the article. He was distracted by the arrival of another man dressed in tweeds and plus fours. He was a burly chap, puffing on a large cigar. His jacket was open and, but for his waistcoat with its buttons strained to their limit, it appeared as though his ample belly might escape over the waist of his trousers. Ignoring everyone, he ploughed through the carriage to the far end. As he passed a steward, he ordered a whisky, three kippers and a pot of tea. Before Jason's attention returned to his magazine, Robert Ventura volunteered the answer to the question that he must have seen on Jason's face.

'That's Jack McCloud, the racehorse owner; he's worth a fortune. He must be going up to Ayr for the races.'

Jason put down his magazine and introduced himself to the actor, enjoying a convivial hour of conversation with him. Jason enquired about his acting career and was given a complete résumé of all his film and stage performances, as well as the female leads he'd starred with, but the actor only showed scant interest in Jason's history, preferring to talk about himself. Not that Jason wanted to be drawn on his wartime experiences by a stranger. As he sat chatting with Robert, he kept an eye open for the author of the cryptic note, who asked to meet him on the train.

Robert Ventura was proving a reasonable distraction to pass the time with until there was a disturbance at the far end of the carriage. Jason got to his feet to peer down the length of the carriage. Jason's curiosity drove him to investigate. He could see a man lying on his back in the aisle. It was Jack McCloud, his face fixed in an expression of shock. The little girl screamed and burst into tears. A steward rushed forward and knelt down alongside the prone racehorse owner, loosening the man's tie and collar. As a crowd gathered, the steward looked about him and called for Dr Stone, one of the passengers he knew to be aboard. The slim doctor with the greased back hair was beginning to back away. Only to be stopped by a second steward, who pushed past the father of the girl.

'Please doctor, I have a patient for you,' said the steward. The onlookers stared at the Doctor waiting for him to perform. Only he seemed reluctant to do so.

'Dr Stone, please, will you take a look at Mr McCloud?' repeated the steward.

The doctor's mouth opened and closed a couple of times without a sound, and then, somewhat tentatively, it seemed to Jason; he knelt down next to Mr McCloud. For a moment, he stared down at the man before making any attempt to feel for a pulse in McCloud's neck or wrist. The doctor chose the wrist, fumbled with it, then laid Mr McCloud's arm down and stood up.

'He's dead, a heart attack by the looks of it.' The doctor stepped away and took a seat, looking somewhat shocked himself. The first steward went to the bar and made a phone call before returning to the body. He and the second steward together lifted Jack McCloud back into his chair. As the first steward offered apologies to the rest of the passengers for the upsetting event, and reassured them that the manager was on his way. The second steward cleared away the dead man's breakfast dishes.

'Astonishing, quite astonishing,' said Robert Ventura over Jason's shoulder. Jason turned to face the actor.

'Yes, it's not what you expect to see on an overnight sleeper to Scotland.' A man Jason assumed to be the train manager brushed past them both and looked at the body in the chair. Two more train attendants quickly arrived and, using a tablecloth, covered the body.

'Ladies and Gentlemen, my name is Mr Dawson. I am the Train Manager, and on behalf of the London and Scotland Railway Service, I would like to apologise for this distressing occurrence. We will take care of everything. First, may I ask that this end of the carriage be cleared with respect to Mr McCloud? The train will be making an unscheduled stop at Bedford for the police to come aboard. I am sure you all understand that the police will need to investigate Mr McCloud's sudden demise. Until we reach Bedford, I will leave a steward with Mr McCloud until the police are able to remove him to a more appropriate location. In the meantime, I will have more tea and coffee served. Please excuse me, I have a lot to prepare before the police arrive. If you have any questions, please ask me now, or if you think of anything later, I'm sure Charles, your Senior Steward, will be able to answer your questions.'

'Er, excuse me, Mr Dawson, but will we be delayed very long at Bedford? Only my husband and I are going to attend our daughter's wedding tomorrow?' asked Mrs Robinson, the elderly lady with white hair.

'I'm sure the police will be waiting for us when we arrive and, as soon as they are aboard the train, we will be on our way again. Any delays will be minimal,' the train manager reassured her. With the main question that everyone wanted to know about out of the way, Mr Dawson was free to leave. The middle and front thirds of the saloon carriage had suddenly become very crowded. The three foreign gentlemen returned to the rear third, as did Dr Stone. Everyone else got as far away from the body as possible. Jason gave up his seat to Mrs Robinson. The steward brought round tea and coffee for everyone. The drinks seemed to be the signal for the chatter to break out, everyone speculating over what had caused Mr McCloud's death. Jason rejoined Robert Ventura. Mr Robinson stayed with his wife. More people came into the carriage, adding to the noise and confusion. The rumour of the dead man spreading amongst the train passengers faster than the staff could cope with. From where Jason stood, he could see the three foreign gentlemen. They had their heads together as though in conference and not wanting what they were saying to be overheard by others. They were no doubt discussing what had happened. Dr Stone sat at the far end of the bar with a large drink in his hand.

As Jason looked around, he suspected the author of his secretive message had not turned up, and he felt that they would be unlikely to do so with all this bother going on. He resigned himself to waiting and signalled to the steward to fetch him another cup of tea.

Jason was lifting the cup to his lips when something in his saucer caught his eye. Using his thumb to slip it aside, he replaced his teacup. Putting the cup and saucer on a small table next to Mr Ventura's chair, he held onto his discovery.

'Excuse me,' without further explanation to the actor, Jason left his seat and moved to the short corridor between the carriages. Unfolding the slip of paper, he read the message.

Come to compartment six. Montrose carriage. Firebird.

Jason slipped the paper into his pocket and returned to the saloon carriage. He called over the steward, who'd given him the tea with the message.

'Who gave you the note?' asked Jason.

The steward looked from side to side before answering. 'Another passenger, sir, and a good tip to ensure I said nothing about it to anyone else.'

'Umm,' said Jason, 'will a pound cover it?' Jason opened his wallet.

'I see nothing. I know nothing, sir.'

Jason slipped the pound note into the steward's hand. 'Make sure it stays that way, and there will be five more for you when we leave the train at Oban.'

'Very good, sir. You can trust Tom Potter.'

Chapter Four

Jason left the saloon carriage and headed towards the front of the train. The Montrose carriage was the second one back from the engine. When he arrived, the carriage corridor was empty. His senses tingled and the palms of his hands became moist in anticipation of the clandestine meeting with the nurse from over ten years ago. He checked off the numbers on the sleeper compartment doors. Cautiously, he made his way along to compartment six and knocked gently on the door. There was no answer. He knocked again, a little harder this time. Using the codeword from the note, in a hushed voice he said, 'it's Firebird.' There was the sound of movement from inside the compartment. Someone fumbled with the lock on the door, and then it opened just a crack. An eye appeared, looking out from between the door and frame.

Jason repeated his code word. 'Firebird?'

The door swung back quickly, and Jason stepped inside. It was shut just as quickly behind him and relocked. The figure of a beautiful young woman, his goddess from the saloon carriage, faced him as she stood with her back to the locked door. Her eyes boring into his, searching his soul.

'What's going on? Who are you?' asked Jason. 'How do you know about Firebird? Where is Nurse Xenia? What has happened to her?'

The young woman didn't respond. Instead, she continued to look him up and down.

'Well?' demanded Jason.

She eased away from the door and crossed to the bed, and sat down.

'The nurse you knew in France, the one who told you the tales of the Firebird, and all the other folktales from Russia, was my mother,' said the young woman in perfect English, with a soft French accent. 'Please, Mr Parva, sit down and let me explain.'

Jason took a seat by the carriage window.

'You already know my mother was a Russian and married to a French Nobleman. What you didn't know then was that she was a Romanov. Her father was the brother of Tsar Nicholas II.' The young woman waited for Jason to comprehend what she had just told him.

'But what has all that got to do with me?' asked Jason.

'While you were in the hospital, you often spoke together. My mother told me she liked you. You told her you had joined the Royal Flying Corp while still underage, thinking the war would be a grand adventure. She told me that once you were out of danger and recovering, how you would talk together late into the night. You would tell her about your dreams for the future and ask her about my father and me. She enjoyed your talks together and how, when you were feeling very low, you would ask her to repeat the tale of the Firebird.'

'Yes, yes, I know all this, but why are you here and not her? Why have you brought me here? Why is being a Romanov important? You no longer live in Russia,' asked Jason.

'My name is Alexandra Natalya Maria Anastasia, niece of Tsar Nicholas II, and I have the honour of being next in line to the throne of the Russian Empire, but you may call me Anna.'

Jason found himself speechless, trying to decide if the young woman was mad or just fantasising about her past.

'Many of my relatives were trapped in Russia during the 1917 revolution,' she continued. 'They were arrested and have never been heard from again. However, my mother was taken to France by her parents when the 1905 uprising happened. To keep her safe, they left her there in case there was more trouble to come. They gave her to a distant relative who had married a Frenchman, so she became French and was taught to be like any other well-to-do French woman. My mother's guardians always reminded her of her parents, and of her royal bloodline, and her connection to Tsar Nicholas. But my mother hid that history from me, hoping that it would protect me. The only hint I had of a possible Russian connection was her name, Xenia. I didn't know the full story of my lineage until very recently.'

'So why am I here? Why are you here?' Persisted Jason.

'There is more to tell. I am on the run. Over the past few months, prominent people of Russian descent, living in France, have been targeted and murdered. One businessman was killed by a speeding car whilst crossing the road in Paris just the other day. The driver was never found. A Russian woman was poisoned in Lyon two weeks ago. At first, I didn't see the connection, not until one evening. I was alone in my flat when there was a knock on the door. When I answered it, I found an old man with a package. He asked my name and then handed me the package with instructions to read the contents carefully and then to leave Paris as soon as possible. I asked him to come in and explain. He said no at first, but I insisted, and he changed his mind. Over the next hour, he told me his name was Albert Stopford and explained my family's links to the Tsar, and about the agents of the OGPU, the Russian Secret Police Organisation. They have been sent to Europe to eliminate all remaining members of the Romanov family who had escaped from Russia during the revolution. The communists want to prevent the Romanov family from raising resistance against the new Bolshevik government. Comrade Stalin fears the rise of Fascism, which is becoming popular in Europe. He believes any surviving members of the Romanov family might try using that political force to start another revolution in Russia. Mr Stopford advised me to leave France and go into hiding. After some thought, I decided the remote parts of Scotland would make a good place to hide, and that's when I thought of you, the heroic fighter pilot my mother talked so much about.'

Jason sat in silence, thinking about the story he'd been told.

'How is your mother? Why isn't she here with you?'

'She died of cancer. It came upon her soon after the war ended.'

'I'm sorry; I would have liked to have met her once more. Why didn't you just go to the police?'

Anna looked at him, aghast. 'Where have you been hiding? These days there are just as many Communists in France as there are Republicans. France could be on the brink of a communist uprising.'

'I've been living in Kenya. I had a coffee plantation there until...well. I arrived home a few days ago; your letter was lucky to find me there. Had the letter been sent to Kenya, it would have been weeks before it found its way to England. Well, I suppose if I am going to help you, you had better tell me everything. Start by reminding me of your name.'

The young woman laughed. 'My real name is Alexandra Natalya Maria Anastasia, but my French mother just called me Anna.'

'Well, you had better call me Jason. Now that we have been properly introduced, you'd better continue.'

Anna took a deep breath and then made herself more comfortable on the bed.

'According to Albert Stopford, Russia's troubles started during the Great War. Tsar Nicholas was a very religious man and, one day whilst at prayer, he saw a vision. It told him he must lead his people to a glorious future. The Tsar assumed the vision had meant him to lead his armies fighting on the eastern front during the Great War. So, he left Russia and his family to take command of his Imperial Army fighting the Germans. Then one night, while he was at the eastern front, he had another premonition; one that foretold of a great disaster that would befall the Romanov family. The vision disturbed him so much that he wrote several letters explain the vision and sent them to all the members of the royal family. The vision of doom affected him so deeply that he also wrote a document of inheritance and a letter of explanation, adding to them a personal family jewel that he had given to his wife. All three items were given to Albert Stopford for safekeeping, with the instructions to pass them on to the new owner when the time was right. The Tsar trusted Albert. They were good friends.

Albert explained to me how he once worked for British Intelligence. How he set up his own antiques businesses in Paris and London to hide his real work for the Intelligence service. Then he set about becoming friends with the rich and famous. He said it was through his antique business that he got to know and love jewels made by Faberge and Cartier. It was while buying and reselling these jewels that he first came into contact with the Russian aristocracy and, later, how he became friends with Tsar Nicholas. Albert is getting old now, and so he passed the Tsar's letter and Firebird Jewel on to me as the rightful heir to the Russian throne. I had no idea about being heir to the Russian throne until Albert gave me these documents. My mother kept that part of my past a secret. Albert would not have come to me so soon, except he knew he was dying. He had no choice but to pass on the documents to me, or risk them falling into the wrong hands!'

Anna retrieved a small case from the wardrobe and placed it on the bed. Opening her jewellery case, she removed a tray of rings from inside. Below the tray lay two documents, each with a large blood-red seal on the top of it into which had been impressed a family crest. The wax seals were attached by two pale blue ribbons to the bottom of each document. Anna reverently lifted the first document from the box. This is the letter the Tsar wrote to my mother, explaining about the document, and this one,' she removed the second, larger document from the box, 'is the inheritance document.' She laid the thick parchment on the bed to unfold it. Once opened, Jason could see the same crest at the top of the document that was also impressed into the seal, but this time, the crest was embossed and illuminated. He looked over the page, captivated by its decoration and formality; it was clearly a document of some importance.

'What does it say?' he asked.

'It is written by Tsar Nicholas II, in his own hand. It explains to the Romanov family who the owner of this document is, and the power it gives to its owner. The document also mentions the Romanov family Firebird jewel, made by Faberge. The jewel must be kept with the document and letter at all times. The papers and the jewel signify the formal handing over of the Russian Empire into the hands of the bearer of the document. The Tsar had the Firebird Jewel made for his wife, Alexandra, and it authenticates the documents and the owner of them as the legitimate heir to the throne of Russia. The papers are not only signed by the Tsar; they are witnessed by his senior ministers and members of the family. The bearer of this letter, and the document, coupled with the Firebird jewel, signify the holder as the closest living relative to Tsar Nicholas. It was Albert Stopford's job to keep them safe and deliver them to the next heir. It is my destiny to own them and, it would seem, it is your destiny to protect them, and me.'

She pulled the Firebird jewel from the bottom of her jewellery box and handed it to Jason. It resembled a bird about to rise into the air and take flight. Only, this precious jewel was made of platinum and inlaid with hundreds of small diamonds of different colours. The head and breast were made from yellow diamonds. The wings, the body and the tail were a mixture of red, purple and yellow semi-precious stones. The bird's crest and wing tips were encrusted with brilliant white diamonds. In the light, it sparkled as though a flame had been lit inside the heart of the jewel.

Anna waited a moment to watch Jason's reaction. He examined the jewel. The craftsmanship was exquisite, but he felt the jewel to be too gaudy, heavy and opulent. On the reverse of the brooch, impressed into the platinum mount, was the Faberge jeweller's mark and, next to it, the crest of the Romanov family. Jason returned the jewel to Anna and then picked up the letter. On opening it, he could see the Romanov family crest at the top of the page, and a large red wax seal at the bottom, but the writing was in Cyrillic, which he could not read.

Anna interrupted his thoughts. 'After my mother died, I went to live and work in Paris. That was where Albert found me. I paid little heed to his warning until I noticed that my flat was being watched and I was being followed. At first, I thought I was just being silly until one night, through my bedroom window, I caught sight of two men watching my flat. Every night for a week, they returned to the same place to stare at the front of my building. When I heard of more and more Russians dying in unusual circumstances, I wrote to you, asking for your help, and made plans to come to England. Somehow, the OGPU, have learned about my inheritance, the letter and the jewel. They are trying to find and kill me.'

'But surely, this is a job for the French police. They can't all be communists.'

'If I bring the police in, my identity will be leaked to the Russian Secret Police. Albert Stopford knew this. That is why he advised me to go into hiding.'

'But why did you contact me? I know nothing about dealing with things like this.'

'My mother told me stories of the brave English pilot who, while recovering from horrific injuries during the war, would ask her to tell him folk tales from her homeland, and that his favourite tale was the one of the Firebird. As you can see, the jewel is in the style of a Firebird. Your friendship with my mother, your love of the Firebird tale, it can only mean one thing - it has always been your destiny to help me. Long before you knew my mother or of me; you were chosen to help us. Oh, don't you understand? My mother liked and trusted you for a reason. She often spoke to me about you when we were alone together. She knew. She felt sure that if I ever needed help in the future, that you would be the one person I could trust more than any other.'

Jason fell silent again for a moment. 'Your mother saved my life during those terrible days. There were times when I had given up. I couldn't see the point in trying to stay in a world that was doing its best to tear itself apart, but she showed me kindness and that the love of life could survive in the darkest of places. I was lucky to have met her. She, more than anyone, gave me the will to live. But, by the time I had recovered enough to fly again, the war was over.'

He fell silent once again remembering back to those weeks in the hospital and the nurse who meant so much to him.

'I owe your mother a great debt. It was only with your mother's encouragement, help, and bloody-mindedness that I survived. The doctors were too busy to care about one airman. She would sit with me during the night until I fell asleep, even though she would have to be on duty again early in the morning. Later, when I was out of danger, I was transferred to a hospital in England, and I never saw or heard from her again, but she has rarely been out of my thoughts. I wish now that I had tried to contact her and thank her for what she did for me, but I didn't know how to find her.'

'She would have liked that. To have seen you once more before she died. It happened so quickly, and there was nothing the doctors could do for her.' Tears pricked at the corner of Anna's eyes before she could wipe them away with a handkerchief.

'I'm sorry, she deserved better than that. She gave hope and comfort to so many, not just me.'

With the death of his own mother and Celia, he now knew the three women who had played the most significant roles in his life had gone forever. His leg began to play up, so he got to his feet and paced the floor a couple of times.

'Are you alright?' asked Anna.

'Yes. I'll be fine in a minute.' He felt very alone and extremely tired for a man of only thirty-two years of age. He reminded himself that he had fought in the war, had nearly been killed in two air crashes, bought and sold a coffee plantation in Africa, and was now on a train to Scotland with a Russian Princess who was being chased by the Russian Secret Police. He had a right to feel tired.

'Your mother showed me kindness when everyone else was too busy to spend time with a flyer on the verge of death. Without her, I would have given up and died in France. I came because I thought it was Nurse Xenia who needed me, because of the debt I owe her.'

He paused as he looked into Anna's eyes. He had no choice. Anna was asking for his help. What else could he to do but say, yes?

'If I'm going to help you, do I call you your majesty or your highness?' Jason gave her a warm smile. She laughed and grasped his hands in hers, letting out a sigh of relief.

'I knew I was right to trust you. Very well, my first royal command is that you call me Anna. Anna Moreau is my adopted French name.'

'Jason Parva, failed pilot and failed coffee planter, at your service.' The couple stared at one another.

'What do we do now?' asked Anna.

'Well, I suppose you had better tell me your plans for Scotland and if you think you were followed onto the train.'

'I booked a ticket to Scotland because of its remoteness, and, I hope, far enough away from Paris for me to be safe. I plan to book into a small hotel and stay there until I can find a place to rent for a few weeks or months. And no, I don't know if anyone followed me onto the train. I didn't even know what you looked like. Once the train left the station, I bribed the steward to give a note to Jason Parva. I didn't know it was you when you were sitting opposite me in the saloon carriage.'

'Who is the little girl?' asked Jason.

'Oh, she belongs to another passenger. He asked me if I would take her for a lemonade while he unpacked and prepared their compartment. She seemed nice enough, and I thought she might help with my disguise.'

'Clever,' said Jason. 'I took the precaution of contacting Thomas Cook before I left home. I have arranged the hire of a cottage outside Oban for a few days, along with the use of a car. I thought somewhere quiet and out of the way would be a useful place for Nurse Xenia and I to hide out. But, I didn't quite realise how much trouble you were in. Well, at least it is booked in my name and not yours. I suggest you use the cottage, and I will stay at the local hotel, that way, I will be able to spot anyone suspicious who comes looking for you.'

'What made you think of doing that?' asked Anna.

'I was expecting to meet your mother and, as the message I received was a cryptic one, I guessed she was in some kind of trouble. If she'd simply wanted to visit me and tell me her troubles, she would have come to my house. So, as I thought she was on the train to Oban for a reason, I made bookings for us to stay near Oban,' said Jason, somewhat smugly.

'What do we do now? We can't stay locked in here for twenty-four hours. After all, I am a Tsarina, and I have my reputation to think about.'

'You are also a very wealthy woman. You could go anywhere you like in the world to hide.'

'No I can't. I may have this jewel and the papers, but I spent most of my savings on this trip to England. Until I am able to claim my inheritance in full, I have very little money left.'

'I suppose you're right. But before we go, I have something else to tell you. Did you know a man has died on the train?' asked Jason.

Anna looked shocked. 'Was he French?'

'No, he was a Scottish racehorse owner. From the size of him, he probably weighed as much as one of his racehorses. A doctor aboard the train attended to him. He said Mr McCloud had a heart attack,' replied Jason.

'Oh, that's terrible,' responded Anna.

'The train is going to have to make an unscheduled stop at Bedford for the police to come aboard. They have to conduct an investigation, but I imagine they will accept the doctor's diagnosis, and we will be on our way again fairly quickly.'

As if to confirm what Jason had just said, they felt the train begin to slow. The train halted at Bedford Station and, through the window of Anna's compartment, they watched two uniformed policemen and two other men, whom they assumed to be detectives, walk towards the saloon carriage.

'I'm starving,' announced Anna. 'I missed breakfast.'

'Come along, I'll treat you to tea and a toasted teacake.'

'Do you think it is safe?' asked Anna.

'If there is anyone on the train who wanted to harm you, they would have done so while you were alone in your compartment. Come on, no one is going to hurt you in front of witnesses and a train full of policemen. Don't leave the papers in your compartment while we are not here. Put them in your handbag and keep them with you all the time.'

Reassured by Jason, she did as instructed. They returned to the saloon car just in time to see two men in black suits and ties carry what could only be Mr McCloud from the train on a stretcher. Further down, in the centre of the carriage, stood two detectives with the two uniformed policemen.

'Very well, Ladies and Gentlemen. After we have taken statements from everyone, the train will be allowed to continue on its way. So the sooner we get this over with, the sooner you can continue with your holidays,' announced the detective in the brown Gabardine Mackintosh.

'My name is Inspector Barrows, Sergeant Duckworth here and the two constables will take your names and addresses along with your statements.'

A murmur of protest and dissatisfaction rippled around the carriage at the announcement of the prolonged delay. The policemen separated, notebooks at the ready, and that was when Anna spotted the three foreign men seated in the corner. She stared at them, and they stared back at her.

'We have to leave; it's them; they are the ones who are after me.' Anna turned to leave the carriage, only to be stopped by Inspector Barrows.

'Excuse me, Miss, you will have to stay until you have given your statement.'

Anna would have ignored him and tried to make her escape but for the entrance of a steward who blocked her escape path. Jason grabbed her by the arm and drew her back.

'Wait, we can use this to our advantage,' Jason whispered to her. Anna paused, looking at Jason questioningly.

Taking a deep breath and pulling Anna closer to him, Jason addressed the Inspector, 'May we speak to you in private? It is very important.'

'Would it have anything to do with Mr McCloud, sir?'

'No, err, no, I shouldn't think so, it's just that...' Jason didn't get the chance to finish the sentence.

'Then I'm afraid it will have to wait until after you have given your statements, sir. Please take a seat and be patient,' insisted the Inspector. He stepped forward, forcing Jason and Anna to step back towards two empty chairs.

'Inspector,' protested Anna, but it was too late, the policeman had turned away to speak to Lord and Lady Holderness. The policemen used the centre section of the carriage to conduct their interviews, so statements could be given in relative privacy. With painful slowness, the police officers made their way through the passengers, enquiring who was present when Mr McCloud collapsed, and what they had seen. They asked if anyone had threatened Mr McCloud, or had they known him before his demise. Time dragged on. Jason held Anna back, ensuring they were left until the last to give their statements. While they waited, Anna kept looking towards the carriage exit, hoping for a chance to escape, but the steward stayed in front of the door, blocking her escape route.

Finally, Jason and Anna were taken to be interviewed by the Inspector. They were the only three people left in that part of the carriage.

'Now sir, Miss, may I have your full names and addresses please,' requested the Inspector.

'Listen, Inspector,' blurted out Jason, 'We are in danger, or I should say Anna here is in great danger.'

'At the moment, sir, the only thing you are in danger of is incurring my lack of patience by not answering my question.'

'My name is Flight Lieutenant Jason Parva, Retired, Parva Hall, Nafferton, East Yorkshire. Now, Inspector, it is important that you listen to what we have to say.'

'And you, Miss, what is your name and address?' asked the Inspector, ignoring Jason.

Anna placed a hand on Jason's arm to quieten him. 'My name, Inspector, is Anna Moreau. I am a French citizen on holiday in England and my address is apartment twelve, Rue Popincourt, Paris 11.'

'Passport please, Miss.' Anna retrieved her passport from her handbag and slipped it across the table to the Inspector.

'Thank you, Miss. Now, in your own words, tell me what you saw happen to Mr McCloud?' The Inspector flicked through the pages of Anna's passport.

'I saw nothing, Inspector. I was in my overnight compartment at the time Mr McCloud collapsed.'

The Inspector made a note in his book and returned Anna's passport. 'And you, sir, what did you see?'

'I was sitting over there,' said Jason, indicating the armchair he had been seated in. I saw nothing until after Mr McCloud had collapsed and the fuss started. There is a doctor on board the train, and he examined the body.'

'Yes, sir, we have spoken to... err, Dr Stone, thank you.' The Inspector began to rise from his seat.

'Inspector,' insisted Jason, 'Miss Moreau is in danger.'

Inspector Barrows sat back down, 'from whom, sir, and why?'

Jason leaned forward and lowered his voice. 'She is really Russian nobility, and there are Russian agents after her.'

'Really, sir,' the Inspector looked from one to the other thinking about his response.

'Has anyone tried to harm Miss Moreau while you have been on the train?'

'No Inspector.'

'Has anyone threatened Miss Moreau while you have been on the train?'

'No Inspector.'

'Do you know the names of the people you say are after Miss Moreau?'

'No Inspector, but Miss Moreau believes those three foreign gentlemen who were sat over there are Russian agents and are going to kill her.'

'Umm really! Mr Parva, we have examined the passports of the three gentlemen in question, and they are Swedish tourists on holiday. So unless you have some hard evidence to the contrary, stop wasting my time. Give your story to the police in Oban; they will no doubt be glad of the excitement.'

Before Jason could protest further, the Inspector left the table and then the train, followed by his police colleagues.

'Looks like we are on our own,' said Jason.

They returned to the rear section of the carriage. Some of the other passengers had taken the opportunity to stretch their legs on the station platform after giving their statements. The steward, who had been guarding the door, came over and enquired if they would like tea or coffee. Anna and Jason declined the offer but, as the steward turned to leave, Jason caught sight of a small automatic pistol in the rear waistband of his trousers. The steward adjusted his tunic as he walked away, and the gun disappeared from sight. Jason stiffened in his seat.

'We have to get off the train,' he whispered to Anna.

Jason led Anna back to her sleeping compartment and locked the door behind them.

'One of the stewards has a gun; it must be him who is after you, just waiting for the train to reach some remote spot where he can shoot you, and then throw your body off the train,' declared Jason.

'What! Why didn't the police see it?' said Anna in alarm.

'I don't know. Pack a few essential things into a small bag, and we'll make a run for it before everyone gets back on the train. I'm going to get my stuff, stay here and lock the door until I return.'

Jason rushed along the carriage corridor to the next car and his own compartment. Drawing down the window blind, he then grabbed his Gladstone bag, emptying the contents onto his bed. His old service revolver tumbled out of the bag along with box of bullets. He checked the gun. Repacking the bag with casual clothes, he placed the revolver on the top and closed it. As he reached the carriage corridor, he heard a whistle blow and, a couple of seconds later, he felt the train pull away from the station.

'Oh damn!'

He tapped lightly on Anna's door and in a hushed voice he added, 'Firebird.' Anna opened the door, and Jason slipped inside.

'What do we do now?' hissed Anna.

'Have you got a bag packed?'

'Yes.'

'Right, I will leave my bag here, then we'll go to the dining car and have lunch. We can ask the train manager what time he expects the train to arrive in Oban. While we eat, we can make plans on how to get off the train before it reaches Scotland. It must make another stop for water or something. I don't think our assassin will strike so soon after departing Bedford. Another body on the train would raise too much alarm and the police would arrest everyone on board and take them in for questioning until they got to the bottom of what was going on. No, we have to stop panicking and start thinking, and I usually do that best when I'm not hungry.'

Chapter Five

At a table for two in the dining car, Jason ordered a warm salmon and potato salad; Anna only wanted a chicken sandwich, though they shared a bottle of Sauvignon Blanc with Jason. The carriage had been empty when they entered, but they were soon followed by Lord and Lady Holderness, who now seemed to be back on good terms with each other. The three foreign gentlemen came in next. Jason eyed suspiciously as they brushed past his table. None of the new arrivals were seated close to Jason and Anna, though the foreign gentlemen kelp glancing toward Jason and Anne's table and talking in low voices. Anna and Jason were just about to order coffee when the train manager arrived and made an announcement.

'I'm sorry to interrupt your lunch, but I have to inform you all that due to being delayed at Bedford, the train has missed its allotted slot along the route to Scotland. So, consequently, there will be a delay in our arrival at Oban. So as not to disrupt the entire main rail network, we are being diverted onto a series of branch lines. The company is deeply sorry for this inconvenience and hope that by way of recompense you will accept our apologies and the hospitality of the train at no extra expense.' The worried look on his face gave Jason the impression that many of the passengers had not been happy with the news he was breaking to them.

'Thank you, Mr Dawson. That will be fine. We are in no hurry,' responded Jason.

'It would seem Mr McCloud has done us a favour,' said Anna.

'Yes, if the train has to keep stopping, it will give us a chance to get off. But it also means that an assassin will have more opportunities to carry out his mission to kill you and make his escape before anyone finds your body.'

'Jason!' said Anna, looking visibly shocked.

Jason and Anna finished their coffee and returned to the saloon carriage. The train continued its journey, but was noticeably slower than it had been prior to arriving at Bedford. The slow travelling speed became irritating. After passing through a small village station, the train finally came to a halt in the middle of nowhere. They were surrounded by fields. The delay brought murmurs of protest and grumbles from the other passengers. Anna began to get fretful, remembering Jason's warning about the assassin having more of an opportunity to succeed in killing her and escape while the train was travelling slowly.

She leaned across to get closer and to whisper to Jason, 'We can't just sit here and wait for him to strike. We have to do something.'

'Well, we can't get off here. We'd be on foot in the middle of God knows where,' Jason whispered back to her. A few seconds later, the steward Jason had seen earlier with the gun, passed by, heading towards the bar.

'I have an idea. I want him to know, that I know, he has a gun. I want to force his hand; make him react and then get him arrested.'

'Are you sure you? You may get hurt. Let's just tell the police he has a gun.' said Anna. Jason rose from his seat, indicating for Anna to stay seated. The train made a sudden jerk forwards, causing him to stagger and catch hold of the seats on either side of him to steady himself. As the train picked up speed, he pursued the steward with the gun to the bar. Jason stopped, and with one hand holding onto the bar, he waited for the steward who was collecting an order of drinks.

'I'll be with you in a moment, sir,' said the barman. Jason didn't respond; he continued to give the steward his full attention. As the steward stepped away from the bar, Jason spoke to him in a low voice.

'Nice day to go shooting, wouldn't you say?'

The steward paused only for a second, but didn't look at Jason before continuing on his way. Jason followed him through the carriage and back into the dining car, keeping close on his heels. The steward delivered the drinks to Lord and Lady Holderness. Jason watched the steward from two tables' distance, and after serving the drinks, the steward returned to the saloon car. Jason stepped aside to let him pass and then followed him, staying three steps behind. Entering the saloon car, the steward continued past the bar, depositing his tray as he went. The steward left the carriage, heading towards the back of the train, with Jason close behind him.

Constantly looking back over his shoulder, the steward passed through the Inverness sleeper, the Kenmure sleeper, never stopping, keeping a steady pace as he continued on. The train slowed a little as it approached Woburn Sands with its large goods yards. The steward, followed by Jason, made his way through the Stirling sleeper. The train continued to slow on its approach to the hamlet station. The steward went through the door at the end of the carriage and entered the luggage car.

Now I've got you. Unless the train stops, you have nowhere else to escape to. Jason hesitated before entering the last carriage, expecting an attack from the steward as he opened the door. Holding his walking stick like a club, he took hold of the door handle, turning it slowly until he felt the door come free of the strike plate. He gave the door a push, watching for movement from inside as it swung open. Inside the luggage car, there was no electric lighting. The only illumination came courtesy of four small windows set into the central loading doors on either side of the carriage. The door swung back and was about to close, when Jason gave the door a prod with his stick. It swung back smoothly on its well greased hinges, slamming against the interior wall. The steward wasn't hiding there. With no plush panelling in this carriage, the noise from the carriages wheels as they rolled over the tracks seemed excessively loud and foreboding.

Jason stepped through into the cluttered interior, his walking stick held aloft, ready to strike. Luggage trunks, suits cases, wooden boxes and crates were stacked and strapped against the walls. A heap of stuffed sacks had been tossed into a corner at the far end of the carriage. Two bicycles stood in the opposite corner, where they had been tied to the wall slats, but there was no sign of the steward.

'Come out. You can't escape,' shouted Jason. A noise made Jason step quickly to the side and into the shadows. A shot rang out, and a bullet slammed into the doorframe where Jason had been standing only a second before. Jason now knew the location of the steward. He was hiding behind some crates about fifteen feet in front of him. Jason crossed to the other side of the carriage; as Jason broke from the shadows another shot rang out. The train ran through a cutting, its whistle screaming loudly. What meagre light had been coming through the windows faded away. Suddenly, the train jerked forward as it picked up speed again. Ahead of him, Jason heard luggage dislodged, followed by a groan of pain. Something hard, heavy, and metallic hit the floor of the carriage and then slide across the floor to hit the wall. Jason leapt from his hiding place, aiming towards the sound of the groaning, hoping to land on top of the steward as he searched for his gun. Unfortunately, Jason only managed to grab the steward by the legs. The steward rolled over, trying to wriggle free, but Jason held him fast. With the steward beating with his fists down on Jason's back, Jason struggled to his knees and, with one great effort, he lurched forward. He was on top of the steward, the two wrestling together, each trying to gain the advantage.

A blow taken across the back of the head caused Jason to black out. When he came to, Anna was by his side, patting him gently on the cheek. The train had stopped and, as Jason regained his senses, he asked Anna what had happened.

'I don't know. You seemed to be gone for a long time. The train pulled into this station, and you didn't come back, so I came looking for you. I saw that the door to the luggage van was open. When I looked inside I found you lying here. I thought you were dead, before I heard you groaning.'

'Did you see the steward?' asked Jason as he rubbed the back of his head.

'No, no one. The steward didn't come back to the saloon car.' She helped Jason to his feet and found his walking stick for him. Leaning against a crate, he straightened his clothing, then together they returned to the saloon car.

Lord and Lady Holderness were sitting together on the sofa, each reading a magazine. Jason flopped into his familiar chair and Anna sat in the one next to his. A new steward came over and, as he did so, Jason gave him a mistrustful look.

'May I get you some refreshment, sir?'

'What happened to the other steward?' asked Jason.

'I don't know, sir. He was new, sir. He disappeared a little while ago and hasn't come back.'

'Two brandy's with soda, please,' responded Jason.

He made himself comfortable, rubbing the back of his painful head while the steward went to fetch their drinks.

'Didn't you notice anyone follow me down to the luggage van?' asked Jason.

'No. After you left me, Lord and Lady, what's it, came through from the dining car. I heard her say that she needed a cardigan from their compartment. His Lordship left to fetch it for her. He was gone a few minutes before returning with a cardigan. I waited for a little while, then went to look for you. That's when I found you unconscious on the floor,' answered Anna. The drinks arrived, and Jason took a sip.

'Well, unless it was you who hit me, we know now there are at least two people working together on this train to get you. And then there are those three strange men you said you'd seen before. One of them told me they are from Sweden. I heard them talking together. They weren't speaking Swedish when I heard them talking. It sounded more like an eastern Slavic language. Did any of those characters pass through the carriage while I was following the steward with the gun?' asked Jason.

'No, I didn't see them. They may have a compartment to the front of the train. I'm sure they are the real assassins. The steward must be working with them.'

Jason looked out of the window. 'Where are we?'

'Bletchley,' replied Anna. 'I saw the station sign as we went past it.' The train manager entered the carriage.

'Ladies and Gentlemen, we will only be delayed for a couple of minutes. We have to wait until a goods train clears the points up ahead, then we will be on our way again.'

As the Oban train waited at Bletchley Station, Jason watched people on the platform pacing to and fro impatiently waiting for their own train to arrive. One of the men on the platform was standing next to Jason's window. He was reading a newspaper. On the front page was a photograph of Anna with the caption, 'Reward offered for information on the whereabouts of a missing heiress.' Jason nudged Anna and indicated to the newspaper.

'It must be a later edition,' said Jason. Their train started to move on again, and the man with the newspaper was left behind.

'Someone must have slipped your story to the press, hoping that the publicity will help track you down,' said Jason in a whisper.

'What are we going to do?' asked Anna.

'Nothing yet. As long as the train doesn't make another stop for passengers to get off and stretch their legs, I don't think there is much chance of anyone on this train finding out who you are. The chap I followed into the luggage van has either gone into hiding or got off the train. But I wish I seen the person who hit me? They are the danger now.'

'Do you think we should go back to my compartment and stay out of sight?' asked Anna. 'Sitting here, I feel like everyone is watching me.'

'No. We'll go back to my compartment. There is something there I need to collect,' said Jason firmly, getting to his feet.

Back in his compartment, Jason opened his Gladstone bag and retrieved his service revolver. 'I won't be caught unprepared next time.' He tucked the revolver into the waistband of his trousers and re-buttoned his jacket.

'We'll get off the train at the next stop. We will still go up to Oban. As you say, it's out of the way but, if we leave the train early, anyone looking for you will think we have abandoned the idea of going to Scotland and hopefully stay local. Are the documents and the Firebird Jewel still safe?'

Anna opened her handbag to show him they were still there.

'Good.' Jason closed his own bag and placed it in the corner of his compartment out of the way.

'If we are getting off the train, I have to go back to my sleeper and pack what I will need on our journey to Scotland,' said Anna, getting to her feet.

'No,' said Jason. 'Carrying unnecessary luggage will slow us down. Once we are free of the train, we'll buy what we need on our way North. If you go back to your compartment now, and the people who are after you see you with a suitcase, it will give away our plan to leave the train. It's far better we stay here and wait for the train to stop and then get off.'

As they waited, Jason and Anna talked about their lives leading up to this point in time. Anna's had been a life of happiness living on a small family-run vineyard with her adopted family. Though she could not remember her real father, she had been told about him and why she had been given away. As she grew older, her real mother would come to the vineyard to see her for a couple of weeks each year. Anna grew to like her mother a great deal and looked forward to her visits. So, it came as a shock when one year Anna's mother failed to arrive. Anna discovered that her mother was dying of cancer, so she travelled to Paris to see her for one last time.

That was when she discovered her mother had left her some money. Anna didn't want to return to the vineyard, so she stayed in Paris after her mother's death, rented an apartment and got a job as a secretary. It was only when Albert Stopford had brought her the documents and the Firebird Jewel that the enormity of her heritage and her ancestry was explained to her.

Jason told Anna about his time growing up in Nafferton before going to Oxford University. How a fellow student had taken him to watch a demonstration flight of a new type of aeroplane. It had fascinated Jason, and he had vowed to learn to fly as soon as he could. When the war started, he cut short his education and joined the Royal Flying Corps as a mechanic and eventually became a pilot. He told Anna about his brother, and how over the generations it had become a tradition for one son in the family to become a doctor or surgeon, and that as his brother had taken that role, he had been able to indulge his liking for all things mechanical.

As they talked, the train had made its way into the Midlands, and it was only when the train began to slow down on its approach to Towcester, that they both looked out of the window.

'Our stop, I think,' said Jason. The train slowed to a crawl as it drew closer to the station. 'I don't think it's going to stop,' said Anna.

Travelling at a snail's pace, the train continued through the station to stop at a signal held aloft by the signalman leaning out of the signal box. The train halted, then began reversing back towards the station platform.

85

'That's lucky,' said Jason, as the train backed slowly along the edge of the platform. That was when they spotted police officers with guns coming out of the station waiting room. As Jason and Ann's carriage passed the WH Smith newsstand, the headline on the poster advertisement read 'Jason Parva Wanted in connection with the death of a man in Paris, and the abduction of a French heiress.'

'I don't understand what is happing,' said Jason.

'I do,' said Anna. 'Communist politicians in France will have contacted the English police and told them a lie about one of the deaths in Paris and that I have been abducted. The police now think you are a murderer and a kidnapper. We have to get off the train and hide until we can find someone to help us sort this out.'

'We'll get off now before the train stops and the police get onboard,' said Jason.

Without giving Anna time to think or protest, Jason picked up his Gladstone bag and went to the door. Anna snatched up her handbag. He opened the door cautiously and looked outside. The corridor was empty, so taking Anna by the hand, they quickly made their way to the end of the carriage and the exit from the carriage. Jason dropped the door window and grabbed the handle on the outside to unlatch the door. The door swung open; the train had almost come to a stop; Jason jumped down to the trackside, stumbled and rolled in the dirt as pain shot through his leg. Anna hesitated for only a second when she saw Jason fall, then followed him. She, too, stumbled and fell, but was the first one to get to their feet.

Grabbing her handbag, she found Jason's walking stick and helped him to his feet. People on the platform opposite watched in amazement as Jason and Anna stumbled across the tracks to the platform on the opposite side of the station. The scream of a train whistle turned their blood cold as a second train approached the station. As Anna attempted to help Jason up onto the platform, two men ran forward, one dragged Jason onto the platform while the other helped Anna to safety, only seconds before the goods train chuffed and clattered over the tracks where they had been.

A man in a railway uniform came up firing questions at them, demanding to know why they had jumped from the train. Jason hesitated a moment, then said in a fake American accent.

'Sorry fella, back home we just step down off the train when it pulls into a station. We don't have any of this fancy platform business.'

Jason gave the man a ten-shilling note, took Anna by the hand, and hobbled towards the station exit. He paused for a moment to look over his shoulder. He could see the police officers making their way through the train as it waited at the opposite platform. It wouldn't be long before they found the open carriage door and would chase after them.

Out on the street, Jason stopped for a rest and rubbing his leg.

'I can't run. I need to rest my leg.'

Anna looked around for a place to hide but spotted a taxi waiting at the kerb a little further up the road. She gave the driver a wave. He started the engine, and drew up alongside them, before hopping out and opening the rear door.

'Where to, Miss?' he asked politely.

'Into town, please; to a doctor. My friend has had a fall,' instructed Anna.

'Very good, Miss. I know just the chap. I hope your young man here is going to be all right.'

With Jason and Anna safely seated in the back of his taxi, the car sedately cruised the half-mile into Towcester. The driver pulled to a stop outside the town hall in the market square.

'You'll find Doctor Hartwell just across the way there,' said the taxi driver, indicating a building on the opposite side of the road.

As Anna helped Jason from the back seat, another man approached the taxi and spoke to the driver.

'The racecourse, Driver, as quick as you can please,' ordered the newcomer.

While Jason paid the driver, the new passenger got in the back of the taxi.

Once across the street, Jason passed Anna his service revolver and asked her to hide it in her bag. He knocked on the door to the doctor's surgery. It was answered by an elderly woman with grey hair held up in a bun. She was dressed in a black top and a long black skirt. 'Yes?'

'We would like to see Doctor Hartwell, please. My friend here has had a bit of an accident,' said Anna.

'Do you have an appointment?' asked the woman.

'No,' said Anna meekly, 'Do we need one?'

'It's always best to make an appointment first,' insisted the woman with a scowl.

A voice from inside called out, 'Who is at the door, Mrs Standish?'

'Two strangers without an appointment wanting to see the doctor,' she replied. She'd no sooner stopped speaking when a man approximately the same age as Jason came to the door.

'Please, come in, I am Doctor Hartwell.'

Jason and Anna followed the doctor to his consulting room, which was off the entrance hall and overlooking the market square.

'Mrs Standish, tea, I think. These two look like they are ready for a strong cup of tea,' said the Doctor. Mrs Standish left the consulting room to do as she had been bid.

'Right, now what seems to be the trouble?' asked the doctor.

'Jason's had a fall and hurt his leg, we were...'

'Our car broke down, somewhere near the racecourse, so we decided to walk into town,' interjected Jason. 'I took a tumble when I put my foot in a pothole. I should have been looking where I was going.'

The doctor asked Anna to wait outside in the waiting room while he examined his patient. Jason lay on the examination couch in his underwear, his wartime injuries very apparent, as well as the minor scrapes he'd picked-up getting off the train.

'You were in the war?' suggested the doctor, as he cleaned a graze on Jason's knee.

'That obvious, is it?' replied Jason.

'I missed it,' said the doctor. 'I hadn't finished my medical training before the war ended. Which service were you in?'

'Pilot,' said Jason.

'Figures. This may hurt,' said the doctor as he flexed Jason's knee. 'Anything else bothering you?'

'No, not really, just a few aches and pains. I'm supposed to be resting, but I got it into my head to come for the racing,' lied Jason.

'Hmm. There's no racing on this weekend. There are just a few trainers putting their new horses through their paces,' answered the doctor.

'Oh well, you can't win them all,' said Jason, trying to make light of his error.

'You can get dressed now,' said Doctor Hartwell. 'Medically, there's nothing wrong with you that time and rest won't heal. On the other hand, the picture of that young woman in the paper, and the headline saying she had been abducted by a man fitting your description, doesn't seem to fit with what I'm seeing here.' The doctor looked for a reaction from Jason, but Jason didn't respond. 'However, as a man of science, I believe in what I see. So what is the truth of it, may I ask?'

Jason sat up and swung his legs off the couch.

'I wish I could tell you, but if I told you everything about her, it would put you in danger as well. All you need to know is yes, we are on the run, and that it is my job to help Anna and keep her safe. I have not abducted her and I have not killed anyone,' said Jason.

As Jason was putting on his jacket, he looked through the surgery window and saw a black car drive into the market square. Four uniformed police officers got out.

'We have to go. How much do I owe you?' asked Jason.

'Nothing,' said Doctor Hartwell, 'all you really need is lots of rest.'

'Do you have a back door?' asked Jason.

'Yes,' said the doctor, 'and you'll need these.' He gave Jason two keys. 'I'm forever leaving my keys in the ignition. You have until five this evening before I report the car stolen.'

Jason thanked him and went to collect Anna.

Parked at the back of the surgery was a blue, open-topped, two-seater Rover 9, a small car with a folding canvas roof.

'There's a Dickie Seat at the back. You can put your luggage in there if you like and there's a travelling rug to keep your knees warm. Take good care of it; I'd like it back when you're finished with it. Good luck.'

Anna kissed Doctor Hartwell on the cheek, and Jason shook his hand one more time.

'Thank you, Doctor. We'll look after it for you, I promise,' with those parting words, Jason drove the little car along the lane at the back of the surgery, around the back of the shops that lined Watling Street and headed north on the A5 as they left Towcester.

'How long will it take us to reach Oban?' asked Anna as they sped along the old Roman road.

'I don't know. I'm not even sure how to get there by road.' Jason looked at the petrol gauge. When we reach a garage, I'll fill the car with petrol and buy a road map of Great Britain. 'There are a few other things I'm going to need. Can we stop in a town to buy some fresh clothes?' asked Anna.

Jason gave a quick look over his own dirty and scuffed clothing, 'Yes, I see what you mean. I'll stop at the next town, but first I would like to put a bit of distance between Towcester and us.'

An hour later, Jason pointed out the signpost for Hinckley. 'We'll stop there. We can buy what we need and stay the night, but first I need to go to the bank to withdraw some money before they close.'

'I think we should stop here,' said Jason, pointing to the Castle Hotel. 'It's not the Savoy, but it will have to do for now.'

After booking in and getting the keys to their rooms, they separated to go shopping. Jason's first stop was the bank to cash a cheque. He got the manager to telephone his home bank in Driffield to confirm that he had sufficient funds to cover his cheque for cash for one hundred pounds. After leaving the bank, he made his way along Castle Street, and found Bradleys, the men's outfitters. After an hour, he had everything he needed to last him a week away from home. The shop assistant informed him that Paynes Garage could supply him with petrol and that WH Smith, further up Castle Street would have a good selection of road maps. Assured that his purchases would be delivered to the hotel before the end of the day, Jason went in search of a cup of tea and a sandwich. By five o'clock, he was ready to return to the hotel. His new clothes and suitcase were waiting for him when he arrived, and a shilling to the porter had them taken up his room for him. A bath and a shave followed before dressing in fresh clothes. A visit to reception informed him that dinner was served from seven till nine o'clock and that he would not need to book a table as there were very few guests staying at the moment. Satisfied that all was in order, Jason wandered through to the lounge and ordered a brandy and soda to wait for the arrival of Anna.

By a quarter to six, Anna had still not arrived at the hotel. Jason was looking at his watch every five minutes, wondering where she could be. At six o'clock, she breezed into the hotel reception with a taxi driver on her heels. He deposited a suitcase and various bags in front of the desk. After paying the taxi driver, she spotted Jason in the lounge.

'Be a darling and order me one. As soon as the porter has taken these up and I've had time to change. I'll be back down in a jiffy.' At a quarter to seven, Anna arrived in the lounge. She was dressed in a simple but elegant yellow dress with a white collar, short sleeves and a pleated drop skirt from the waist to just below the knees. With it, she also wore a slim white belt that highlighted her waist and matched the white collar of her dress. She had also refreshed her make-up and combed her hair. That image of the stunning beauty Jason had first seen on the train earlier that morning was standing right in front of him once again.

'Are we eating in or dining out tonight?' she asked him.

'I thought we would eat here at the hotel. The menu is simple but acceptable and then we can have an early night.

With an early start in the morning, we should break the back of our journey before we stop tomorrow night.'

Anna crooked her arm, 'you had better take me through to the restaurant; I'm starving. For some reason, shopping always makes me hungry. I hope you approve of what I bought. I've tried to be practical. You do like this dress, don't you?'

'Yes, you look wonderful,' said Jason.

Chapter Six

The sound of knocking on his bedroom door roused Jason from his dream.

'Your early morning call, sir,' came the male voice from the other side of the door.'

'Thank you, replied Jason.'

By the time he had donned his dressing gown and reached the bathroom at the end of the corridor, it was already occupied, so he returned to his room, laid out his clothes for the day, and opened the road map of the British Isles. It didn't take him long to see that they could continue along the A5 all the way to Chester. From Chester, they would travel up the A69 to Carlisle and then on to Glasgow. Happy that he knew where they were heading today, he returned to the bathroom just in time to meet Anna, leaving it after having a bath. Her hair wrapped in a towel, her face was fresh, pink, and puffy and her silk dressing gown showed off the contours of her body.

'Good morning, Jason, I won't keep you waiting too long. I'll meet you downstairs for breakfast.' Anna walked back to her bedroom and was gone. Jason stood speechless as she floated past him. He hardly knew her; he was eight years older than she was and yet she was making him feel like an infatuated schoolboy. Celia came to mind. It had only been three months since that fatal crash. They had spent seven happy years together, so why was Anna affecting him this way? He entered the bathroom feeling guilty.

True to her word, Jason had no sooner ordered his breakfast when Anna arrived wearing navy blue slacks, a navy blue cardigan hemmed in white over a pristine white shirt. She ordered coffee and toast after giving up on her first choice. The waiter had given her a strange look when she'd asked for croissants. When Jason's breakfast arrived, she looked at him in amazement.

'You're really going to eat all that?' she asked. Jason looked at his plate: fried egg, bacon, black pudding, sausage and tomato, 'I have to keep my strength up; doctor's orders.' He smiled at her guiltily and cut off a section of sausage before dipping it in his egg yolk and then savouring the delights of an English fry-up.

By the time they had both finished breakfast, the porter had brought their luggage down to reception. The car was loaded and with a stop at a garage to check the oil and water levels and fill up with petrol, it was ten o'clock by the time they set off again. It was a lovely morning with a blue sky and only the occasional passing car as they sped along. Crossing the Coventry Canal at Atherstone, Anna pointed out the brightly painted narrow boats passing below. Having never seen one before, she remarked at how jolly they looked. They reached Shrewsbury just before one o'clock and stopped for lunch. Jason parked outside the King Charles Hotel and went straight to the restaurant. He ordered a brandy and soda for each of them while they perused the menu. They settled for the lobster salad as they both fancied a light lunch. After a coffee for Anna and tea for Jason, they were ready to continue their journey. While Anna went to powder her nose, Jason paid the bill and wandered out to the car. However, before he stepped outside the hotel, he spotted a policeman checking their car and taking notes. Jason stepped back a couple of paces and waited for Anna, pointing out the curious policeman to her.

'What do we do?' asked Anna.

'I'm not sure,' said Jason. 'We can't get to Scotland without the car. We can't go by train; they'll definitely be watching the railway stations. We need that car, if only until we can get a different one.'

The police officer put away his notebook. Looking towards the hotel entrance, he began to walk towards them.

'Quick,' said Jason, 'out the back!' He led her past the kitchen and out into the rear delivery yard of the hotel. Hurrying through a gate in the wall, it led them into a narrow alley. Turning left at the end, they were back on the street.

'This way,' said Jason.

'If we are quick, we can get back to the car and set off before that policeman knows we've left the hotel.'

Jason spotted the little blue Rover parked at the kerbside.

'Don't run to it,' said Jason. 'We'll just casually walk to it as though we don't have a care in the world. We don't want to attract attention to ourselves.'

With a careful eye on the front door of the hotel, Jason helped Anna into the car and dropped his walking stick in the back. Switching on the ignition, he walked round to the front of the Rover and turned the starting handle. Hoping and praying the car would start the first time, he swung the handle a full turn, and the engine burst into life. They had just pulled away from the kerb when the policeman came running out of the hotel. Seeing the car drive away, he pulled out his whistle and blew.

The narrow streets of Shrewsbury were confusing, and it was a few minutes before Jason found his bearings and spotted the signpost for Wrexham and Chester. Once clear of the town centre, they were soon travelling along a road lined with trees and hedgerows on both sides. Jason increased the speed of the little blue Rover. With the wind rushing over the windscreen as they sped along, it wasn't long before they got their first glimpses of the Welsh Hills.

'We need to get rid of this car,' said Jason. 'When Doctor Hartwell reported his car stolen, the police must have put two and two together and sent out a nationwide alert for it.'

Back on the A5 heading north, they were an hour's drive from Chester. Up ahead, a motorcycle came rushing towards them. As it drew closer, it began to slow down until the rider, a policeman, had sufficient time to view the passengers of the Rover.

Jason pushed his right foot to the floor, and the Rover picked-up speed once again. The speedometer pointer registered fifty miles per hour and kept climbing. The policeman on the motorcycle did a U-turn on the road behind them and was following, catching up on the Rover. As Jason grasped the steering wheel, the chase was on. With the wind and the noise of the engine in his ears, it brought back memories of his RAF days. His heart raced as he concentrated on the road ahead. The policeman, all dressed in black, was his enemy, trying to shoot him down. He, the English pilot, trying to shake off the faster, more manoeuvrable German plane. The Rover's speedometer read fifty-five mph, only the car's acceleration was increasing more slowly now. The little car was struggling to go any faster. The police motorcycle was sure to catch up and overtake them in the next few seconds. The Rover reached sixty mph. Anna crouched down in her seat behind the windscreen to protect her from the wind. The car engine was screaming under the strain of being pushed so hard. The car flashed past one junction signposted Oswestry. The A5 continued towards Wrexham. A second turning for Oswestry flashed past. Jason stayed on the A5. The police motorcyclist kept pace with them, seeming happy to follow the Rover rather than trying to stop it.

Anna spotted a train to her left, leaving Oswestry. It was gathering speed, seeming to keep pace with the car at first, then slowly dropping behind the Rover. A shrill cry from the train's steam whistle cut in above the noise of the Rover's engine, warning of danger ahead. Jason spotted a roadside sign for a level crossing up ahead. If he stopped, the policeman would have them. He glanced across at the train. It was only a little way behind them. His only hope of escape was to beat the train to the crossing. Appling more pressure on the accelerator, he prayed they would make it. The wind buffeted the windscreen, making it shake and rattle. The smell of hot oil filled their nostrils. Tyres rumbled as the car bounced over the ill-kept road surface, but Jason kept his foot to the floor, forcing the car to maintain its speed. The train whistle cut through the air, once again screeching in alarm. The white-painted railway gates just ahead of the car were plain to see. The gate on his side of the road began to close and so did the one diagonally opposite it. Jason slewed the car across to the opposite side of the road and headed for the still open gate. The train whistle screamed loud and shrill, and so did Anna. With the crossing gateman waving at Jason to stop, the Rover shot across the half closed railway crossing, just before the second set of heavy wooden gates closed completely. The police motorcyclist pulled to a halt on his side of the crossing and watched as Jason and Anna continued on towards Wrexham, while the train from Oswestry passed between them.

'We need to get off this road fast. That policeman will follow us the second the gates open,' shouted Jason over the noise of the car engine and the wind. At the next junction, Jason slowed the car and turned right.

'Where are we going?' asked Anna.

'I don't know yet. I want to stop, hide the car, and then think about what we should do next.' As they sped along the narrow roads on the Welsh Borders, they passed numerous stone buildings. They were too small and simple in design to be houses, as they also had no windows. When they came upon a junction in the road, Jason read, Overton 1 mile. He stopped the car and reversed it back to a gated field entrance. There, in the corner of the field, was another one of the simple structures which seemed so popular with the local farmers. He opened the gate and drove across the field, stopping at the entrance to the stone building. On closer inspection, he recognised it as a small barn. Opening the double wooden doors, he looked inside. The interior was dark and musty; the floor made from rough-cut stone. At the back of the barn, he could make out a stack of hay. *It must be a food store for the farmer's flocks during the winter,* he thought. After driving the car inside, he closed the barn doors. To his surprise, it didn't become completely dark. Looking for the light source, he found slender vertical openings evenly spaced within the walls. He smiled to himself, *'of course, they were for ventilation, to keep the hay dry and prevent it rotting.'*

'Jason, I don't feel well,' said Anna. They were the only words Anna had spoken since they turned off the old Roman road of Watling Street. Anna scrambled from the car and out of the barn into the field just in time to vomit up her lobster salad lunch. Jason apologised for his driving, thinking it was that which had upset Anna, but it was only after she collapsed, when they went back inside the barn, that he realised it was something far more serious.

Picking her up, he carried her to the back of the barn, placing her on a bed of hay. The movement must have upset her stomach again because, as she rolled onto her side and vomited up the last remnants of the lobster salad. She heaved again, but nothing more came up. Jason gathered up the foul smelling mess in a handful of dry hay and disposed of it outside. Returning, he touched Anna's forehead. She was burning up.

'I'm cold,' she said in a weak voice. So Jason covered her with the travelling rug from the car.

'You need a doctor,' said Jason. 'I'll drive you into the village up ahead.'

'No,' pleaded Anna. 'They will find us. Let me stay here for a little while. I will be alright when this passes. Just let me sleep for now. I'll feel better later.'

Jason wasn't entirely sure that it was a good idea. But she was right about the risk of being discovered. In the shaded stone barn, away from the sun, the air was cool, and there was nothing to stop the breeze blowing through the slotted ventilation holes in the walls, so he piled some hay on top of the travelling rug to provide her with extra warmth. Going to the barn door, he looked outside. The field gate was open. In his haste to get to the barn, he had forgotten to close the field gate; that was bound to attract the farmer's attention, telling him someone had entered his field.

As Jason closed the field gate, he heard a powerful car coming towards him. Stepping back behind the hedge, he watched the car approach. It was being driven by someone he recognised; it was one of the constables from the train and in the back of the car was the police inspector. *The motorcycle policeman must have spotted us turning off towards Overton, then gone back to report his car chase. But why had this police inspector, who'd got on the train at Bedford, got off the train to follow me and Anna to Wales? Why hadn't it been left to the local police to find us? If the inspector hadn't been interested in our story back then, what's happened to change his mind? What is going on?* As the sound of the car fell away in the distance, Jason made his way back to the barn full of questions.

Anna was asleep, so he went over to the car. He was hungry despite having had his lunch only a couple hours earlier; the salad had not been very filling. He searched the car to see if there was any food in it. It was pointless. He needn't have bothered. He already knew there was nothing there, but the urge to look for something, anything to eat or drink, was overpowering. *I should have thought to buy something to eat or drink for our journey.* With Anna incapacitated and unable to travel, there was only one option. *I'll have to wait until it gets dark. We will need something to and drink if we are going to spend the night here.* As he lay in the hay next to Anna, he fell asleep.

Jason awoke with a start, sat up, and listened for the noise that had disturbed him. Silence. As he looked around, it was pitch black inside the barn. He leaned over and felt for Anna's forehead; she was still hot and didn't respond to his touch. Then the sound came again, 'too-wit' followed quickly by 'too-woo.' He sighed, relieved at recognising the sound. It was Tawny Owls calling to one another. From the sound of it, one of them must be perched on the barn roof. Standing up, and with his arms outstretched before him, he searched for the car. By running his hands along the side of the Rover, he made his way to the back of it, and then, a couple of yards further on, he found the barn doors. As he stepped outside, the night air was cool on his face. The sky was a bluish-black and was filled with stars. The openness of his surroundings, and the clarity of the view, reminded him of the African sky over his farm in the Kenyan hills.

He followed the track back to the field gate and onto the road. He knew the village was less than a mile away, so, providing he took it easy and didn't strain his recovering leg, the distance wouldn't be beyond him. A glance at his watch with its illuminated dial told him it was twelve-thirty, plenty of time to get back before daybreak. He would have the road to himself.

He'd only been walking for about fifteen minutes when he spotted the dark outline of a house on the roadside. He stopped and studied it before getting any closer. Slowly, he drew nearer, silhouetted against the sky. He could make out its shape more clearly. It was a small isolated house with outbuildings. The village must be further on. The barn he'd hidden the car in probably belonged to this farmer. Making his way around to the back of the house, he found the back door and felt for the latch. Working the latch slowly and quietly, the door opened. Suddenly, he felt ashamed. The people in these parts, so trusting in their nature, still left their doors unlocked at night, and he was about to take advantage of them.

Pushing his guilt aside, he crept into the kitchen and stopped. It was too dark to see, and if he bumped into anything, the noise would alert the owners. He struck a match and looked about him. On the windowsill stood a candle; he lit it. Candle in hand, he looked for the pantry and found it in the corner. Inside on a shelf, he found the remains of a pork pie, some white cheese, half a loaf of bread, and most of a fruitcake. As he stepped forward to break off a piece of cake, his walking stick hit something on the floor that rattled. Looking down, he spotted a row of dark beer bottles and, next to them, a wicker basket. Loading the basket with two bottles of beer, the cake, cheese, bread and the pork pie, he backed out of the pantry. Leaving the candlestick on the kitchen table with a pound note tucked beneath it, he removed the candle from the stand and took that as well. With his basket of illicit supplies in hand, Jason made his way back to Anna.

Leaving the barn door open gave Jason sufficient light to not stumble when he entered the barn. He put the basket on the driver's seat of the car, removed and lit the candle, and then secured it to the bonnet of the car with some hot wax. After closing the barn door, he checked on Anna. She was still asleep and still very hot. With no other option but to wait for the morning, Jason ate some cake, washing it down with half a bottle of beer, before settling to sleep the rest of the night away.

The noise of the barn door swinging open and scraping on the earth as it caught fast on the uneven ground outside woke Jason. A man's voice filled the interior of the barn.

'Hoy, what you doing in my barn and stealing the food from my house?'

It took a couple of seconds for Jason to gather his thoughts and for his eyes to adjust to the day light. As he got to his feet, he saw a man silhouetted in the open barn entrance, but it was the shotgun the man held that grabbed Jason's attention. Jason didn't know what to say, so said nothing. He just stared at the shotgun.

'Come out here, where I can get a better look at you,' demanded the man in the doorway. Jason stepped forward into the open with his hands in the air. As Jason came out of the barn, the farmer took a few paces backwards, stumbled and fell flat on his back, his arms flailing outwards and back with his shotgun still in hand. The gun went off, firing into the air. Jason instinctively ducked away and then turned back to see the farmer still sprawled in the grass. Ignoring the pain in his leg, Jason leapt forward and grabbed the shotgun as it lay on the ground and turned back towards its owner. He thumbed the release catch, ejecting the two spent cartridges, and handed the gun back to the farmer.

'I'm sorry,' said Jason, 'I hoped the money would compensate for the inconvenience and cost of what I took.' It was the farmer's turn to remain silent as he took possession of his firearm. Jason extended his right hand to help the farmer to his feet. The man accepted his help and got up.

'What happens now?' asked Jason.

'I don't know. This is not what I expected to happen,' said the farmer. Jason offered his right hand again, 'Jason Parva.' The farmer looked at Jason's hand for a moment and then shook hands with him. 'Ifan Jenkins.'

'Who else is with you?'

Jason hesitated a moment, 'my wife; well...er...she will be my wife, soon. We are on our way to Gretna Green to get married – my family did not approve, so we eloped. My father's a bit old-fashioned that way. Anna was our maid. You know what some families are like,' Jason dissembled.

'Ohhh, it's like that, is it?' said Ifan, his eyebrows climbing higher and higher on his forehead as Jason concocted the story of two runaway lovers.

'She's hiding at the back, is she shy like?' asked Ifan.

'No, no,' said Jason, 'she's not well. I think she ate something yesterday that has upset her. She has a bit of a fever, and we just stopped to let her sleep it off.' Ifan looked a bit puzzled at Jason's not sure if he should believe his feeble excuse for them sleeping in his barn and breaking into his house. So he went to take a look at Anna for himself. As Ifan and Jason rounded the car, Anna sat up, looking very pale, somewhat bedraggled, with hay caught in her un-brushed hair and her clothing. Jason stepped in front of Ifan. 'How do you feel this morning, dear?'

Anna managed to raise a smile. 'A little better thank you, dear, though I still feel a bit weak and dizzy. I woke up when the gun went off. I heard your voices. Is everything alright?'

'Yes, Ifan and I seem to have come to a peaceful settlement. Ifan gave Jason a quizzical look.

'Good morning, Miss. Are you unwell?' asked Ifan. Would you like to come to the house? Megan will have a pot of tea on the table by now.'

Anna looked up at Jason, who nodded his consent.

'Thank you, Ifan, that sounds wonderful, though my legs feel a bit shaky,' said Anna.

'You help the lady into the car, young fella, and I'll go open the gate.' Ifan paused as if thinking, then turned to Jason. 'She's French, if I'm not mistaken?'

'Yes, I had noticed,' said Jason.

'Oh, that's all right then; I'll go open the gate.' Ifan wedged his shotgun between the suitcases stored in the back of the Rover and headed off towards the field gate.

'How do you feel?' Jason asked again.

'Terrible, but you sounded like you needed help. Where is Gretna Green?' Jason's face turned a deep shade of crimson. Anna chuckled at his embarrassment.

Mrs Jenkins came to the door to get a better look at the unexpected visitors as the car rolled up to the front of the farmhouse.

'Who's this then, Ifan?' Mr Jenkins had cut across the field, and come up the back garden path to explain what he had found in the barn to his wife.

'This couple are on their way to Gretna Green of all places, Megan, my love.'

'What were they doing in our barn then, Ifan?'

'Looks like the young lady has been taken ill and needed somewhere to stop over for a sleep.'

'They're not local then?'

'No love, they've come all the way from London, and the young lady is French,'

'What's she doing in London, then?'

'Seems like she was working for this fella's da, and they fell in love.'

'What, this fella's da, and the young lady?'

'No, Megan. This ere fella, and the lady have fallen in love, and his da is not happy about it, see, so they've run away together.'

'Right, I'm with you now.'

All the time the couple were going through their questions and answers, Jason and Anna were left standing at the gate. Anna gave a gasp and slumped against Jason. He caught her before she fell to the ground.

'Now look at what you've done with all your silly questions. The lady has taken bad,' said Ifan.'

Megan rushed forward, looping her arm around Anna.

'Go put the kettle on, Ifan; I'll make some fresh tea.'

Ifan shot indoors, while Megan and Jason helped Anna into the kitchen, sitting her at the table. Anna doubled forward, holding her arms across her stomach. She retched, but nothing came up. Her face, pale and sweaty, clearly showed the discomfort she was in. As the pain eased, she leaned back in the chair.

'I'm sorry,' she said. 'I don't feel well at all.'

'Don't you worry none, I have just the thing for a touch of stomach trouble. Get me the Kaolin and Morphine down Ifan. A couple of spoons of this will have you right again in no time.' After Anna had been given the medicine, Megan went upstairs to make up the spare bed for Anna.

'Do you think I should fetch the doctor?' asked Jason.

'Oh, no need for that. We don't hold with all them fancy modern ideas. Megan knows best. Just leave it to Megan. She'll have your young lady ripe as nine-pence before you know it,' said Ifan confidently.

Megan returned to the kitchen. 'Come on, young lady, what you need is some sleep in a proper bed.' She hoisted Anna to her feet, and half carried, half dragged her up the stairs. After removing Anna's dress, she laid the invalid on the bed and covered her with blankets.

'You sleep now, my lovely. You'll feel a whole lot better when you wake up.' Megan was about to leave the bedroom when she turned back for one last question.

'Just between you and me. Are you expecting?' Anna blushed, bright red, 'No, I really am ill. I've just eaten something that disagreed with me, that's all.'

'You have a sleep, now. I'll come up later to check on you, later.'

As Anna listened to Megan's footsteps going down the stairs, her eyes began to droop, and she fell asleep on the soft feather mattress, wrapped in the warm woollen blankets.

Megan entered the kitchen, sitting down at the table. Ifan had made a fresh pot of tea and had poured three cups ready for her return. Megan asked Jason for a full explanation of what the couple was doing, and Jason responded with the tale he had given Ifan.

'Well, all I can say is that you have a strange way of doing things in London,' said Megan.

Having seen Jason limp into the house, Ifan asked him, 'Got the limp during the war, did you?'

'Ifan, that's none of your business,' scolded his wife.'

'That's all right, Mrs Jenkins. No, it's from my time in Africa.' On hearing the exotic-sounding name, Megan and Ifan leaned forward, eager to hear more. So Jason gave them a brief description of his farm in Kenya and his plane crash, but left out the part about Celia.

'Well I never,' exclaimed Ifan. 'You've certainly done some travelling. Megan and me have never been further than Chester, and that was only the once. We didn't take to the big city life it was far too confusing.'

'Speaking of travelling, as you and Mrs Jenkins have been so kind as to take us in until Anna is feeling better; I need petrol for the car. May I leave Anna with you for a few hours so I can go find a garage and fill up the Rover?'

'Aye, for sure. You'd best go towards Wrexham. Gwynn Jones has a garage out that way. You'll pass him on the way. He'll sell you some petrol.'

Megan got to her feet. 'You're not going nowhere until you've had your breakfast. Ifan says it's the best meal of the day, don't you, Ifan?'

An hour later, and with detailed directions from Ifan, Jason set off in search of petrol. After a few miles, he spotted the garage sign and pulled in. A young man in blue overalls, sporting a cloth badge with Castrol emblazoned on it, came out to greet him.

'Good morning, sir; petrol is it?'

'Yes please, and would you also give the car a quick once over? I have a long way to go?'

'No problem at all, sir. Staying local like are we?'

'Sort of. We are staying at Ifan Jenkins farm just up the road.'

'Oh, nice bloke that Ifan, known him and Megan for years. If you would be kind enough to just drive your car over the inspection pit, I'll look at it right away. We don't get many cars out this way, it's mostly tractors see, and when they break down, the farmers get a horse to tow them in. You can take a seat in my office if you like. There is a newspaper you can read while you're waiting.'

The office was no more than a partitioned-off corner of the garage, home to an old kitchen table for a desk and a stack of cardboard boxes as a filing cabinet. Jason was about to sit in the chair until he noticed it was smeared with old oil stains. He resolved the problem by covering the seat of the hard-backed chair with the newspaper. He passed the time by looking around while he waited before closing his eyes for a moment. The sound of the mechanic working on the car, and the smell of oil, dirt and grease brought back memories of his time in France. He felt as though he was flying again. A vision of the battlefield trenches came into view. He opened his eyes, shouting, 'NO!' He found himself gripping the sides of the chair to stop himself from falling, and then he heard Gwynn Jones calling to him.

'Everything all right, sir?'

Jason stood up. 'Yes, thank you, Mr Jones. Everything is fine; I must have dozed off for a moment.' Jason had no sooner retaken his seat when he heard the honking of a car horn from outside. Looking through the dirt-encrusted window, he spotted a large black car with three heavy-set men in it. Mr Jones went to the driver's window.

'Petrol is it, sir?' An accented voice responded.

'No, we are looking for a man and a woman travelling together in a small car. Have they stopped here in the past day or two?'

'Oh, no, nothing like that. I'd remember anyone such as that coming by this way. I've got the only garage between Chester and Wrexham, you see, so…'

'Thank you for your time.' The black car sped off, the wheels throwing up gravel as it pulled away.

Gwynn Jones re-entered the garage. 'Bloody foreigners coming over here asking questions. Killed my brother, they did, during that war. I don't trust 'em see, don't know what they'll be up to next. You mark my words; we'll be at war with them all again one day.'

He went back to the front of the car and put his head under the bonnet. 'I won't keep you long now, sir, she's full of petrol. I've changed the spark plugs and topped up the oil for you. I just need to check the water in the radiator, and you can be on your way. Business or pleasure, sir; your drive, that is? You said you had a long way to go?'

'Oh, er, pleasure. I'm taking a bit of a holiday in Snowdonia.'

'Very nice, sir. It can be a bit bleak this time of year, but you may be lucky with the weather.'

The garage owner closed the bonnet on the Rover, 'There you are, sir, all done and dusted. She'll be good for another couple of hundred miles now. No one ever complains after I've worked on their car. That'll be three pounds, nineteen shillings and sixpence if I may be so bold, sir. I hope you don't mind me saying, if I were you, I would hide the young lady's luggage a little better than that if there were foreigners looking for me. They'll soon spot the lady's cases. There are more of them, and they are smaller than yours, you see, showing that there are two people travelling in the car.'

'Thank you for the advice, Gwynn. I will make a better job of disguising them.' He handed the garage owner a five-pound note, 'Please, keep the change.'

'Thank you, sir, you're a gentleman. It's been nice doing business with you, and I wish you and the lady a safe journey.'

Jason arrived back at the Jenkins' farm a little over an hour after he had left it. Mrs Jenkins was making a fresh batch of bread dough on the kitchen table.

'Oh, there you are. I thought Gwynn was going to keep you talking all day. I've been up to look in on the young lady, and she's sleeping soundly. Sit yourself down, and I'll make us some tea in a minute. Ifan has just popped out to check on some ewes in a field across the way. He'll be back soon.'

'You are both being very kind and understanding, considering I broke into your house last night.'

'Well, at first we were both quite angry about it. But we noticed it was only food that went missing and you did pay for it. After giving it some thought, we realised that had you been a real burglar, you would have taken more than that, and you wouldn't have left the money in payment. So Ifan reckoned that you were in some kind of trouble and needed help. When he went to look in the barn, he took his shotgun just in case like, not sure what he might find. He would never have used it in anger. He got too much of that during that dammed fool war. You see, we used to live in Wrexham when we first married; Ifan was a fine shoemaker in those days, still is. It was during that time that he got called up. Well, as you can see, he survived to tell the tale but, when he came home at the end of it, he wasn't the same. He said he needed space and some peace and quiet, so we came here. It's hard work, just the two of us, but I don't mind. I'm just thankful he came home in one piece when so many didn't.'

'Thank you for your understanding, Mrs Jenkins. I too was in France during the war.'

'Think nothing of it. You must call me Megan now you're in my house.'

'Thank you, Megan. My name is Jason Parva, and it is Anna you have safely tucked up in bed. Is there somewhere out of the way I can park the car? It's on a narrow road, and I would hate for it to get in anyone's way.'

'If you wish; you can put it back in the barn where you slept last night.'

Chapter Seven

Anna awoke early the following morning. Looking around the strange bedroom she wondered where she was for a moment until she recalled the events of the previous day. *Should I get up, or stay where I am until someone comes to find me?* The decision was made for her, nature was calling. She looked at the chamber pot beside the bed, but she didn't fancy the prospect of facing its contents after she'd used it, so she made her way to the stairs and down to the kitchen. A look through the kitchen window soon located the outdoor privy.

By the time she returned to the kitchen, Megan was putting coal in the range to bring it back to life. 'Good morning, my dear, how are you feeling today?'

'Good morning, Megan, much better thank you. I sorry, I hope I haven't been a burden to you. I just felt so desperately ill yesterday, that all I wanted to do was sleep the pain away.'

'No, no trouble at all. Ifan and I have had a good natter with Jason, and he's explained everything. Sit down, it won't take a minute for the kettle to boil, then there'll be some hot water for a wash before the men get up and we'll be able to have a nice cup of tea in peace.

Anna washed and freshened up while Megan made and poured the tea. She kept to the story about her being an eloping maid and marring Jason against his family's wishes.

Half an hour later Ifan joined them, after which he went to wake Jason who was sleeping on the sofa in the other room. By the time Jason came through to the kitchen the smell of frying bacon was wafting through the house. There wasn't any coffee and sweet rolls, so Anna made do with tea and some plain bread and butter.

'We cannot thank you enough for your kindness, but we will have to leave after breakfast,' said Jason.

'I think we will be sorry to see you go. We don't get much excitement around here do we Ifan? Promise us you will call in the next time you are passing. I know you were only with us for a day and a night, but I get the feeling you are nice people…'

'Now, now, Megan,' interjected Ifan. 'Don't you go embarrassing them like that. They have more important things to do and places to go than to come back here.'

'No, Megan's right,' said Anna. 'I will not forget your kindness and, if we are ever in North Wales again, we will be sure to call in and see you.'

An hour later Jason and Anna waved goodbye to Megan and Ifan as the Rover headed off towards Chester along the A5.

'Yesterday, when I was getting petrol for the car, I saw those three big guys from the train,' said Jason.

'What happened? Did they see you? Did you speak to them?'

'No. I was waiting inside the garage while the car was being serviced. They stayed in their car. They asked the garage owner if he had seen us, but he said no and they drove off.'

'What are we going to do?'

'I've thought of that. We will go to Chester, but we'll leave the car parked outside a hotel and get a coach to Lake Windermere. Hopefully, when those men find the car, they'll think we are still in Chester and waste time searching for us, whilst we slip away.'

'Do you really think it will work?'

'Yes, all we have to do is find the Thomas Cook's ticket office, and arrange for our tickets to Lake Windermere and book a hotel for when we arrive. We leave our luggage at the ticket office. We then buy some new suitcases and book into a hotel in Chester. After we have checked into the Chester hotel for a week, we leave the empty suite cases in the hotel, and return to the ticket office tomorrow to get the coach to the lakes. Leaving the car behind should throw those guy's off our scent.'

'Maybe, if I'd done something like that in Paris, I wouldn't have been followed to England.'

'Ha, when I was a lad at boarding school and we needed to escape for a few hours at the weekend we learnt all sorts of tricks to avoid the teachers and put them off what we were really doing.'

In less than an hour, Anna and Jason were entering the old roman city of Chester. As they crossed over the bridge on the River Dee. Chester Castle was to their right and the race course to their left. The city, with its defensive wall and mixture of Georgian and Tudor architecture, reminded Jason of York, only Chester retained more of its black and white, wood-framed buildings. He turned the car on to Watergate and stopped outside a tea shop.

'We'll have a cup of tea and ask for directions to the Thomas Cooks office.' suggested Jason.

As they got out of the car, they noticed the entrance to the old tea rooms was below street level. Anna and Jason descended down two steps and entered the tea shop.

'What happens when it rains,' asked Anna, 'does everyone inside get their feet wet?' she sniggered holding her hand in front of her mouth to hide the giggles. They were met by an elderly lady dressed in black and wearing a white apron.

'Good morning, sir, Madam. I'm afraid we are not quite ready yet, it's still a little early. But if you do not mind waiting a few minutes until the water comes to the boil, I'll come back and take your order. Would you like a menu while you are waiting?'

She left two menus on the table and returned to the kitchen at the rear of the premises. Anna read the menu. Jason watched the expression of surprise on her face as she did so.

'I never knew there were so many different types of tea. I have heard of Breakfast Tea, Earl Grey, Darjeeling and Chamomile, but there is Bukhial Tgfop Assam, Ceylon

Gunpowder Green Tea, and Chunmee Taipan Superior Green Tea. The list goes on and on, and then, last of all is coffee. The coffee is listed as black, with milk or with cream. What's wrong with you English? Why don't you like coffee? And they only serve toast, teacakes, crumpets or muffins, but no Croissant or Pain Au Chocolat.'

'Well it is a Tea Room, and we are in England,' said Jason. 'The English prefer tea. How easy is to get a cup of tea in Paris?'

'Umm, maybe you have a point,' conceded Anna.

The woman returned, this time sporting a freshly starched waitress hat. 'Are you ready to order, sir?'

'Yes, tea and crumpets for two, please.'

'Would that be the breakfast tea, sir?'

'Yes please, breakfast tea will be fine.' The waitress scratched the order on her notepad and returned to the kitchen.

'When she returns I'll ask her the whereabouts of Thomas Cook's,' said Jason. 'I would also like to get a newspaper to see if they are still spreading the story about us being on the run and all that nonsense.'

As they waited for their tea to arrive Anna looked out of the window at a double fronted shop on the opposite side of the street. It was a toy shop with a window full of teddy bears, aeroplanes, cars and metal construction sets. The window next to it was displaying toys for girls and a man was looking in the window at the girls toys. Anna didn't take much heed of him at first, but he stayed where he was, just looking in the window for far longer than Anna expected. The waitress returned with cups and saucers. The next time Anna looked out of the window the man was still there. But, even though the man had his back to the tea shop, Anna could see that he was small, slim and had greased back hair. There was something familiar about him, but Anna could not bring the memory to mind. The waitress placed a silver teapot, milk jug, sugar bowl and butter on the table within easy reach of Anna and then set a plate of freshly toasted crumpets between the couple.

'Looks like you have to be mother,' said Jason.

'Pardon?' said Anna.

'Ha, ha, just a little English humour. The teapot is closer to you. The waitress is expecting you to pour the tea for both of us as if we were at home.'

'Why? Don't you know how to pour the tea for yourself?'

'Yes, of course, I do. It is just an English custom for the woman to pour the tea.'

'Well, as I said before, in France we drink coffee, so you can play mère if it's important to you.' When it came to the crumpets, Anna only took a couple of small bites, wrinkling her nose at the taste and left the rest saying they were too stodgy.

'I've just noticed,' said Anna. 'Look across the street, it is on two levels. We don't have anything like it in France.'

Through the tea shop window, Jason admired the Tudor style frontage of the buildings. Above the shops at street level ran a wooden covered walkway allowing a second row of shops above those at ground level.

'Two rows of shops one above the other, it must have been like that for hundreds of years,' said Anna enthralled by the historical scene. 'I wonder if the whole city is like this.'

'When we go to the ticket office we can have a wander about and see if you wish.'

'You didn't ask the waitress the whereabouts of the ticket office,' Anna reminded Jason. Having eaten four buttered crumpets and drinking two cups of tea, Jason called for the bill.

'Would you happen to know where the Thomas Cook ticket office is, please? He asked the waitress.

'Yes, sir. Go towards the cross at the end of the street, turn right, and carry on along Eastgate. It is on your left, just before you get to the clock. You can't miss it.'

'Thank you.' Jason left the waitress a two-shilling tip and led Anna to the street.

'What a wonderful city. There is nothing like this in France. It's as though we have gone back in time,' declared Anna, as they walked up the street.

'Yes, it's a pity we will not have more time to explore and look around. Look, the Thomas Cook office is just over there.'

As they headed towards the Thomas Cook ticket office, Jason saw a sign for the Grand Hotel.

'There, that hotel fits our needs perfectly.'

After purchasing two coach tickets to Bowness-on-Windermere, with a stopover at the Lake Windermere Hotel, Anna and Jason proceeded the extra few yards up the street to the Grand Hotel. They booked two rooms, telling the desk clerk they would return shortly with their luggage.

Returning to the car, they drove up to the ticket office and deposited their luggage ready for the coach the following morning.

'It looks like you are going to get your wish to do a little exploring,' said Jason. 'We have some shopping to do for our overnight stay in Chester. Get a large suitcase to make it look as if we are staying the week. But just buy enough clothes and things for tonight and tomorrow.'

'Jason, wait. Buying more clothes will use up the last of my money. I didn't expect to get through my savings so fast,' lamented Anna.

'Don't worry, you can pay me back later by making me the Duke of Siberia or somewhere else. I'll go to the bank and arrange more funds.'

An hour later with their new purchases in the back of the car, Jason drove up to the front of the Grand Hotel.

'We've already checked in, our luggage just needs taking up to our rooms,' Jason informed the porter who met them as he switched off the car engine. The porter helped Anna from the car and then went around to the boot to retrieve the luggage. As he tugged the near-empty cases from the back seat, he almost fell backwards off balance, expecting the cases to be heavier than they were. He gave Jason a strange look.

'Sorry about that,' said Jason. 'We expect to do a lot of shopping while we are here.' The porter responded with an enigmatic smile. Jason retrieved their keys from the receptionist and led the porter upstairs to their rooms, giving him a tip for his trouble.

'I going to have a bath and freshen up,' said Anna. 'I will telephone you when I'm finished. It was all very pleasant and friendly staying with Mr and Mrs Jenkins, but there wasn't much in the way of modern conveniences and privacy whilst we were there.'

'Not quite like this, you mean?' said Jason as he held his arms out indicating the plush room and private bathroom Anna would now have to herself.

'I think I will do the same, and then read the newspaper while I'm waiting for you to finish dressing.'

Two hours later the telephone rang in Jason's room. It was Anna announcing that she was ready and suggesting that they go explore the delights of the old city. As they dropped off their room keys at the hotel reception, they both heard trumpets playing outside on the street. Jason turned to the hotel receptionist, about to ask a question, only the receptionist responded before Jason could ask. 'It is the Lord Mayor's Parade, sir.'

'Come on Jason, I want to see it,' said Anna.

As the couple emerged from the hotel, they were in time to see the front of the parade coming towards them along Eastgate. At the front of the procession was a military brass band. The musicians were wearing red jackets, white pith helmets, black trousers with a red stripe down the seam, and highly polished black shoes. The soldier at the front wore a black and gold coloured sash and carried a long black staff with a silver top.

Crowds lined the street, cheering. More people were coming from side streets to join the excitement and see the parade. The military band marched past and was followed by a troop of smartly turned out boy scouts, followed by the Lord

Mayor himself. He was wearing his ceremonial robes over a black suit with a white frilled shirt and a black cloak with gold trim. On his head, he wore a black tricorn hat with gold braid and around his neck hung his badge of office on an elaborate gold chain. Following the Lord Mayor was a company of soldiers from the Cheshire Regiment, and they were followed by various horse-drawn drays displaying different crafts and businesses from Chester and the surrounding villages.

As Jason and Anna watched from outside the Grand Hotel an elderly couple asked if they might squeeze past them to enter the hotel.

'I beg your pardon,' Jason apologised and stepped away from the hotel door.

'Come this way Anna, we'll walk down the street a little to get out of the way of the hotel entrance,' suggested Jason.

As they did so, they came face to face with a man Jason recognised from the train.

'Doctor Stone, how unexpected, I didn't envisage meeting you in Chester.'

The small man struggled to speak for a second before saying.

'Good day, er, forgive me, I am terrible with names.'

'Mr Jason Parva. We are visiting this enchanting city as part of our holiday. Are you doing the same?'

'Good day to you, Mr Parva, and in answer to your question. Yes, I am also here on holiday to see this wonderful city. It is quite a coincidence for us meeting like this. Are you staying in Chester long?'

'We have rooms at the Grand Hotel,' said Jason. 'We plan to stay the week before heading down to Warwick, and then back to London before Miss Moreau returns to Paris.'

'I don't understand,' said Mr Stone. 'Why would you take a train, a sleeper train to Scotland if you did not intend to go there?'

There was an overlong pause before Jason came up with an answer.

'Because of the delays to the train caused by the death of that unfortunate man, we lost our hotel booking in Oban and missed the cruise around the Scottish Islands. So I suggested we hire a car and come up to Chester before driving back to London,' continued Jason.

'Oh, I see,' said Doctor Stone. 'I hope you both enjoy the rest of your holiday.'

'Why didn't you continue on to Scotland, Doctor?' asked Jason. 'Are you here on your own?'

'Oh, a similar story to yours, I was going to a doctor's conference. The delays meant I missed it, so I decided that as I would be away from home anyway, I may as well do some sightseeing. Yes, I am on my own. I never married. I never could find the time.'

'Then please, join us for dinner tonight at the hotel,' Anna pointed to the Grand just behind her. 'Shall we say seven?'

'That is very gracious of you, but I would not like to interpose into such a charming couple's holiday.'

'Think nothing of it, Doctor. We would love to have your company tonight.' Anna flinched as she felt Jason poke her hard in the side.

'Thank you, I would be delighted. I will see you at seven then. Goodbye for now. I am going to visit some Roman ruins that have been uncovered on the other side of the city.' Doctor Stone disappeared into the crowd which was following the Lord Mayor's procession. Anna turned to Jason rubbing her side where he had jabbed her with his thumb.

'That hurt,' Anna protested.

'What are you doing arranging for us to have dinner with the doctor? We are supposed to be keeping our location and movements a secret until we can find somewhere safe to hide and the Russian Secret Police give up looking for you. We know they are not far away,' Jason scolded her.

'He is a doctor. He went to help that man who collapsed on the train. It is the three big men that are looking for me, not him. And besides, having dinner with him at the hotel will help keep up the pretence that we are staying longer than we are doing. As you said before, there is safety in numbers.'

'I still think you should have consulted me first. There was nothing in today's newspaper about me kidnapping you, but what if the doctor has seen the article, he may turn us in,' protested Jason.

'Don't be silly, that was a terrible photograph, and who,' she said, lowering her voice to a whisper, 'would expect to see a Russian Princess with a French accent, walking the streets of Chester, with an ex Great War pilot? Come; show me around this fascinating city.'

It was four o'clock in the afternoon before Jason and Anna returned to the Grand Hotel after an exhausting day roaming the streets of Chester. Both of them were ready for afternoon tea, or in Anna's case a coffee. The afternoon had been uneventful with Anna buying souvenirs of Chester, and Jason enjoying Anna's company and the sights of the city.

By six-thirty, they had both freshened up and changed ready for their evening dinner date with the doctor. They were in the lounge about to order an aperitif before dinner when Doctor Stone arrived.

'Good evening, Doctor. Would you care for a drink before we go through to the dining room?' asked Jason.

'That is very kind of you, Mr Parva. I would like a Bloody Mary if I may.' Jason finished giving his order to the waiter with a glass of Pernod and water for Anna and a gin and tonic for himself. The threesome chatted briefly about what they had seen during their respective sightseeing trips around Chester, when a waiter informed them that their table was ready, and asked if they would like to take their seats. They decided to start their meal with a selection of hors-d'oeuvres as it would give each of them a varied selection of dishes to choose from. For their main course Anna selected Chicken Veronique with sauté potatoes and asparagus, Jason chose Tornado Rossini served with a green salad, whereas the Doctor decided on Beef Stroganoff. The conversation continued from where they had left off in the lounge until the doctor asked about their plans for the future.

Jason became defensive, 'As I said earlier, we plan to visit Warwick before returning to London. Anna will finish her holiday and go back to Paris.'

'Ah yes, I remember you saying. Warwick is another wonderfully historic English town, I believe, though I have never visited it myself, you understand.' The doctor slurred his words and then suddenly stopped speaking, put down his glass of wine.

'This wine is very nice, but a little potent compared to what I am used to, being a humble country doctor.'

'Where is your practice doctor, you never did say?' asked Jason.

'Didn't I? I'm sorry; I have a surgery in the east end of London, administering to the poor.'

'That is very noble of you,' interrupted Anna. 'That must give you a lot of satisfaction, helping those in the greatest need?'

'Thank you. Yes, indeed it does, but it does not pay well. However, you might say I am lucky. I have a private income that allows me to indulge my desire to treat those less fortunate than myself. I only need to rely on one or two wealthier patients to supplement my income to enable me to maintain a modest income. Now, that's enough about me. Tell me, how did you two meet?'

Jason and Anna looked at each other, unsure of how to answer.

It was Jason who spoke, 'I met Anna's mother during the war. She was a nurse who helped me when I was injured. After the war, Anna's mother told her about me. Anna wrote to me and said she wished to come to England for a holiday, and asked me if I would be willing to escort her.' Jason figured keeping the story as truthful as possible would be safer than trying to remember a fully made up one.

'Your mother must be a remarkable and fine lady, Anna. Able to remember one patient out of so many, Mr Parva must have made a real impression on her. And, a simple nurse, able to send her daughter to England for a holiday, she must have a substantial private income?' The doctor's tone was boarding on rudeness with its implication.

Jason was just about to answer for Anna when she put her hand on his arm to stop him.

'My mother married a farmer. It is not a big farm, but it supplies what we need, and we grow a few grapes to turn into wine and provide a little extra income. I paid for my own holiday. I am a secretary in Paris. I worked hard and saved up for a few years to enable me to come to England.'

'Then, you are very fortunate. I don't know many French businesses that pay their secretaries well enough to enable them to go on foreign holidays,' sniped the Doctor, again slurring his words.

'What would you know about French businesses and how much they pay their secretaries?' interjected Jason in Anna's defence.

'I'm sorry. I did not mean to be rude. It is just that as a doctor, I get used to asking questions. I also like to travel abroad when I can. I have been to Paris once or twice on holiday. It is a beautiful city. Have you been there, Mr Parva?'

'No, I haven't had the pleasure as yet.'

'You must, it is a very romantic city, the perfect place for a young couple like yourselves.' Anna blushed at the inference.

She looked at Jason, and he at her, both searching for a response to the doctor's innuendo.

'We, er, are not romantically linked, we are just friends,' answered Jason. Anna nodded her enthusiastic agreement. The doctor gave a devilish smile.

After they had finished their main course, a waiter cleared their table. 'Would sir like to see the dessert menu?'

'Not for me,' responded Anna. 'We have a lot of sightseeing to do tomorrow, so I will say goodnight.'

'I too have had a long day,' said the doctor. 'Thank you for dinner. I hope I get the chance to return the compliment sometime.'

'My pleasure,' said Jason. 'I hope you enjoy the rest of your holiday.'

'What an insufferable person,' said Anna, as they climbed the stairs to their rooms. 'I regret asking him to dine with us now.'

'Yes, I agree, not a gentleman at all. Did you notice how he shovelled his food into his mouth, and the wine went straight to his head. Forget about him, we begin our trip tomorrow.'

'I suggest an early night,' said Anna, 'we have to be up early tomorrow.'

Back in his room, as Jason undressed and washed before getting into bed, he couldn't help but remembering the reference the doctor had made. *Paris is a romantic city, the perfect place for a young couple like yourselves.* The thought had been playing on his mind ever since the doctor had said it.

131

Anna was a beautiful young woman. From the first time he spotted her on the train, he had been attracted to her. But, since learning that she was the daughter of the nurse who had saved his life and that she was the heir to the Russian throne, he had put all notions of a personal relationship with her to the back of his mind. But, if they were to pull off this subterfuge of being a couple on holiday; in public at least, they were going to have to show a little more interest in each other of a romantic nature. He buttoned up his pyjama jacket and got into bed. Tomorrow, he decided, he would have to talk to her about it.

It proved to be a long night for Jason. Finding it difficult to sleep. The doctor's words kept going around and around in his mind. Yes, Anna was very attractive, but he hardly knew her and he still missed Celia. His feelings towards Anna made him feel guilty. In his mind's eye he kept seeing the little white wooden church in Kenya and the grave with its little wooden cross where he had said goodbye to the love of his life. He got up and finished reading the newspaper he'd bought earlier in the day and then turned to the various magazines left in his room to advertise places of interest in Chester.

The next time he looked at his wristwatch it was five fifty-five am. He had fallen asleep with the light on and his bed was covered in discarded magazines. His eyes were stinging, he had a mild headache and his mouth was dry. He brushed aside the magazines and dropped his feet to the floor. He didn't feel as though he had slept at all. After a drink of water, a shave and a shower he felt a little better. He dressed quickly then went along the corridor to Anna's room and knocked on the door. He was just about to knock again when the door opened just a crack, 'Oh, it's you,' came a tired voice from inside the room. The door swung open. Anna turned her back and headed for the bathroom dressed in a silk, ankle-length ivory coloured nightdress. He suddenly felt like an intruder and once again the doctor's words came to mind. He gingerly went over to the bathroom door knocking lightly upon it. Without waiting for a reply he said, 'sorry, I just thought we had agreed to make an early start. I'll leave you to get ready. Meet me downstairs for breakfast.'

Jason was just finishing his first cup of tea when Anna arrived. She had dressed quicker than he had expected.

'Sorry Jason. You were quite right. I know we have a busy day today. You could have waited in my room if you had wished to,' said Anna. The thought of it made Jason feel uncomfortable as he felt himself blush a little. Moments later, Jason's fried breakfast arrived followed by Croissant, Pain Au Chocolat and coffee for Anna.

'I took the liberty of ordering your breakfast for you,' said Jason with a smile.

'I'll be sad to leave such a wonderful hotel,' said Anna.

'Shhh,' hissed Jason. 'We are here for the week–remember?'

'Yes, yes I know. You don't need to shush me. Apart from the hotel staff, we are the only guests here at this ridiculous hour.'

'I can't help that, the coach trip to the Lake District leaves in an hour,' said Jason with a hint of mild rebuke in his voice.

Just as they were about to leave the restaurant, the elderly couple they had seen yesterday outside the hotel entered the dining room. The lady gave them both a warm smile and the man greeted them with, 'good morning.' Jason returned the greeting and paused for a moment watching the old man assist his wife to a chair. The stiffness of her movements a sign of her mature age, whereas he still seemed reasonably agile. Jason lingered for a second; there was something familiar about the couple.

Outside the hotel, Anna buttoned her jacket against the morning chill.

'What do we do now it is still a little too early to set off for the coach?'

'We'll take a stroll along the top of the city wall for a few minutes. Then we'll make our way to the Thomas Cook Ticket office to wait for the coach. The direction they took along the wall led them past Chester Cathedral. From their elevated vantage point on the Roman wall they got a magnificent view of the cathedral before descending a flight of steps to the cathedral gardens. At that hour, they had the gardens to themselves, enabling them to admire the building in the beauty of the early morning sunshine. As they passed through the grounds, it was only a short walk to St Werburgh Street, before turning onto Eastgate and making their way to the coach stop.

As they approached the ticket office they were surprised to see the elderly couple from the hotel sat on a bench outside.

'Good morning, we seem to have had the same idea,' said Jason.

'Quite so,' said the old man. 'Great minds think alike, so they say.' More people turned up and soon after, the coach arrived. The conductor assisted the old man to get his wife on board the coach so they could have the front seat. Once the elderly couple were seated everyone else climbed aboard and spread about the coach. Jason let Anna select a window seat about halfway down the coach before sitting next to her. His knee momentarily brushed against hers lifting the hem of her dress an inch or two. He quickly apologised, moving his leg away before Anna noticed. A few more people arrived and then the driver started the engine. The conductor closed the coach door, and a couple of minutes later the conductor checked his watch.

'It's time Fred.'

The driver put the coach into gear and they were off.

Chapter Eight

Once the coach had passed through the more industrialised areas around Warrington, Wigan and Preston, it took a more meandering route through the Cheshire and Lancashire hills and then along the edge of Lake Windermere, making for a pleasant journey.

The coach made only one stop outside Lancaster Castle for an hour to exchange drivers, and this allowed the passengers a refreshment break at a tea shop opposite the castle gates. The stop was just long enough for a brief look around the outside of the 11th-century castle.

The well-fortified structure was now a prison, and they could see inmates at some of the small, thickly barred windows. The elderly lady, who Jason and Anna now recognised from the train and at the Grand hotel, stayed on board the coach whilst her husband went to fetch her a cup of tea. When it came time to leave, thankfully everyone returned to the coach on time, and the bus set off with no delay.

The coach passengers remained silent as they left Lancaster. But, by the time they were half-way to their final destination, the melancholic atmosphere brought about by the prison had passed, and the passengers were once again chattering to each other.

After four hours, the coach pulled up outside the Lake Windermere Hotel in Bowness-on-Windermere. It was a two-story building in the Victorian style and made from the local dark grey granite. Jason sighed with relief as the coach stopped at the hotel. Being sat on a cramped bus for such a long time had made his leg ache, and he longed to lie down and rest it on a comfortable bed. He impatiently waited alongside the coach for the conductor to unload their luggage, and for the hotel porter to come with a trolley to take it inside.

Anna went into the hotel to register with the receptionist. The only other passengers with luggage were the elderly couple who had gone straight into the hotel and not waited for their luggage to be unloaded from the coach. By the time Jason reached the reception desk, the elderly couple were nowhere in sight.

The rooms Jason and Anna were allocated were next to each other. Each had a small balcony with a wrought iron rail around it, allowing views out over Lake Windermere. Their rooms shared an adjoining door, and also a bathroom. The rooms were clean and comfortable, though the furniture was getting that well-used look about it. The porter delivered their luggage and Jason gave him a shilling. While Jason was unpacking, there was a knock on the adjoining door.

'I hope you do not mind,' said Anna. 'I must take a bath and freshen up. After which we could have lunch and then go for a cruise on the lake. Have you seen the boats from your window?'

'Yes, I have. Good idea. Do you expect to be very long?' responded Jason.

'No, well, maybe. What do you call very long?' She smiled at Jason.

'It doesn't matter. Take as long as you like. There is a W.C. at the end of the hall should the need arise.' Anna closed the door, and moments later, he heard her enter the bathroom. His bathroom door rattled as she checked that the door locked, then came the sound of rushing water as Anna filled the tub. He sat in an armchair by the balcony to read a magazine. The sound of Anna humming a tune and pottering about on the other side of the wall made it difficult for Jason to concentrate on the magazine. The magazine struggled to hold his interest as the sound of running water finished and a vision of Anna stepping into the bath came to mind. He turned the pages looking for an article to read but found nothing to cloud the image of Anna in the bath. With a sigh of frustration, he dropped the magazine on an adjacent table, grabbed his jacket, and went down to the bar for a drink.

'Gin and Tonic, please.' Jason took his drink to the window to look out over the lake. The vista of Windermere's vast expanse ran to the horizon. The placid water reflected an azure sky. From the lakes shores, steep hills rose to meet fluffy pillows of cloud which cosseted their summits.

Across from the hotel, in the centre of the lake, was a large wooded island. On the lake, pleasure craft ferried day trippers and holidaymakers back and forth from the Bowness pier. A little further along the shoreline, he spotted a forest of small white masts, a marina, he presumed. The thought of getting away from crowds of people onto a boat was an appealing one but, with no experience at handling a yacht, it was just wishful thinking.

While he was watching the boats, he caught sight of a thin puff of smoke passing the moored yachts. The smoke gave the impression that a small train was travelling over the water, as the uppermost part of the black chimney was all he could see. Moments later, the vessel came into sight as it passed the end of the pier. The boat was about thirty feet in length and powered by a steam engine set in the centre of the craft. The front portion of the boat had a raised deck with two portholes in the side. Jason assumed these indicated some kind of day cabin. A man stood in front of a large spoked wheel, steering the boat. The engine itself, all black with highly polished brass tubes fitted around its exterior was in the centre section of the boat. The rear section of the boat was covered by a white canopy fitted to four posts. This was where the boat's passengers were sitting, admiring the scenery.

He finished his drink and left the hotel to investigate the boat pier. As he got closer to the water's edge, he felt the wind on his face as the long narrow lake funnelled and exaggerated the strength of even the slightest breeze as it passed over the water. Drawn by the relaxing atmosphere of the view and the water, he bought two tickets on a large cruiser for a tour of the lake the following day. He thought about Anna, and how he had been captivated by her beauty and playfulness. Then he reminded himself that they were on the run from the Russian Secret Police and the three foreigners claiming to be Swedish tourists. Luckily, since leaving Ifan's and Megan's farm, there had been no sign of them and he hoped that he had given them the slip. He was sure it would only be a matter of time before they turned up in Chester to look for them. Jason smiled as he imagined them watching the car and the hotel, waiting for Anna and Jason to step through the hotel doors and fall into their trap; maybe to kidnap or murder Anna in some dark alley.

The ship's steam whistle interrupted his thoughts. He watched the large white cruiser reverse gracefully away from the quay. Its passengers standing at the rail waving to the people on the shore as though they were leaving their loved ones behind to go on a long sea voyage, and not just for an hour's cruise around the lake. As Jason continued watching, the steamer glided away over the water. He turned and wandered further away from the hotel to explore the shoreline. Once he was beyond a few large boathouses, he could see the forest of white yacht masts he'd spotted from the hotel window.

The lakeside marina was full of yachts of all sizes, and Jason contemplated learning to sail one day. He could afford to buy a boat, keep it, and sail it from Bridlington. Sailing around Bridlington bay on a summer day seemed very appealing. But then he dismissed the idea. He hadn't decided what he was going to do next week, never mind a year from now. The quintessential and idyllic scenery of the lake was alluring, but memories of Kenya were still pulling at his heartstrings. As he walked along the jetty, admiring the boats, he heard someone calling. Jason turned around to see a man in a white yachting jacket and wearing a white hat with a black peak coming towards him.

'Good day, sir. Interested in hiring a boat?'

Jason smiled politely. 'No, I'm sorry. I have no experience of sailing boats. I'm just out for a walk.'

'We also have motor cruisers for hire, sir. I could teach you all you need to know about sailing one of those in a few minutes. Imagine, surprising your good lady wife by taking her cruising on your own private boat for an hour or two. What would she think of that?' said the man, hopefully. 'The cruisers are kept on the other side of the marina. Come with me, I'll show you around.' Jason dutifully followed the man along the jetty.

When they arrived at the second part of the marina reserved for the motor cruisers, Jason was surprised to see so many different sizes, shapes, and styles of the boats for hire. Some were tiny, only large enough for two people and clearly meant for an hour or two cruises on the lake, whereas some others were grand affairs with fore-and-aft cabins and a covered cockpit in the centre from which to steer the boat. The salesman stepped aboard a medium-sized boat with a large cabin to the front, a small steering wheel was attached to the outside bulkhead of the cabin, and the rear section of the deck had seats for the passengers to sit and enjoy their sailing experience.

'We'll take this one out for a few minutes. The principles behind controlling the boat are the same regardless of the size of the boat. The larger boats simply require more space in which to manoeuvre. To start the boat, you first ensure the engine is in neutral with this lever. It needs to be pointing straight up.' He indicated a large chrome lever with a black handgrip on the top. 'Then you turn the key and press the starter button.' The engine started with a rumble and a puff of black smoke from the rear of the boat. The salesman jumped ashore, untied the mooring ropes from front and aft, then hopped back on board. Turning the wheel to the right, he eased the chrome lever forward a little. The note of the engine changed from a rumble to a smooth purr, and the motor cruiser slipped away from its moorings, heading towards the open expanse of the lake. Once clear of the marina, the wind picked up and Jason could feel the slight buffet of the boat as it sliced through the chop on the water.

'Come and try the steering,' called the salesman. Jason stepped forward and took the wheel. 'Just turn the wheel in the direction you wish to go. Be patient. It takes a second or two before she responds.'

Jason turned the wheel to the left and then the right, feeling the boat respond to his commands.

'Now, use the throttle to increase the speed. It's simple: the further forward you push the lever, the faster you will go. To stop, pull the lever back to neutral and then pull it back a little further, the engine will go into reverse and slow the boat down. It's just a matter of getting the feel for it, and allowing yourself enough time and space to manoeuvre the boat. You're doing great. Head back to the marina. You can tell me what you think of her in the office.'

Jason gave the salesman a smile and a nod but didn't respond to the obvious sales implication behind his statement. Jason deftly brought the boat to a stop alongside the marina jetty and the salesman jumped ashore with a mooring rope.

Once in the marina office the salesman took his place behind his desk and removed some brochures from a draw.

'Now, sir, what do you think of these beauties?' he placed the leaflets and brochures in front of his potential customer. Jason sifted through them, more out of curiosity, than seriously looking at them. He gave brochures back.

'I'm sorry, I'm not looking to buy a boat, but I would consider hiring one for a few days. Do you hire out boats?' The salesman's face dropped a little with the disappointment of a lost sale, but he soon recovered.

'Yes, sir. How long would you like to hire one for, a couple of days, a week maybe?'

'At least a week,' said Jason. The salesman beamed.

'Sir would need a boat a little larger than the one we took out just now if you were planning to sleep on board each night, or did sir plan to return to the marina each evening?'

'I hope to cruise the lake and moor up where ever we fancy. Get away from it all for a few days you might say.'

'Then I would suggest this boat here, sir,' he sifted through the brochures to find the one he was looking for. She sleeps up to six passengers in three cabins. Jason asked for a price to cover a fortnights hire.

'That one looks excellent, just what we need. Do you accept banker's cheques? I can arrange to have a cheque written out in the Marina's name and let you have it tomorrow.'

'A banker's cheque would be perfectly acceptable, sir. From when would you like to hire the boat?'

'How about tomorrow?' asked Jason.

'No problem at all, sir, and I shall ensure the boat is well provisioned for a week.' The two men shook hands and Jason headed back to the hotel.

As he entered his hotel room, he found the door leading to Anna's room had been left ajar. He knocked lightly on it before entering. Anna was sitting in an armchair reading a magazine. She was wearing a dark blue short-sleeved dress with white buttons from the waist to the neckline. The style and colour suited her perfectly, the colour combination giving her a nautical look. Jason smiled to himself as he said, 'Hello.' Considering where he had just come from he found the coincidence amusing.

'Been anywhere interesting?' she asked him.

'Down to the marina, I took a boat out for a sail on the lake.'

'You never said you liked yachts, how nice. I wish I'd been able to go with you. Maybe we can go sailing while we are here?' said Anna, looking enthusiastic at the idea.

'Well, it wasn't a yacht, it was a cabin cruiser. However, before I found the boat and took it out for a test run, I bought tickets for us to go on steamship for a lake cruise. It was only after I'd bought the tickets that I found the marina. Whilst I was out on the cruiser I had an idea. I could hire a boat for a couple of weeks and we could hide out, here on the lakes. I've just come back to see if you are ready to go out. All I need to do is go to the bank to arrange funds for hiring the cruiser.'

'That sounds splendid, much more fun than a ride on a big boat.' Anna dropped the magazine on a side table. Standing up, she picked up her jacket that had been hanging on the back of the chair. It matched her dress perfectly. She headed for the door.

'Come on, I'm keen to see this magnificent boat you've hired.'

Jason found a branch of his bank on the high street and arranged for a cheque to be made out in the marina's company name, before taking Anna to the boat.

The salesman spotted them as they arrived on the jetty and came across to greet them.

'Hello again, Mr Parva, I see you've brought your lovely wife along so she can give her approval to your choice of boat.'

Jason was about to explain their relationship but before he could, the salesman had taken Anna by the arm and was leading her along the jetty, extolling the virtues of Jason's choice of boat. He enthusiastically explained what a wonderful time they would have on holiday in such a picturesque and tranquil part of England. The boat would take them where ever they fancied, in first class comfort.

The boat Jason had chosen was much bigger than the one he'd taken out for a trial run. The salesman described the cruiser to Anna.

'As you can see, the Morning Star is a fifty-foot motor cruiser with a covered central cockpit, that's the place from where you drive the boat. There is lots of space in there for you to sit if the weather should turn a little damp, after all this is the Lake District and we wouldn't want you to get your hair wet, would we? But equally, there is space on the foredeck, that's the bit at the front. You can lounge out there on a sunny day and enjoy the scenery. Shall we go inside? Mind your step.' He slid open the door to the cockpit allowing Anna to step through. 'I've already gone over the controls with your husband so there is no need for you to trouble yourself with those. If you would like to follow me, I will show you the cabins.' He waited at the bottom of the steps ready to take Anna's hand in case she needed assistance. 'As you can see, this is the saloon area. There is a kitchen area just here. The table in the centre of the deck can be removed and stored away to give you more space when you don't need it and there is plenty of comfortable seating.' He led Anna further forward through another door.

'This is the master cabin.' He opened the door to show a spacious bedroom with a double bed, 'and just here is the bathroom. It's a little small for a bath but there is a shower, a wash-hand basin and the other usual facilities you would expect.' Jason stayed in the saloon waiting for them to return. As Anna went past him she raised her eyebrows as though wanting to ask a question. But the salesman took her arm again and led her to the back of the saloon.

'Just down here we have two more cabins, each with bunk beds. As you can see they are much smaller than the master cabin, but they serviceable enough for anyone with children. Not that I expect a lovely young couple like you will need them.' He turned towards the next door. 'And last of all, a second bathroom. A little larger than the one up front, but it is for four people.' He closed the door and took Anna back to the saloon.

'What do you think of her? I think you'll both have a wonderful holiday.' The salesman waited for a response from Anna, but Jason beat her to it.

'Thank you very much for showing Anna around the boat, Mr Longbottom. I have the banker's draft ready for you.' Jason reached inside his jacket and removed an envelope. 'I take it the boat will be ready tomorrow?'

'Yes, sir. It will be fully provisioned and fuelled as requested.'

'Very good. I will make arrangements with our hotel to have our luggage packed and brought down to the boat,' instructed Jason. 'Come along, dear, I'm sure we have some last-minute shopping to do.' Jason encouraged Anna towards the steps which led up to the deck above.

Once away from the marina Anna came to an abrupt stop. 'You told that man we were married; how could you? And the way he spoke to me. He was horrible. I just wanted to put him in his place.'

'Yes, I agree. I'm sorry but, we are supposed to be in hiding. Hiring a boat seemed like the best way of doing it, and letting him think we are married will help the subterfuge we are creating.'

She gave the matter some thought. 'Maybe you are right, but what about Scotland? I thought we were making our way up there.'

'Yes, we will, but the opportunity to disappear completely for a few days, and throw anyone following us off our scent, is too good an opportunity to miss.'

'Um, I suppose you may be right. But I do not want to meet that insufferable man again?'

'Agreed. I will deal with him. I had hoped to just show you around the boat without him being there, but he must have wanted to meet you.'

'Very well, what about this shopping you were talking about? I will need to buy some suitable shoes and some slacks. I can't wear a dress if I have to climb ladders and jump on and off boats. I will also need some sweaters and a waterproof jacket and...'

'All right, all right. You have made your point. We both need sailing clothes. I will ask the hotel to pack our luggage and put it into storage until we send for it. We can get our sailing clothes delivered to the boat directly from the shop.'

They spent the rest of the day visiting all the best shops in Bowness-on-Windermere that sold sailing clothes, with a break for lunch to rest tired feet.

It was as they were walking to the marina the following morning that Jason spotted a black car drive past with three familiar passengers in it. He pulled Anna to one side, holding her close, hoping that the occupants of the vehicle hadn't seen them.

'It's the Russians. They just went past in that car,' said Jason, in a low voice.

Anna looked alarmed, twisting in his embrace to stare after the car which was just turning a corner. 'Are you sure? What do we do?' she said anxiously.

'We stick with my plan and take the boat. The hotel will keep our luggage until we return for it or I will ask for it to be forwarded on to another address. I didn't tell the hotel manager about the boat. Come on, the sooner we get out on the lake the better. We have some serious thinking to do about how they seem to know where we are and how to find us.'

An hour later Anna and Jason were on their own, directing the Morning Star south, away from the busy Bowness marina.

Chapter Nine

'We should be safe out here,' said Jason, just before killing the cruiser's engine.

They had sailed south from Bowness-on-Windermere and were now moored outside the village of Lakeside at a jetty, which was a couple of hundred yards away from the village railway station.

As they drank coffee and ate sandwiches on the deck of the Morning Star, Anna was lost in her thoughts.

'I don't understand how the Russians are able to stay one step behind us all the time. It's not even as if we know where we are going until we get there,' said Anna.

'They must have someone following our every move, someone we haven't spotted, someone so clever at staying out of sight that we haven't noticed they are watching us,' said Jason.

'Who could it be?'

'I don't know,' snapped Jason, a little more aggressively than he had meant to.

'Well, we can't stay on this boat forever,' said Anna.

'We should be safe for the time being, at least. No one can get close to us out there on the water, without us seeing them. We have to think as they do. How would we track someone? We have to assume the Russian Secret Police will discover which hotel we were staying at in Bowness. But that will only bring them to a dead end. I didn't tell anyone at the hotel where we were going, or when we would return. Next, I suspect the Russians will check the bus and railway stations, and discover we haven't left the area that way. That leaves the only other means of leaving the lakes: car, or walking. Hopefully, they will waste a lot of time trying to find where we hired a car. Checking the ferries that run from one side of the lake to the other, won't help them. There are hundreds of people using the ferry every day. The operators wouldn't remember us even if we had escaped the area that way. If we get really lucky, they will assume we have stolen a car, and have moved on; still heading for Scotland. So by the time we return the boat in two weeks, we should be free of them,' said Jason.

Anna became thoughtful again.

'Maybe I should go to the police. Tell them the whole story and that I'm being followed.'

'You've tried telling the police you are in danger. If you told them everything, the press would get to know and you would never be free of them. No, the police can't help us, not yet anyway,' countered Jason.

'Should I go home? My family has more experience at avoiding communists than the police do.'

'That would just raise more problems. If the secret police know who you are, they will know the identity of your adoptive family and be watching them. No, you are better off staying in England with me. We just have to give the Russians time to think they have lost you. If we give them enough time, they will move on to look somewhere else.'

'What do we do now?' asked Anna.

'We may as well stay here for the night. It will be dark soon and too late to go in search of new moorings.'

After an evening meal, made from the contents of a few assorted tins and a bottle of wine, they played a few hands of cards before retiring for the evening. Anna, as Jason had expected, took the larger fore cabin, and he moved into one of the stern cabins with bunk beds.

The combination of a long day, fresh air, wine, and the gentle rocking of the boat soon sent them to sleep, listening to the ripple of the water against the boat's hull.

The following morning dawned dull and grey. A drizzling rain fell from the low cloud, creating a thick screen around the boat. Visibility was down to twenty yards. Anna peered into the gloom through the porthole above her bed. She shivered. 'Merde,' she said to herself, her breath fogging the glass in front of her nose. Pulling the blankets up under her chin, she looked at her watch: six-thirty. Hearing movement from the saloon, she threw back the covers and grabbed her jacket, putting it on over her nightdress, before going to the tiny bathroom to wash her hands and face. The water from the hot tap ran cold. 'Oh non,' she sighed. After quickly splashing her face with the water, she returned to her cabin.

Opening her cabin door, she saw Jason. He was wearing a thick cable-knit sweater and navy-blue trousers.

'There is no hot water,' she said, pulling her jacket closer about her.

'Oh, I'm sorry. I didn't want to wake you by starting the engine. We need the engine running to get hot water. The kettle has just boiled; you could use the water from that for washing if you like.' Anna held out her hand and Jason passed the kettle across to her. Fifteen minutes later, she emerged from her cabin having washed and dressed, but she was still wearing the warm jacket.

'What happened to the weather? I'm freezing,' shivered Anna.

'Yes, it rains a lot in the Lake District. Don't worry, it'll probably brighten up later in the day. Would you like some toast and coffee? It's only instant coffee, I'm afraid.'

'Coffee first please,' she wishfully looked out of the window for any sign of improvement in the gloom and drizzle.

'I've lit the gas heater,' said Jason. 'It's a bit on the small side, but it should warm the place up soon enough.'

Anna gave him a look of disbelief, then sipped her coffee, which she held in both hands.

'There's nothing we can do about the weather. At lunchtime, I'll treat you to a nice lunch at the hotel that's near the station. After that, if the clouds have blown away, we can cruise the lake for a bit,' suggested Jason.

153

Anna responded by shrugging her shoulders. So Jason went up to the cockpit, leaving Anna sitting in the saloon, staring out of the window. In the locker with the waterproof clothing, he found a fishing rod. He enthusiastically assembled it and made bait by tearing bits of bread to put on the hook, but after an hour of the fish nicking the bait without taking the hook, he gave up. It was one of those strange days you get around water. It's cold. The mist is so thick you can barely see where you are going. But, if you look directly upwards, you can see the sun and blue sky.

Eventually, eleven-thirty arrived. Anna and Jason left the boat, making their way to the Waterside Hotel. With a gin and tonic, and Pernod with lemonade in hand, they settled in front of a roaring log fire, their spirits reviving in the cosy warmth and glow of the flames.

'I'm sorry,' said Anna. 'The weather is so dull, and I was so cold this morning, I didn't feel like talking.'

'That's all right. It has been a depressing morning sitting on the boat with nothing to do and unable to appreciate the scenery. Though, when the weather improves, the lake around here is supposed to be beautiful. It's just our bad luck this mist has closed in. Let's have a good hearty meal and a bottle of wine to cheer us up.'

The rustic, informal atmosphere of the country hotel gave the place a homely feel, and they relaxed into a conversation about their homes and Anna's mother. It was two hours later when they ventured out of the hotel and headed back to the boat.

'Couldn't we stay at the hotel tonight, instead of being cramped up on your little boat?' asked Anna.

'It's hardly a little boat,' protested Jason. 'No, I don't think that would be wise. If we stay at the hotel, they will keep a record of our names and addresses. The whole point of hiring the boat was so we could stay anonymous and keep moving. Look, the mist is lifting, and the sun is breaking through. We should move on and find somewhere else to stay for the night.' Jason looped his arm through Anna's. 'Once we are sure we have lost the Russians, we can think about creating a new life for you. You may not have realised it, but I don't think you will be able to go back to your family home in France. They will have it under constant observation...' Anna pulled Jason to a stop and looked up into Jason's face.

'I hadn't considered that at all. I thought. I don't know what I thought - I just hoped that if I could escape for a while; tell the police about everything. Maybe the Russians would go away. I wish that old man had never brought me those papers and the jewel. I don't want to be the Empress of Russia. I've never been to Russia. I don't even speak Russian very well. I'm going to destroy the papers and sell the jewel, then I won't be able to claim who they say I am and they will leave me alone.'

'I'm afraid it's not that simple. The secret police won't let you. What if you change your mind later on? They won't take the risk that you have more evidence of your true inheritance hidden away. Papers or no papers, there will be others who will know your true identity and seek to use you for their own political agenda. I've been thinking about it. You only have two choices: claim your birthright, overthrow the communists in Russia and take your place as Tsarina or disappear, change your name, your life, your home, everything, and start again outside France as a new person.'

Anna broke awake from Jason and walked ahead of him back to the boat. Once on board, she went to her cabin and shut and locked the door. Jason heard her sobbing inside. He wanted to go to her, comfort her, but what could he say that would change anything or make matters better? He had made Anna see a reality she hadn't wanted to face up to. She needed time to come to terms with it. Jason untied the boat and set off to find a new mooring spot for the night.

*****

Unseen and unheard by Jason and Anna, as the Morning Star headed smoothly over the water, there was a screech of tyres in the car park of the Waterside Hotel. On the boat, the throbbing boat engine drowned out the sound of the car's tyres shredding rubber on the newly tarmacked hotel drive. The slamming of a car's doors and running feet as men ran into the hotel.

*****

A mile further up the bank of the lake, Jason spotted a jetty which ran out into the water. It led to a group of buildings surrounded by trees. Jason got the impression it was a neglected farm. There was no sign of life and in need of a secluded place to stop for the night, Jason brought the boat alongside the jetty and switched off the engine. After ensuring the boat was securely moored, he set off to search the buildings. The old farm buildings looked as though they had been abandoned for a long time. The farmhouse was boarded up, and the barns stood empty. Jason looked up at the sky. The light was fading faster. Clouds had rolled in; the drizzle had turned into heavy rain. Jason cast a final look around with one thought in mind: *that bloody war.* He'd seen things like this before around his home village of Nafferton; young men, leaving home for an adventure, leaving their parents at home to run the family farm. For many, their sons did not return from war or they were too severely crippled to carry on the family farming tradition. When this happened, the smaller farms would get sold off to neighbouring farmers. But the unwanted farm buildings were left to fall into disrepair. Eventually, as families died out or moved away, even the old family home would be abandoned.

By the time Jason returned to the boat, Anna was sitting in the saloon. The kettle was coming to boil on the stove. She looked up at Jason for a second as he came down the saloon steps. Then, embarrassed at the way she must appear, she turned her face away and wiped a final tear from her cheek. Jason paused at the bottom of the steps, looking at the steaming kettle, then back to Anna, 'coffee?'

'No-let me,' Anna shuffled from her seat and, avoiding looking directly at Jason, she fumbled with the cups and the filter for the coffee. 'Would you prefer tea?' she asked without turning around.

'Coffee, please. I've pulled in at an abandoned farm. We have the place to ourselves.'

She didn't respond but carried on making the coffee. Anna set two cups of coffee on the table.

'I'm sorry. I've been a bloody fool. I've been treating this as some kind of holiday adventure, but it's not, is it?' Jason didn't answer. 'I will send the papers and the jewel back to Russia. I will put it in writing that I give up any claim to the Russian throne. I'll tell them anything they want me to say.'

'Are you sure that's what you want to do? If so, we can return to Bowness and send the Jewel and papers to the Russian embassy in London. We'll have to stay in hiding for a few more days to give the Russian ambassador time to contact his agents and tell them to back off, but I suspect by the end of the week, it will be all over. Is that what you want to do?'

Anna stared blankly at Jason. 'What's the matter?' asked Jason.

'I don't have them with me,' said Anna, slowly.

'But you showed them to me on the train.'

'Yes. I had them on the train. But do you remember when we stopped in Hinckley to buy some new clothes, and stayed the night in that hotel? Well, when we separated to go shopping, I went to a bank arranged for them to keep the papers and the jewel in their safe. I didn't say what how important they were or what they represented. I just said I would return and collect them in a few weeks because I didn't want to carry them around with me and risk losing them.'

Jason was about to respond when there was the sound of a bump from the other side of the jetty, followed by footsteps on the wooden boards. Jason went up the steps to the cockpit to see who had arrived. All Jason could discern in the gloom and rain was the outline of two people standing on the jetty, one male and the other female. They were looking in his direction. Jason opened the wheelhouse door and stepped through onto the deck. A male voice called across to him.

'I'm sorry, we didn't mean to disturb you. It's just that the weather is too bad to stay out on the lake and we needed somewhere to pull in. I saw your boat's lights and then the jetty and thought we'd join you. I hope you don't mind?' Jason moved closer to the couple. They were young, early twenties, he thought, their waterproof clothing hiding most of their appearance. Their small boat with a tiny fore cabin and an outboard motor was about the size of a floating caravan for two people.

'No problem, please do,' responded Jason. Hearing voices, Anna came up behind Jason to see who he was speaking to. After a few seconds, Anna gave Jason a dig in the ribs.

'Ask them if they want to come aboard. They look frozen out there.'

'What, you don't know who they might be,' hissed Jason.

'Well, they don't look or sound like Russians, that's for sure.'

Jason humphed, before turning back to the couple on the jetty.

'Would you like to come aboard for a hot drink?'

'Thank you,' came the keen response. 'If it's no trouble? We'll just take our oilskins off and we'll be right over.' Anna went down to the saloon to make more coffee; she also pulled a bottle of Scotch from the cupboard.

'I thought we were going to stay out of sight for a while?' hissed Jason.

'They hardly look like Russian Secret Police, do they? And, anyway, I remember Mr and Mrs Jenkins taking us in when we needed help. It's the right thing to do.'

'They don't need help. They just stopped because the weather turned bad,' retorted Jason.

'I know-I just need some company to take my mind off things. After all, we are going to be on this boat together for a week.'

The sound of feet on the deck above their heads, and a shout of 'ahoy there', ended the heated debate brewing in the saloon.

'We are down here,' Anna called up to the visitors.

Jason stood away from the steps to allow their guests to come down. The man came first. He was young, good-looking, with blond hair and athletically built. The girl looked about twenty, slim, and beautiful. She also had blonde hair.

'This is very good of you. My name is Barry, and this is Felicity. We are new to this boating lark and thought we'd better stop for the night before we ran into something in the dark.'

'Fliss. My friends call me Fliss.' Fliss shook hands with Anna and then Jason. Barry produced two bottles of wine from a shoulder bag.

'I didn't want to come aboard unarmed, so to speak. Not after your kind offer.'

'I'm just making coffee and was going to put a tot of whisky in it to warm us all up, but if you'd rather have wine, I don't mind,' said Anna, defensively.

'No-that sounds great. We can have the coffee and whisky to warm us up and the wine to keep the conversation flowing,' said Barry, placing the bottles on the table. Jason looked on in silent disapproval.

'Take a seat, please. The coffee won't be long. This is my cousin Jason and I'm Anna. We are on holiday. Jason wanted to show me the lake. It's just our bad luck the weather isn't better than it is.'

'Yes, it can be beastly around here, even in mid-summer. The weather over this lake seems to have a mind of its own. Have you been here long?' questioned Fliss.

'No,' said Anna. 'Just a few days. It was Jason's idea to hire the boat, and...'

While Anna chatted to Fliss, Jason finished preparing the coffee by pouring a tot of whisky into each of the four mugs, and then topping them up with the steaming black liquid.

'Sugar and cream, anyone?' announced Jason.

'Not for us, thank you,' responded Barry, as he put his hand into his pocket. Just for an instant, his fingers fastened around something hard and metallic. He hesitated, then released his grip.

Jason joined Barry at the table and for the rest of the evening, the conversation revolved around boats, past holidays, and where they hoped to visit next. Once the two bottles of wine were finished, they started on the whisky. So it was close to midnight when four very drunk people parted company. On deck, Jason and Anna steadied themselves against the boat's guardrail as they said farewell to their visitors. Barry, surefooted, jumped to the jetty, ready to help Fliss, who was a little unsteady as she stepped off the Morning Star. After much-protracted hand waving and many goodnights, Jason shut the wheelhouse door. Anna went below first whilst Jason checked all was secure for the night. He was about to turn the boat's deck lights out when he was distracted by a scream from below. Jason rushed to the top of the steps. Anna was lying in a heap on the saloon floor.

'Anna, are you all right?' he called down to her. He got no response. Quickly descending to her side, he stood over her.

'Anna, Anna. Are you hurt?'

'Only my pride,' came the slurred reply, followed by a fit of giggles. 'I think I missed a step.' More giggles followed. Jason bent down to help Anna to her feet.

'I think I will sleep right here,' she slurred, her eyes unable to focus on Jason's face.

'Oh, no you won't,' muttered Jason. Scooping her up in his arms, he carried her through to her cabin and dropped her unceremoniously on the bed.

Anna giggled again. 'I told you they were nice people. I like Fliss. I like the name Flissss. Should I change my name to Flissss, Jason?'

'If you like. But do it in the morning.' He pulled off her shoes, hesitated about what to do next, and then threw a blanket over her. 'Sleep well; I'll see you in the morning.'

After entering his own cabin, Jason was hit by a wave of tiredness. His head was aching, the alcohol and the long day overtaking him. Sitting down on his bunk, he ran his fingers through his hair and yawned. Lifting his bad leg onto the bed, he lay back. He was asleep within seconds of his head hitting the pillow.

Jason opened his eyes and blinked. His head pounded, his eyes struggled to focus, and his stomach felt like it was full of sour cream. He lay still, wondering what time it was. But it was his bladder that forced him to get up. He staggered to the bathroom.

When he was finished, he washed, and then drank four glasses of water. He hoped there were some aspirin tablets in the first aid box. With two painkillers and another glass of water in hand, he slumped onto the bench seat, which ran along the wall in the saloon. Resting his head in his hands, he wondered why he had allowed himself to drink so much, and why he had been foolish enough to finish the evening drinking whisky after two bottles of wine. He looked at the door leading to Anna's cabin. There was no sound coming from within. S*erves her right if she's suffering. She shouldn't have asked those two onboard.*

After ten minutes of feeling sorry for himself, he tried to fill the kettle with water, but the water pump barely had enough power in it to force any more than a dribble out the tap.

'What the hell is the matter with you?' he muttered to the tap. He gave up on the water and decided to check on Anna. He knocked on the door but got no reply. He knocked again and was rewarded with silence. Jason slid the door open a touch and peeked through.

'Anna, are you awake?' Silence. He opened the door fully and saw Anna was missing from her bed. Crossing to the bathroom, he found her lying on the floor alongside a vomit-splashed toilet bowl. The light in the bathroom was on, just. The bulb burned dimly. He looked up at the cabin light. It too was on, but also shone very dimly.

'Oh great, we've run the boat's battery down,' he exclaimed as he slammed his hand against the light switch to turn it off. Leaving Anna where she was, he went around the saloon, switching off every electrical item he could find. Then, returning to Anna, he grabbed a towel and rolled her onto her side to wipe her face. She moaned a little and curled up on the floor, shielding her eyes from the light that came through the frosted glass porthole. Jason picked her up and placed her back on her bed before returning to the kettle. He gave it a shake, listening to the water slosh around inside. There was probably just enough to make a cup of tea each. By the time the kettle had boiled on the gas stove, Anna was making moaning noises in her cabin.

'*Serves you right,*' thought Jason. '*Serves us both right.*' Tea made and with two heaped spoons of sugar in his, he took a sip and then two more. That felt better. He took a cup through to Anna. She took a sip and cringed. 'Coffee,' she croaked.

'There isn't any,' said Jason. She opened her eyes and looked at him, confused by his answer. He offered her two aspirin tablets.

'I'll explain after you have taken these.' She sipped the tea slowly until it had all gone, saving the last bit for the two aspirin.

It was close to twelve o'clock - noon before they were sat side by side in the saloon. Jason explained to her how the lights had been left on all night and that now the boat's battery was flat.

'What do we do?' asked Anna.

'I'm going to ask Barry if we can borrow the battery from their boat to start our engine, so we can recharge our battery again.'

'Can you do that?' asked Anna.

'What, ask them if I can borrow their boat battery, or use it to start our boat's engine?'

'You know what I mean. Stop making fun of me. There's a little man in my head trying to crack his way out with a hammer.'

'Yes. If they haven't done the same stupid thing that we have.' Jason drew back the curtains and looked outside.

'They've gone,' he exclaimed. 'They must have left during the night or early this morning.' He left the window and headed for the steps up to the wheelhouse. Jason scanned the jetty. Their visitors from the evening before had gone and were nowhere in sight. As Jason turned back towards the cockpit, he noticed how the deck and upper structure lights had been left on all night. They too glowed weakly on the low power.

'Oh no. What else can go wrong?' He looked at the boat's control panel. The ignition key was in the on position and the needle on the battery power indicator was in the red zone. 'What? How did that happen?' After flicking all the switches to their off position, he looked at the battery dial again. It still indicated no power. There was no point in trying to start the engine and draining it further.

Going back to Anna, he explained the situation. 'Barry and Fliss are nowhere in sight and all the deck lights had been left on. With no battery power, we can't start the engine, and until we can do that, we are stuck here.'

'What does the instruction manual say?' asked Anna.

'What?' said Jason, looking confused.

'You know; the boat instruction book. It's over there in the drawer.'

Jason looked at where she was pointing.

'What's the point? If the battery is flat, I can't start the engine. If I can't start the engine, I can't charge the battery. What is the instruction book going to say that differs from that?'

'I don't know. Read it. It may tell you where you can find a spare battery.'

Jason reluctantly flicked through the pages. Sure enough, there it was on page sixty-three. In Case of Loss of Battery Power. You will find a second battery in the compartment next to the wet weather clothing locker. Included are all the tools necessary to swap the battery over. Jason closed the book and tossed it on the table.

'I'll be back in a few minutes.'

After some banging about and a few choice swear words, all fell silent from Jason. He came down the steps from the deck above.

'We need to get off the boat!'

'Did you find the new battery?' asked Anna, smiling.

'Yes, and that's not all. There is a bomb attached to the engine. If the battery hadn't failed, when I tried to start the engine, the boat would have exploded.' Anna's face dropped. She went very pale.'

'Who could have done it?' she asked.

'Who the hell do you think? Our two guests from last night. Who else?'

'No, but, but...'

'Pack a small bag with essentials and get ashore. I have an idea.'

An hour later, standing at the entrance to one of the empty barns, Anna and Jason, each with a small bag, watched as the Morning Star exploded in a giant ball of flames, black smoke and splitters of wood. Anna let out a cry of shock at the size of the explosion, pulling back behind inside the neglected barn for cover. When she re-emerged, fragments of burning boat had been blasted across the lake. Debris was falling from the sky like burning confetti, settling on the water and shoreline for a second before being extinguished by the water of the lake. The explosion had been so intense there was nothing left of the Morning Star above the waterline and the jetty to which the boat had been moored had been cut in two.

'What do we do now?' asked Anna.

'We walk,' said Jason, feeling for his service revolver in his coat pocket. 'That explosion will have been seen and heard for miles. The police will be here soon and the person who planted the bomb will be back to check on his handy work. It won't take the authorities long to figure out there was no one on board. We must leave now; get out of the area and find somewhere else to hole up.'

Chapter Ten

Leaving the abandoned farm, Jason led Anna north through the trees. He didn't know where they were going, only that they had to get away from the hire boat before anyone came to investigate the explosion. They couldn't go east because of the lake, south would take them back towards the hotel and the railway station. If they went west, they would have to cross the road that led to the village of Lakeside, the railway station and the hotel, and risk being seen. North was the only direction left open to them.

The day was dry and clear but, because of rising late, and being delayed by the bomb on the boat, the afternoon was passing quickly. The woodland through which they stumbled was dense and waterlogged. Hidden roots beneath the water hindered their progress as their feet snagged on every unseen obstruction. After a couple of hundred yards of hard slog, the trees thinned out, and Jason could see a small open stretch of ground as the land rose slightly towards the road and up to the hill on the far side. Beyond the open ground grew more stunted trees and tangled undergrowth. It was too greater an obstacle in their path. They had no choice. Jason turned towards the road. As they reached it, they could hear shouting coming from the abandoned farm behind them. It hadn't taken long for people to come from Lakeside to investigate the source of the explosion. When Jason and Anna reached the road, it was clear of traffic.

'This will be our best chance to cross the road. Come on,' said Jason in a hushed voice. They rushed across the narrow road and into the tree line on the far side. The ground rose immediately, taxing their lungs as they struggled over rocky outcrops while they tried to keep under cover of the trees. The wooded hillside seemed to have set traps for them with every step they took. As they made their way over loose rocks, patches of mossy ground full of water and around thorny bushes which stabbed and pricked through their clothing or tore at their hands as they climbed the hill. It took them an hour to reach the summit, where they found another smaller lake. They both dropped to their knees at the water's edge and scooped up handfuls of the cold, clear liquid to wash the grime from their hands and faces.

'I'm hungry and tired,' complained Anna.

'Eat half a sandwich and a couple of biscuits; we'll rest for ten minutes and then move on.' Jason sat on a rock and massaged his complaining leg. 'We need to put as much distance between us and the farm as quickly as we can before we find shelter for the night.'

'But where are we going?' begged Anna.

'I don't know,' confessed Jason. 'Another thing we need to do is change our appearance. As soon as we can, we need to get some clothes that make us look like locals or hikers. These boating clothes show we've come from the lakes.'

'I'm frightened. How are the Russians keeping up with us? They always seem to know where we are. What happens when we can't get away?' Jason looked at Anna as she sat on the rock at the water's edge. He knelt down beside her, cupping her cheek in his hand and wiping crumbs from his mouth.

'We *will* get away from them. I promise.' As he stared into her eyes, there was a look of vulnerability that added to her beauty.

For the rest of the day, they tramped on relentlessly until Anna sat down.

'I can't go any further. My feet are bleeding and I'm tired.'

'I'm sorry, I wasn't thinking.' Jason scanned the surrounding countryside.

'Look down there. Do you see? There's a farm down there. We'll rest for the night in one of the barns, only this time, we won't have a car leaving tracks in the mud to give us away. We'll rest here until it gets completely dark. Look, we can follow that farm track down to the farm. We won't have to clamber over this rough ground to get there. Let me have the first aid pack from the boat and I'll bandage your feet.' Jason removed Anna's deck shoes and socks to reveal blisters on her heels and toes.

'The best I can do for now is to wrap a bandage around your feet to stop them rubbing in your wet shoes. Before you go to sleep tonight, put your socks inside your clothes next to your skin, and you'll find that by morning they will have dried out, the same with the bandages.'

As darkness fell, they could see lights in the valley below. 'Right, come on, we'll follow this track down to the farm,' said Jason.

Anna staggered to her feet. The blisters on her feet complained bitterly, with stabbing pains at every step she took. She limped on, with only the promise of somewhere safe to sleep, giving her the incentive to put one foot in front of the other. The stars were bright and, with only a faint glow from the moon to give them light to see by, it took them longer than Jason had anticipated to reach the stone wall which surrounded the farm.

'Wait here. I'll see if there is a hayloft for us to hide in.' Jason tiptoed up to the first outbuilding. It was too small to be a barn; it seemed to be some kind of tool shed or workshop. Past the tool shed stood a larger building. Keeping in the shadows, he crossed the yard to the side of the building. He could just make out the large open doors of what must be the entrance to the barn. Satisfied he'd found their bed for the night, he returned to Anna.

'It's this way, not far now.' He picked up both of their bags and set off, with Anna limping behind him. Once inside the barn, Jason pointed to a ladder. 'We go up there.'

'I can't climb up there,' hissed Anna. 'My feet hurt too much.'

'You have no choice. There is nowhere else. We can't risk knocking on the farmer's door and asking him to put us up for the night. I'll help you up, it's not far.' Jason took up their bags first and returned for Anna.

'Start climbing. I'll follow close behind and assist you.' One painful step at a time, Anna made her way up the ladder to the hayloft. She was just coming within reach of the top when her legs wobbled.

'Jason, I'm not going to make it. The pain is too much.' Jason didn't reply. He took a couple of steps up the ladder to get as close behind her as he could. Holding on to the ladder with his left hand, he placed his right hand on Anna's bottom and shoved as hard as he could. Anna stifled a scream as she felt Jason's hand lift her off the ladder and launch her skyward. She landed in a heap on the hayloft deck. Scrambling across the floor of the hayloft, she moved away from the ladder. As Jason reached the top of the ladder, he could hear Anna complaining bitterly in French about the way he had manhandled her. Jason understood some of what she was saying. As he reached the platform, he put his finger to his lips and went, 'Shhhh. I'm sorry. I had to do it or you were going to fall.' He stifled a laugh.

'It worked though, didn't it?'

Anna glared back at him for a moment before letting her face break into a smile.

'You took me by surprise. You should have told me what you were going to do.'

'There wasn't time,' protested Jason. 'Come on. Shuffle towards the back and get some sleep; we need to be on our way at first light. We can't risk the farmer finding us.'

A crowing cockerel awoke Jason as the first signs of daylight dimmed the stars. The pungent smell of straw in the barn reminded him of the time they'd spent in North Wales with Megan and Ifan.

'Anna, Anna, wake up. We need to get going.'

Anna groaned. 'What? Do we have to? I've only been asleep for a few minutes.'

'You've had nearly six hours' sleep, according to my watch. We have to leave before the farmer starts work. Once we are safely away from here, we'll stop and finish the sandwiches and biscuits. When we find a village shop, we can buy some bread and cheese or something.'

Anna gingerly re-bandaged her feet and removed her dry, warm socks from inside her clothes. Jason descended the ladder first. Anna dropped their bags down to him and followed.

'I can't keep up the same pace we did yesterday. My feet hurt too much,' complained Anna, as limped towards the barn door.

'Yes, so I see. We'll stay on the roads today. It'll make walking easier for you. Anyway, we need to find a road sign to figure out where we are going.'

As they walked, they watched the sun come up over the hillside and listened to the dawn chorus. Rabbits and pheasants searched the fields for food. The world around them was at peace and the events of the day before felt more like a bad dream than the reality of their life. By mid-morning, they had reached Penny Bridge, a small village with a shop. They stopped to buy a pie each and a pint of milk to share. The locals eyed the strangers with curiosity, dressed in their boating clothes. Jason thanked the shopkeeper politely before joining Anna as she looked around the store.

'Don't say anything,' Jason whispered to Anna, 'or your French accent will really give the shopkeeper something to get interested in.' Jason ushered Anna out of the shop. It didn't take them long to finish the pie and the milk as they walked along.

'We're attracting too much attention dressed like this,' said Jason.

'Yes, I know what you mean. I was beginning to feel like a specimen on display,' said Anna. Jason laughed.

'I suspect they don't get many strangers in a little village like that, especially dressed as we are.'

Their pace slowed. Jason, too, was feeling the strain as his leg complained painfully, and Anna's blistered feet were making her limp worse. The next village they came to was Greenodd. It was larger than Penny Bridge. Main Street had a variety of shops, one of which sold clothing suitable for farm workers.

'This will do,' said Jason, pointing at the shop. 'We'll buy a change of clothing from here. We'll get boots, socks and durable trousers and a couple of shirts. They have backpacks as well, so we'll be able to dump these small cases. We'll look more like a couple of hikers rather than two stranded sailors.'

'I don't care what we have to wear so long as I get a chance to sit down and rest,' said Anna.

It didn't take long for them to find new clothes and to change. A short local bus ride took them into Ulverston, a market town.

'Are we stopping here for the night?' asked Anna. Jason looked at his companion. He could see she needed more rest.

'Yes, all right, but we'll find a bed-and-breakfast for the night. No more hotels for us from now on.'

'I don't care, so long as my room has a bed,' sighed Anna. As they walked along King Street, at the corner of Lower Brook Street, they found a notice board pointing towards Mrs Graham's Bed and Breakfast. A little way down the narrow street they found Mrs Graham's teashop, B&B, vacancy. On entering the teashop, they were greeted by a lady with a lean face, thin lips and a narrow bony nose. She was wearing a white apron that matched the colour of her hair.

'Good afternoon, we are looking for a room for the night,' enquired Jason. The woman looked them both up and down.

'We don't have any unmarried hanky-panky in my house. It will have to be separate rooms unless you are married?'

'Separate rooms are what we are looking for,' said Jason as agreeably as he could muster.

'Very well then, it is five shillings per night, each mind you and breakfast is from seven till half-past. I can't be doing with people sleeping in. There's always lots of work to do; I have to get the teashop ready for opening time.' 'Mavis – will you keep an eye on things for me while I take this couple up to their rooms?'

A woman stuck her head around the side of the kitchen door. 'Yes, Agatha. I'll be right there.'

The head which had appeared in the doorway was a carbon copy of Agatha's. Mavis Graham stepped into the teashop and smiled at Anna and Jason. The two ladies were clearly twins, but one got the immediate impression that, though they may look alike, their personalities were completely different. Agatha led them through to the back of the teashop and then up a set of steep, narrow stairs. At the top was a small landing with three doors leading off it. A white oval enamel plaque with blue writing on it indicated which room was the bathroom.

'These are your rooms. If you come down to the shop when you are ready, you can have a cup of tea and a fruit scone. I like to make my guests feel welcome. You can pay for your rooms at the same time.' Agatha turned about and descended the stairs.

'I take it hanky-panky means what I think it means?' sniggered Anna.

Jason whispered back, 'It does indeed, so mind you behave yourself and no sneaking into my room in the middle of the night.' A moment of silence passed between them, where they both flushed red. Jason cleared his throat.

'We'll drop these bags off, and then go down for tea, shall we?' Anna simply nodded, opened the door closest to her and went inside.

A few minutes later, they were both seated in the teashop. Mavis, carrying a tray, came out of the kitchen. 'I made these this morning.' She placed a plate of fruit scones in the centre of the table, followed by dishes of butter, jam, and cream. 'I'll just go get your tea.' When Mavis returned with the tea, Anna looked up and asked, 'May I have coffee instead?' Mavis looked at her with a confused expression for a moment, before replying slowly, pronouncing each word carefully.

'We – don't – sell – coffee – dear. We – are – a – teashop – but – I – expect – you – don't – understand – that – being – foreign?' Mavis smiled and nodded at Anna before returning to the kitchen.

'They obviously don't get much call for coffee up here,' sniggered Jason. Picking up a scone Jason, cut it in half. It was hard and dry and crumbled into large lumps on the plate.

'Is it supposed to do that?' It was Anna's turn to laugh at Jason.

'Only in the best of English teashops,' he replied. Not giving up on his scone, he buttered the lumps and put jam on the larger pieces. With the other scones, he found a sawing action with his knife managed to separate the two halves without them falling apart in his hands. But the dry confection needed all the help it could get from the butter, cream, and jam to make it palatable.

Later, as Anna and Jason walked the streets of Ulverston, they felt less out-of-place wearing their new clothes and looking more like hill walkers or day trippers.

'Let's go to the bus station. When we leave here, we'll get a bus to our next destination,' said Jason. 'However, I still think we should head for Scotland to hide out for a few weeks.'

'But they know we are heading to Scotland?'

'I know, but the original plan was to go to Oban. That is where the train was going and where I've booked a cottage for a week's stay. The Russians will know about it by now and will have had the place under surveillance in case we turn up late. So we keep heading for Scotland, only we won't go to Oban. When I was a child, during the school holidays, the family spent some of their summers in a little fishing village called Maidens. I also did some of my flight training during the war nearby. It's on the west coast of Scotland. It's isolated, but it's a beautiful place. If it's not too cloudy or raining, when you look out to sea, you can see the Isle of Arran. Our cottage was just yards from the beach, so we spent every day outdoors, playing in the sand or else we'd walk along the beach to the grounds of Culzean Castle. We weren't supposed to go onto the estate, but it was a good place to play amongst the trees. The gamekeepers didn't seem to mind so long as we kept out of their way and away from the house.' Jason fell silent for a moment, lost in boyhood memories of holidays in Scotland.

Anna let him have his memories before asking. 'It sounds ideal. How do we get there?'

'Bus to start with.' Arriving at the bus station, Jason led Anna to the ticket office. In the window were posters advertising day trips to various parts of the Lake District and the Isle of Man. Inside, Jason enquired about buses going north. Anna perused a stand full of leaflets, advertising places to visit. When Jason returned, she showed him a leaflet about the Isle of Man.

'I hope we get the chance to come back one day. There seem to be so many lovely places to visit. Why is this place called the Isle of Man? Is it for men only?' She pointed to the poster on the wall.

'I'm sorry, I don't know,' replied Jason, thrown by the strangeness of the question. 'But I'll make a point of finding out one day.'

'Is there a bus going to Scotland?' she asked.

'No. However, there are two buses per day to Carlisle, one at 8am and one at 3pm. We've missed today's afternoon bus, so I've bought two tickets for tomorrow morning.'

'What do we do until then?' asked Anna.

'I saw a cinema further down the street. They are showing an old Marx Brothers film. We'll watch the film and then I'll treat you to a fish supper.'

The film proved a great distraction, and Anna loved it. Darkness had fallen when they came out of the cinema. A handful of fish and chips wrapped in newspaper brought back memories of his childhood for Jason, though Anna wasn't keen on the greasy fat chips and the battered cod, dropping hers into a bin after trying a few chips and a mouthful of fish.

Back in the bed-and-breakfast, Jason lay on his bed, having enjoyed the evening. One remark Anna had made played over in his mind. *I hope we get the chance to come back one day.* Was it just a slip of the tongue, or did she really mean *we*? He stared up at the ceiling, imagining a possible future for them both.

He must have fallen asleep while imagining himself as the Tsar of Russia because when he awoke, the room light was still on and he was still dressed, lying on top of his bed. His watch was showing 02:10. Memories of Celia and the farm in

Kenya returned. He felt guilty. Undressing, he got into bed, but his thoughts belonged to Anna. She must be about ten years younger than him, the heir to the Russian throne, and with her own life in France. No, there could be nothing in the remark she had made earlier. It was a slip of the tongue. She was simply someone who had asked him for help, someone her mother had mentioned from the past.

He awoke again at 06:40 covered in sweat and shaking after reliving another wartime nightmare. Only this time, it was a more confused version of the usual nightmare. The face of the German pilot who had shot him down was someone off the train from London. But his memory had blurred and he couldn't fully recollect the image from his dream. Throwing back the covers, he sat on the edge of the bed, his body aching, reminding him of the injuries he had sustained in his aeroplane crash and the long walk of the previous two days. A bath and a shave would help ease away the tension. A wave of sadness suddenly hit him. Celia wouldn't be there to massage his neck and shoulders and to reassure him all was well. He spent a few moments with his eyes closed, reliving her laugh, her touch, her love.

Shortly after returning to his room, he heard Anna going to the bathroom. Suspecting she may be some time before she was ready to join him, he finished dressing, packed his rucksack, and went downstairs for breakfast. Mavis had already set a table for them, and he could smell the aroma of frying bacon coming from the kitchen. Mavis put her head around the kitchen door, 'MORNING! I'll just be a minute.' True to her word, she emerged from the kitchen with a tray of toast and tea.

'Where's your friend? A bit of a sleepy head, is she?'

'Good morning, Mrs Graham. Anna will be along shortly.'

'Oh, I'm not a Mrs, that's just my sister, Agatha. She married just before the war, but he didn't return. So I moved in with her and that's the way it stayed. We started this teashop to provide a bit of extra income, never expecting it to become so popular.' Just as Mavis finished speaking, Anna entered the room and sat down opposite Jason.

'Good Morning, Young Lady,' said Mavis, giving Anna a cheery smile. 'I've just brought the tea and toast. I'll have some nice fried egg and bacon for you in a minute.'

'No breakfast, thank you. The tea and toast will be fine,' said Anna defensively. Mavis looked hurt at the rebuffal.

'That's not a problem, Mavis. Just put it on my plate. There's no better meal than a good English breakfast.' Mavis brightened up a little at Jason's suggestion and, by the time she brought his plate of double eggs, bacon, sausage, black pudding, fried bread and mushrooms through, she was back to her normal cheerful self. Jason's face dropped when he saw the amount of food on the plate.

'I'm sorry,' said Mavis, 'I seem to have run out of tomatoes. I hope you don't mind?' She left the plate on the table in front of Jason and went back to the kitchen. Anna looked at the breakfast swimming in grease and stifled a snigger.

'Do you intend to eat all that?' she asked.

Jason picked up his knife and fork, 'I've got to haven't I? I said I would, and besides, we don't know if we will get a chance to stop for lunch once we are on the bus.' Jason almost choked on a piece of sausage when Mavis brought more toast, but Anna volunteered to eat it.

After the enormous breakfast, the couple staggered out of the bed-and-breakfast teashop to make their way to the bus station, arriving with only a couple of minutes to spare. The bus was only half full, and the passengers looked like local people on their way to work.

From Ulverston, the bus headed south to Barrow-in-Furness, stopping for five minutes before heading north to Broughton-in-Furness. By the time the bus had reached Broughton, they had been travelling for over an hour and were still only ten miles from their point of departure. After leaving Broughton, the road climbed through the Cumbrian Hills. They travelled through rural villages, past fields full of sheep on the hilltops and cattle in the lowlands. Occasionally, the bus passengers were treated to a view of the sea from the top of a hill, but it was a further two hours before the bus made its gear grating way into Whitehaven, where it stopped outside the railway station.

'We'll be stopping for half an hour. You can get lunch from the station buffet and stretch your legs,' the bus driver informed his passengers before getting off the bus himself.

'Are you ready for some lunch?' asked Anna, with a smile on her face.

'No, but I, er, do need to stretch my legs, if you know what I mean,' responded Jason as he held his bloated stomach. 'I'll meet you in the buffet. Get yourself a coffee, don't wait for me.'

Anna followed the rest of the bus passengers into the station buffet and bought a coffee and a cheese and cucumber sandwich. She finished both, but there was still no sign of Jason. So, with only five minutes of their scheduled stop remaining, she went to stand next to the bus. All the other passengers filed aboard except Anna and Jason. He was nowhere in sight. The bus driver arrived, viewing Anna suspiciously; before saying, 'If he's not here on time, Miss, I have to go. I have a schedule to maintain.' He took his seat behind the wheel and filled out a log sheet attached to a clipboard. After finishing logging his time, he looked at Anna and started the bus engine. 'Well?' said the driver.

'Just one more minute, please, driver.' Anna went around to the rear of the station buffet and stood outside the gents' toilets. Embarrassed, frustrated, unsure of what to do next, she called out to her missing companion.

'Jason, the bus is about to leave. What do I do?' Jason appeared from the door and together they rushed back to the bus, thanking the driver for waiting. Dropping into their seats, she turned to Jason and hissed in his ear, 'what took you so long?'

Not wanting to go into detail, he replied firmly, 'there was a queue.'

Two hours later, they arrived in Carlisle. The bus crossed the bridge over the River Caldew, turned right onto Castle Street and stopped in the market square, close to the cross. After alighting from the bus, Jason and Anna walked to the railway station to enquire about a train to Maidens in Scotland. The booking clerk informed Jason that trains no longer ran to Maidens and that the closest they could get to the village by train was Ayr. Jason bought two tickets for Ayr on the following day's train.

'We'll spend the night in Carlisle,' said Jason, 'I couldn't stand another day cramped up on a bus journey.' He explained to Anna.

'So long as it's not another Mrs Graham's Teashop, Bed and Breakfast,' insisted Anna. They looked at each other for a moment, then both broke out laughing.

'No, I couldn't face another breakfast like the one I had this morning. But, I have to admit, it's coming on for four o'clock and I'm still not hungry. Mind you, I could do with a cup of tea. I missed out at lunchtime.' After taking tea in a teashop facing onto the market square and enquiring about a place to stay, they were directed to the Crown and Coronet Hotel by the waitress. Suitably refreshed, they made their way across the market square to the hotel.

'I thought we were going to stay clear of hotels,' said Anna.

'That was the plan but, after a night in a barn and that last bed-and-breakfast place, we'll risk a hotel for one night. No one followed us onto the bus in Ulverston, who didn't get off many miles back. I bet we've lost our bloodhounds for the time being.'

Before entering the hotel, they viewed the smart-looking exterior and then looked at the clothes they were wearing. 'We won't exactly fit in, will we?' said Anna.

'We don't need to,' answered Jason. 'It's not how you dress that matters, it's how you project yourself. I learnt that in the Royal Air Force. One can spot an officer even when he is not in uniform. Ask any enlisted man.' Jason straightened his clothing, put his knitted hat in his pocket, and stiffened his back.

'Confidence is what you need.' Taking Anna by the arm, they marched forward together. The doorman looked them up and down as they approached the hotel and at the last moment took hold of the door handle, holding the door open for them, snapping his feet together and lifting his hat in greeting as they entered the hotel. They continued up to the desk where Jason, without waiting, asked for two rooms with baths for the night. The hotel receptionist immediately stopped what he was doing and attended to him. Jason completed the hotel register using false names and addresses. Two keys were produced and a hotel porter stepped forward. After being shown to their rooms, Jason tipped the porter well. The Porter asked if they would require a table for dinner.

'No, thank you. Our evening dress is being transported to our next hotel. We will dine in my room this evening. Have two menus sent up,' said Jason. After the porter had gone, Jason turned to Anna. 'See, it's easy.'

Anna laughed. 'You wouldn't have got away with it in a Parisian hotel. I'm going to my room to freshen up and rest.

I'm tired and dirty after that bus ride. I'll let you order dinner, but no fish.'

Later that evening, in Jason's room, Anna was dressed in a clean shirt but still wearing the brown corduroy trousers she had bought in Ulverston.

'I've ordered a light supper rather than a dinner,' said Jason. 'I hope that will be agreeable? It should arrive within the next few minutes. While you were resting, I used the hotel telephone to contact Thomas Cook and asked them to find us a cottage in or close to Maidens. They said that they would phone back in the morning with the address of the cottage.'

A knock on the door announced the room service waiter with his delivery of a trolley laden with various covered dishes. Anna jumped up from her seat to investigate the dishes while Jason tipped the waiter, informing him he wouldn't be needed as they would serve themselves. There was melon cocktail for starters, followed by lamb cutlets, buttered potatoes, carrots and peas, and for dessert, there was a selection of pastries with a dish of whipped cream. A bottle of red wine had also arrived with the meal.

'This is delicious, 'said Anna, as she took her first taste of a dish of melon.

The evening passed in a relaxed and convivial atmosphere. Anna and Jason shared stories from their childhood. However, Jason steered the conversation away from his wartime experiences, except when Anna pressed him for memories of her real mother. Jason delighted in Anna's company; as she was educated and charming, just like her mother had been. Secretly, he dared to hope, to dream, that once Anna had finally escaped her pursuers, they could still spend time together, even if there was no romantic entanglement.

The following morning, Jason was awoken at eight o'clock by a knock on the door. It opened and room service arrived with his breakfast.

'Your early morning call, sir. There is also a note for you, from Thomas Cook, I believe. Would you like me to pour your tea for you, sir?'

Jason read the note. A cottage had been arranged for them just outside the village. It had a live-in housekeeper by the name of Annabelle Summers, who would cook and clean for them during their stay. There was a P.S. to the note. Due to the demands of finding a cottage at short notice in such a remote location, Thomas Cook hoped that Miss Summers' love of cats wouldn't mar their holiday.

'Do you like cats?' Jason asked Anna over breakfast.

Chapter Eleven

A porter greeted them as they stepped aboard the train in Carlisle station.

'Good morning, sir. May I show you to your seats?' At first, Jason was taken aback by the unusual civility of the station porter. However, after showing him their tickets, the porter took them to an empty compartment in the centre of the carriage. Jason tipped the man a couple of bob, and the porter left them to settle in.

'How far is it to Maidens?' asked Anna.

'Not as the crow flies, but we have to go to Ayr first, where we'll catch a bus to go the rest of the way.'

Around lunchtime, the train pulled into Ayr station. They had an hour to use up before the bus for Maidens arrived, so they went for something to eat at a Lyons café across the street. The journey to Ayr had been an uneventful one, with the train stopping at only three stations en route. However, Jason noticed that at each station, the porters had been ready to escort passengers from the platform to their seats. A very different practice compared to station porters on the southern railways. He had also been grateful that he and Anna had managed to retain their compartment and not had to share it with strangers. As Jason looked at a distracted Anna, he couldn't help comparing her with Celia. Celia had been full of self-confidence, spontaneity and fun. With Anna, he felt he needed to be more protective towards her, as though she was precious and needed to be kept safe. A vulnerability that drew him to her and he knew he never wanted to leave her. He no longer felt as though he was acting as a guardian to the daughter of someone to whom he owed a debt of gratitude. She was special–special to him.

By the time they'd finished their tea, sandwiches and cakes, it was time to meet the bus. It arrived on time and they boarded, buying two one-way tickets to their destination. Apart from two elderly ladies and a family of five, there were no other passengers. There were three stops along the way, after which the bus delivered them to the harbour front in Maidens. The tide was out and small crab, lobster, and herring boats littered the wet sand inside the harbour wall, waiting for the sea to return and set them free. Beyond the harbour, out on the horizon, the mountains of the Isle of Arran rose majestically from the sea. The mountaintops, surrounded by low cloud, seemed to have a mysterious aura about them. Off to the left, standing proudly from the sea with sheer cliffs, was a much smaller island, Ailsa Craig. From his vantage point on the mainland, Jason could see nowhere to land a boat on the island. In his youth, the shape of the island had always reminded him of a giant cupcake floating on the water. It looked a lonely place. As a boy, he had imagined the island to be ruled over by the King and Queen of a thousand sea birds, undisturbed for thousands of years by humans on their cupcake fortress.

As they turned away from admiring the view, they spotted two fishermen sitting on fish boxes with their backs to the harbour wall while they mended fishing nets.

'Can you tell me where I can find Sea View cottage?' asked Jason. The two men stopped working and eyed Jason and Anna curiously. One gave a great puff on his pipe, blowing the smoke in their direction before answering.

'Up there, yer see yon place all painted white.' Pipe in hand, he pointed to a house just outside the village and part way up a low hill. 'The old wida woman lives there. I hope yer fond of a cat or two.' The two fishermen shared a knowing glance and returned to their work. As Anna and Jason looked towards the house on the hill, they spotted a single-story building with white-painted walls and blue painted window frames and backdoor. The dark slate-covered roof sprouted two sets of chimneys, one lot on the right-hand side of the building, and the main cluster set in the centre of the roof.

'Looks like we have a bit of a hike to get there,' said Jason.

It took them half an hour to walk from the village back along the road and then turn right along a narrow track up the hill. The trek was worth it, if only for the views out over the village, to the sea, and across to Arran. Off to their right, they could see the Scots Pines of the grand Scottish estate of Culzean Castle, where Jason played as a lad.

In contrast to the white-painted cottage, there was a wall surrounding the garden. It was made from the local stone and covered in thick lichen. The gate was long gone. Just two rusty hinges hung uselessly from a rotting gatepost.

'You take me to all the best places in town,' said Anna playfully as she made her way along the path to the front door. The garden, in contrast to the gate, was an array of colours and well kept. Before Anna could knock on the front door, it was opened by a stockily built woman in her late thirties, with blonde hair.

'Welcome, welcome. I've been expecting you. Do come in.' Jason had to duck his head as he entered through the low front door.

'I hope you like cats?' the woman continued. 'My aunt does like her little furry friends. She's not here at the moment. I'm her niece. She's been taken ill and gone to live with her sister for a while, so I'm here looking after the cats and the house. Thomas Cook sent a telegram saying you were desperate for somewhere to stay and, as auntie used to run the house as a bed-and-breakfast, they asked if she would be willing to put you up for a week or two. My name is Annabelle Summers, but please call me Belle.' She showed Jason and Anna around the cottage.

'This is your half of the cottage; I have two rooms through here.' Belle pointed to a door off the entrance hall. 'I will take care of all the cooking and cleaning. All you have to do is enjoy your holiday. I'm afraid there isn't much I can do about the cats being here, but they are pretty friendly and won't give you any trouble. The cats look after themselves most of the time. There is just one to be wary of, Samson. He's a big Persian and can be a bit funny with strangers. But he keeps himself very much to himself, so you may not even see him at all. Would you like of cup of tea? Sit down; sit down while I put the kettle on.' The sofa and two armchairs were covered in tartan travelling rugs, no doubt to protect the fabric beneath them from the cats. Anna and Jason dropped their packs to the floor and sat next to each other on the sofa. A black cat with a white chest and forelegs eyed them from the fireplace.

'Do we have to stay here?' whispered Anna.

'It will do for now. No one would think to look for us here. Just remember what happened to the boat. This is better than being dead.'

Anna fell silent for a while until Belle brought the tea things through. She spotted the strained expressions on the faces of her guests.

'You must be tired after a long day of travelling. Help yourselves to the tea and biscuits. I'll pop your bags into your rooms for you. I'll run a bath for the young lady. You'll feel much better after you freshen up.' Before they could answer, Belle had picked up their bags and was exiting the room.

'See, it's not all bad,' said Jason. 'We have a servant.'

Anna glared at him and picked up a large piece of shortbread. As she bit into the sweet buttery confection, she relaxed a little, lying back on the sofa to finish the biscuit. Jason poured two cups of tea. Before he'd finished pouring the tea, Anna leant forward and took another piece of shortbread. Belle returned and sat in a straight-backed chair near the fireplace.

'The bath will just take a few minutes to fill up, so you've time for one cup of tea now; you can take another one with you. I always think it's the height of luxury to drink a cup of tea in a hot bath. Now then, are we formal or not? Do I call you Mr Parva and Miss Moreau, or is it to be Jason and Anna?'

The couple on the sofa looked at each other and Jason spoke for them both.

'Anna and Jason, as we are guests in your house.' He smiled at Belle. Anna nodded in agreement.

'I love these biscuits; are they a Scottish delicacy?' asked Anna.

'Aye, you might say. Later, if you would like to, I'll show you how to make them. That bath should be ready by now.' Belle led Anna to the bathroom.

'Would you like me to stay? I could scrub your back and stay to chat a wee while?' suggested Belle.

'No. I'll be fine, thank you. I'd just like to clean up and put on some fresh clothes.'

Belle returned to the living room and Jason.

'That's a nice wee lassie you have there. How did you two meet?'

'Oh, you might say we had a mutual friend. This is Anna's first visit to Britain, so I volunteered to show her around,' dissembled Jason.

'She's French, is she not?' probed Belle. 'She must be wealthy to be able to come to Britain for a holiday in these times of hardship?'

'No, not wealthy. Her family has a small farm and a vineyard. It provides for their needs, and Anna has a job in Paris.'

'That sounds nice.' Belle stood up. 'I'd better be getting on with making tonight's supper. We're having fish and tatties,' said Belle, changing the subject.

Left to his own devices, Jason went out into the garden. He wanted to hide his service revolver. If he left it in the house, he was sure Belle would find it and ask questions. A pile of discarded rocks which had been brought up from the seashore looked to be a likely location to hide his revolver. Rolling one aside, he placed his gun, wrapped in its oiled cloth that he used for cleaning it, inside the space before replacing the rock. Standing up, he looked at the view before him. The land sloped gently down toward the sea. The fields were full of unripe wheat and barley swaying in the breeze. Some of the steeper fields held sheep and in other low-lying fields, cattle. He sat on the wall. Memories of his childhood flooded back, playing with the local lads or watching the boats come and go from the harbour, of baskets full of crabs, lobster and fish. To the south of the harbour, he could see the edge of Turnberry Golf Course. Instinctively, he looked up into the sky over the golf course. There was nothing there except a few seagulls soaring on the breeze. He recalled the days when the golf course had been part of the Royal Flying Corps Turnberry. The flying school that had taught him aerial gunnery practice before he was shipped out to the western front. Jason's head swam as reminders of his training days mixed with memories of being shot down during the war. He placed his hands on top of the wall to steady himself as his world spun out of control and before all went black.

Anna came out of the bathroom wrapped in a thick woollen dressing gown and went straight to her bedroom. Picking up a comb, she went through to the living room. It was empty. Hearing someone in the kitchen, she went to see what was happening. Belle was rolling out pastry on the kitchen table.

'Where has Jason gone?' asked Anna. Belle stopped what she was doing.

'He's in the living room.'

'No. He's not,' answered Anna. 'What are you making?'

Belle wiped her hands on her apron and went through to the living room as though she hadn't believed what she had been told. 'Now; where has he got to, and supper will be ready soon?' She called his name but got no reply. Anna followed Belle to Jason's bedroom. It, too, was empty.

'Jason!' Belle called, a little louder than before. There was still no reply. She crossed to the front door, her pace becoming more urgent, and looked outside. At first, she saw nothing but the garden, but then her eyes were drawn to two booted feet sticking out across the path on the far side of the wall. 'Jason!' She yelled.

Belle ran forward, with Anna close behind. They found Jason unconscious in the grass on the far side of the wall. As Anna stood dumbfounded looking on, Belle dropped to Jason's side and lifted his head, feeling for the pulse in his neck. As she did so, Jason groaned and his eyes fluttered open.

'What happened?' he mumbled.

'I don't know, you tell me,' answered Belle. As Jason regained his senses, he pushed himself into a sitting position.

'I'm sorry. I'll be all right in a minute. Help me up. I feel stupid lying here in the dirt.'

'But what happened to you?' asked Anna. As Jason gradually regained his feet, he leaned on the wall.

'Nothing. It was nothing, just a bad turn. I must be more tired than I thought.' Jason brushed himself down and returned to the house, flopping heavily onto the sofa.

'I'll fetch you a medicinal brandy,' said Belle. 'Do you need a doctor?'

'I'd rather have a single malt,' answered Jason. 'Don't bother with the doctor.'

Glass of whisky in hand, Jason took a large mouthful and swallowed it slowly. He sighed and silently wished Celia was there to massage his neck and shoulders.

'Feeling better?' asked Anna.

'Yes, thank you,' he lied.

'If you're sure you are alright, I'll finish getting dinner ready,' said Belle.

Belle's fish and tatties supper turned out to be pan-fried salmon steaks with sauté potatoes and steamed asparagus with a Dill, Basil and Tarragon white wine sauce, followed up with a large glass of single malt whisky.

'Please, excuse me, ladies. I am suddenly very tired. With your permission, I will have an early night.'

'That's probably a good idea,' said Belle. 'I'll wake you just before breakfast.'

After Jason had gone to his room, Belle and Anna cleared the table and together they did the washing up.

'Coffee?' asked Belle.

'Please.'

'Go sit down. I'll bring it through when it's ready.' When Belle brought through the coffee, she sat opposite Anna. They sat in silence for a moment before Belle asked, 'How did you meet Jason?'

Anna thought a moment before answering. 'He's an old friend of the family. Do you have any more of that delightful shortbread?' Belle got up to fetch some from the kitchen. When she returned, Anna was ready with a question of her own.

'What do you do when you are not looking after your aunt's cottage full of cats?'

'I'm a nurse at the Glasgow Royal Infirmary,' responded Belle, without hesitation. 'What about you?'

'Oh, I'm just a secretary for the manager of a bus company in Paris.'

'You speak English very well for a bus company secretary. Did they teach you English at school?' probed Belle.

'No, my mother taught me. She spoke a few different languages.'

'Oh, that's nice. Which languages could she speak?'

'Er, I can't remember just now. You know, I'm also feeling rather tired. I think I will go to bed and read for a while.'

Belle couldn't keep the disappointment from her face as Anna said, 'Good night.' Belle remained seated, watching Anna as she retired to her room.

It was dark and silent when Jason abruptly awoke from his nightmare. He lay still, trying to remember where he was as his brain slowly made sense of his surroundings. He shivered and switched on his bedside light. Getting up, he went to sit in a chair. Wide awake and getting cold, he dressed in his day clothes before returning to the chair. He selected a book from the shelf on his bedside table and tried reading, but he was too edgy to concentrate on it. He didn't feel like sleeping, but it was too early to go through to the living room and risk waking the others by pottering about, so decided to go for a walk.

Sneaking out of the house, he walked along the road back towards the village. Arriving at the harbour, he spotted a couple of boats with lights on and men preparing fishing nets on deck. He watched them, thinking how their hours of work were governed by the tides and weather and not by clocks like everyone else. It was a hard life, but one that gave them the freedom to come and go as they please. Turning left, he continued towards the spit of land that stuck out into the sea and which helped to provide one side of the safe mooring within the harbour. His eyes, now accustomed to the near darkness, could make out the dark hillside. He continued on a little further, finding the footpath to the top of the hill. He smiled to himself, reassured by finding something familiar from long ago, from happier days. At the top of the path, he could make out the undulating landscape of the golf course.

After a short walk across the green, he felt the crunch of concrete beneath his feet. It was still here, or at least some of it was, the old runway of the airfield.

'A bit dark for a game of golf, isn't it?' Came a familiar voice from behind him. Jason spun around to face the voice in the darkness.

'Why have you followed me?' he snapped.

'I heard you leave the house. By the time I'd finished dressing, you were gone. It seemed logical that you would come down to the harbour, so I followed you. When I saw you under the streetlights, standing at the harbour wall, looking at the boats, I hung back a moment before following you up here. Do you know this place?' asked Belle.

The first rays of the morning sun were appearing in the sky, and more of the disused runway was now visible as it ran through the length of the golf course. Jason shivered as he felt the ghosts of the past swirl about him.

'Yes. I know this place.' He turned away from the runway and headed back down the path towards the harbour without saying any more to Belle. She let him go, following behind, only catching up when he stopped again at the harbour wall.

'I would spend hours here as a kid, talking to the fishermen, marvelling at the crabs and lobsters they caught in their baskets. They would stack the baskets against the harbour wall, ready for shipping off to market.' As he spoke, a crab boat left the harbour heading out to sea, its deck stacked high with crab pots.

Turning to Belle, he said, 'I think I'm ready for a cup of tea about now. I'm afraid my bed is a bit of a mess.'

'That's all right. There's plenty of spare linen. If you have any washing that needs doing, just put it with the sheets.'

By the time Anna came into the living room, Belle and Jason were on their second cup of tea.

'Sleep well?' asked Jason.

'Yes, thank you. What got you up so early?' asked Anna.

'We went for a walk to blow some cobwebs away,' answered Jason.

Belle just smiled and said. 'Good morning.'

Anna looked at them both for a moment, then shrugged her shoulders and returned to her room to dress.

She returned to the aroma of frying bacon drifting into the living room.

'Belle has made you some coffee.' Jason pointed to the tray on the table.

'What are we going to do today?' asked Anna as she poured herself a cup of the morning pick-me-up. She sat in an armchair with the cup cradled in both hands and took a sip of the black, bitter liquid. She sighed, 'That's better.' Looking up at Jason, she waited for him to answer to her question.

'We'll go for a walk along the beach and up to the wood where I used to play as a boy. There's not much else to do around here except walking, fishing and birdwatching.'

At that moment, Belle entered the room to announce that breakfast was ready. As Anna sat at the table, Belle placed a bowl of off-white mush in front of her. She looked at it for a moment before turning to Jason.

'It's porridge,' said Jason. 'A Scottish delicacy. You can eat it the way the Scots do, with salt, or you can have honey with it, the way Sassenach's eat it.'

Anna tasted a little first without either. Deciding a bowl of hot oats was not for her, she put the dish to one side.

'I'll just have some toast, please.' Jason smiled at her and finished his porridge before Belle brought through the bacon and eggs with black pudding. Anna picked up her coffee and left the table.

After breakfast, Jason took Anna down to the harbour. Most of the boats were out at sea, with just one old boat remaining, tilted at an obtuse angle as it sat on the sand, while the tide was out. Dark green tentacles of damp seaweed hung from its hull. The upper parts of the structure were covered in peeling paint and rust. Forgotten and neglected by its owner, it was a sad sight tethered by a chain to the seawall. Jason imagined it as a chained animal beaten and misused by a neglectful owner. For some strange reason, he felt sorry for it. Turning, he led Anna away, following the wall as they headed north towards the beach. The wind was blowing off the sea. On the horizon, the Isle of Arran looked crisp and fresh in the morning light. A ship, tiny in the distance, was heading towards the island from the mainland. Looking inland, a couple of hundred yards from the shore, stood a row of single-story cottages which belonged to the fishermen. Passing the cottages, they soon reached the edge of the village before continuing on towards a small headland covered with trees. When they reached a stream draining onto the beach, they found a path leading up into dense woodland.

'This is the way I used to come when on holiday as a lad.' Jason led Anna onto slightly higher ground as they followed the path into the wood. Once amongst the trees, they were sheltered from the wind, with only the rustle of the treetops to remind them of the wind off the sea. The path continued upwards at a gentle slope until they came out of the trees onto a wide green.

'Come and look,' said Jason, as he led Anna to a low wall of about knee height. On the far side was a lake.

'This is Swan Pond,' said Jason. 'It's easy to see how it got its name.' Dozens of swans swam gracefully over its surface. Their brilliant white plumage contrasting with the dark water and the green of the Scottish pine trees on the far bank. Jason sat on the wall and Anna joined him, together, watching the swans as they glided effortlessly and peacefully over the water. A sudden voice from behind them made them jump and turn away from the pond.

'Hoy, what are you doing here? This is private land.' What looked like a gardener was coming towards them from a shed hidden in the trees. Jason stood up and waited for the man to arrive.

'This is private land. Be off with ye before I call the gamekeeper.' Jason smiled at him.

'Mr MacIntyre, don't you remember me?' The old man studied Jason's face for a moment before recognition brought a smile to his own face.

'Well, I never. I didn't think I'd be seeing ye again, me lad,' said Mr MacIntyre.

'Aye, there were times when the same thought crossed my mind,' said Jason.

Jason introduced Anna and explained that they were staying locally for a while.

'The Laird and his family are away down south in London for the summer and he's let part of the house to strangers for a few weeks, so I see no harm in ye wondering about down here. Just dunna go up to the house.'

'Thank you, Mr MacIntyre, we won't.'

'Well, I'll be about me business, now. Come over to the shed later on for a mug o' tea and ye can tell me what ye been up to and why ye stayed away so long, young Jason, me lad.'

'Thank you, Mr MacIntyre. We may well do that.' The old man turned and headed back to the shed.

'He was nice,' said Anna. 'I thought he was going to chase us back to the beach.'

'Oh, he did that often enough when I was a lad. One day, he caught me sneaking around here with my pals. I was standing on this wall at the time and fell into the pond when he shouted at us to clear off. Mr MacIntyre fished me out and dried me off in his hut before sending me home. After that, he always turned a blind eye when he saw me come up here. I liked to come up here on my own and sit on the wall to watch the swans.'

'You must have changed quite a bit since you were a boy. I'm surprised he was able to recognise you?'

'Ah. Well. I've been here once or twice since them.' Jason turned and walked back towards the trees before Anna could ask another question. Jason was lost in his memories when Anna caught up to him and they walked in silence back to the beach. Once out of the trees, Jason stopped, took a deep breath, and released it slowly.

'I don't think coming here was a good idea,' he said mournfully, before setting off again in the direction of the village before Anna could ask why.

In Maidens once again, Jason went to the shop and bought a newspaper. The front page showed a photograph of the newly completed Empire State Building in New York. Lower down the page, there was speculation on who the winner might be in the forthcoming French Presidential Election. He bought a bar of nutty chocolate for Anna as a means of an apology for being a bit withdrawn on their return walk from the woods. As they headed back to the cottage, Anna reminded him of their luggage still at the hotel in the Lake District.

'Yes, I'll arrange to have it delivered.'

As they walked up the cottage path, Belle was hanging the washing out to dry at the rear of the house. She waved to them as they drew closer and, leaving her washing basket on the ground, went into the house to greet her guests.

'Did you have an enjoyable walk? I'll make you some tea as soon as I've finished hanging out the washing.'

'Yes, thank you, Belle. There is also something else we need. Would you arrange for our luggage to be brought here from The Lake Windermere Hotel in Bowness-on-

Windermere? We only have the one change of clothes that we brought with us in those backpacks,' explained Jason.

'The Lake Windermere Hotel, you say. I will telephone the hotel for you and get them to put your luggage on the next train to Ayr. I can get it picked up from the station and delivered here by one of the local hauliers,' said Belle.

The following afternoon, their suitcases arrived by van from Ayr station. Each suitcase carried the remains of a large white label which had been stuck to its lid and had later been torn off.

'It seems strange for someone to tear off the delivery address from our luggage. What was the point of that?' asked Anna.

'Maybe it simply shows they have delivered the luggage,' said Jason as he carried the cases to their rooms.

Three days later, life at the cottage had settled into a routine of walks, reading and talking. Each morning Jason would go for a walk and on the way back call in to the local shop to buy a newspaper. Anna helped Belle with the cooking and learned how to make shortbread. The day before, Jason and Anna had even taken a boat trip to Arran for a day out.

On the morning of the fourth day Jason walked along the seafront. The sun was low, only slightly above the gentle rise of the hill. It was a warm, early morning sun, salmon pink for a few minutes before it transformed into a bright golden globe, giving off heat and light to sea and land below. As the sun warmed his face, he spotted flashes of light from the hillside.

At first, he ignored them, but when they came again, they reminded him of something sinister from the past. He stopped for a moment and scanned the hillside, but the flashes of light stopped. Dismissing them, he carried on walking. The flashes started up again, making him stop and look toward the hillside again. A long, high-pitched scream from behind him made him turn toward the sea. A flock of Gannets sawed over the water before folding back their wings and diving into its depths to capture fish. Jason shook his head. Was he becoming paranoid? he wondered. He dismissed the flashes. They were probably sunlight reflecting off the lenses of a birdwatcher's binoculars as they enjoyed the spectacular display being given by the Gannets.

He carried on with his walk. His thoughts taking him back to his old farm in Kenya. He missed the warm sun and the happy smiling faces of the farm workers who sang as they worked. Before he knew it, he was on the path through the woods heading towards the hut where he hoped to find Mr MacIntyre. The ageing gardener was sitting on an old, upended beer crate watching a kettle boil on an oil-burning stove.

'I heard you coming, so I put the kettle on. You'll never make a poacher the way you snap every stick you tread on.'

'Aye, you're right, not like when I was a kid sneaking up here with my mates.' Jason sat on a rickety stool that Mr MacIntyre had set for him. Nothing was said until the tea was made, and the two of them had a mug in their hands.

'Have you seen any strangers about?' asked Jason.

'Only them that's taken up at the house while the laird is away in London. Why what's up?'

'I don't know, something. It's a kind of feeling. Ghosts maybe.' Jason didn't elaborate on his real reason for being back. 'The peace and the quiet here have given me time to think. It's strange being here after so long. First on holidays and then when I came to do my flying training. Now I'm back again. I never expected to see this place again once I went out to Africa.' Silence fell between them before Jason continued.

'Troubles coming. I read in the newspapers about unrest in Europe. You never know, we could be at war again in a few years' time. Am I going mad? Is the world going mad or is it what happened during the war? I don't know,' said Jason.

Mr MacIntyre sipped his tea before speaking.

'Why are you here? Why have you come back? That's what you've got to ask yourself. That wee lass you're with; who is she? What is she to you?'

'It's a long story and a strange one, but I owe her mother a debt and my life. Anna is in trouble. I've promised to help her. I suppose that's why I brought her here. It's somewhere I know. I have fond memories of this place.'

'Are the police involved?'

'Yes, but that's the strange thing about all this. Anna asked them for help. When she told the police about her troubles, they refused to believe her story. When we were on a train coming to Scotland, a passenger died delaying the train. In the confusion, Anna spotted the men who were chasing her, so we ran. The police now think I had something to do with the death on the train and that I've kidnapped Anna.'

'Do you know if she is telling you the truth, Lad?'

'Yes, she is. Someone *is* after her. I spotted one of the stewards on the train was carrying a gun in the waistband of his trousers. He shot at me when I followed him.'

'What are you not telling me? There's more to this tale than you've told so far.'

'There is one thing, and it explains why Anna is in so much danger,' Jason hesitated before continuing. 'She is a Russian Princess. She is on the run from the Russian secret police. They want to kill her and anyone else who has a link to the Russian throne.'

'Umm, I dunna think I can help you this time, Lad. This is more trouble than just falling into yon pond and helping you dry off to save you from a spanking off your Pa.'

'Yes, I know, Mr MacIntyre. But you know what they say about a trouble shared. Thank you for the tea and the talk. I think it's time I went back to Anna. We need to figure out what we are going to do next.'

On the way back to the cottage, Jason collected his newspaper and read the headlines. There were photographs of him and Anna on the front page. The pictures were fuzzy and grainy as though taken in a hurry, but they were good enough for Jason to recognise Anna and himself. The headline simply read

Fugitives needed to help police with their enquiries.

The headline was followed by a vague article outlining the death of the man on the train and a young couple who had gone missing in the Lake District.

Chapter Twelve

'As there's just the two of us; come through to the kitchen. I'll show you how to make a Dundee Cake. Jason won't be back for an hour or so. It's easier to talk freely without a man around.'

Anna looked up from the book and thought about the suggestion for a moment.

'Yes; that would be nice. I'll be able to take the recipe back to France with me.'

Belle smiled and headed off to the kitchen, with Anna close behind her.

'You'll need one of these,' said Belle, as she passed Anna an apron. 'You'll find mixing bowls in that cupboard over there. I'll get the ingredients.' She lifted down packets of flour and another of sugar but, when she opened the stoneware butter dish in the pantry, she only found half a pack of butter.

'I'm sorry, Anna, I don't have enough butter. I'll just pop down to the shop and get some more. You weigh out a pound of flour and five ounces of caster sugar for each of us. You'll find the jars of dried fruit on the top shelf in the pantry. I'll be back in a few minutes. Annabelle stripped off her apron and headed for the door.'

Anna did as she had been told and busied herself weighing out the flour and sugar.

By the time Belle reached the village shop it was unusually full of customers, each one spending more time chatting with the shopkeeper instead of buying what they needed and leaving, so Belle, much to her frustration, had to wait her turn to be served.

*****

As Jason turned into the road which ran down through the village to the harbour, he caught sight of a black car speeding into the distance. His pace quickened, a sense of urgency running through every fibre of his body. However, the faster he tried to go, the more the pain in his leg reminded him of his recent injuries. Pushing the pain aside, he carried on until he reached the path to the cottage.

'Anna!'

By the time he'd reached the garden gate, he could see the front door was open.

'Anna, Belle!'

The living room was empty. Rushing into the kitchen, ingredients were scattered across the table and over the floors.

'Anna, Belle!'

Desperately, he checked the bedroom; it, too, was empty. Returning to the living room. As he looked for clues about what had happened, he spotted a note on the mantelpiece.

Hands trembling, he picked up the paper and read the message written in pencil.

Stay in the house.

Do not inform the police, or she will die.

If you want Anna back, bring the documents and the jewel to me.

I will get word to you later as to where and when to bring what I want.

Come alone, or she will die.

Just as Jason finished reading the note for the third time, Belle returned.

'Where is Anna?' Jason thrust the note at her. She read it.

'We have to inform the police.'

'No!' insisted Jason.

'Why?'

'You don't understand. I cannot tell you.'

'What is that supposed to mean? Of course, you must inform the police.'

'No! I need time to think first.' Jason marched into Anna's bedroom and searched through her possessions.

'What are you looking for?' asked Belle.

'Nothing! Something. It doesn't matter, there's nothing here, anyway.' Jason left the bedroom, his leg throbbing, his mind racing as he tried to piece together what had happened. Lastly, he went outside to check the ground around where the car had been that he saw leaving. Belle followed him.

'Do you know where she might be?' asked Belle.

'Where were you?' snapped Jason, changing the subject. He didn't wait for an answer, but returned to the cottage and eased himself into an armchair. Belle stood before him.

'I' went to the shop to buy some butter; Anna and I were going to make a Dundee Cake.' Jason looked at her questioningly.

'I did, look. It's there on the table where I left it when I got back.' Jason glanced at the table against the wall. Three half-pound rectangular bricks of butter, wrapped in greaseproof paper, were scattered across its surface.

'Call the police,' insisted Belle.

'No!'

'Why not?'

'You wouldn't understand, and because the note says not to. If there is any chance of getting Anna back unharmed, I will do what they say. I know what the kidnappers want. I just can't get it. Even if I did call the police, they wouldn't be able to help Anna. It's down to me to get Anna back.'

'Well, what do we do now?' asked Belle.

'We? You do nothing. I wait until they tell me what to do next.'

The rest of the day passed slowly. Belle made them some sandwiches and coffee for lunch, but neither of them felt much like eating.

Hour by painful hour, they watched the clock's hands crawl around its face. Unable to leave the house, unable to settle or read, Jason and Belle did their best not to look at each other as the frustration of waiting clawed at their nerves while they worried about what was happening to Anna.

*****

Anna felt herself being dragged from the back of the car. The hood over her head hindered her breathing and added to the dizziness induced by the drug-soaked cloth they had forced over her face to render her unconscious. Supported on each side by someone tall and strong, she found it hard to keep pace with her assailants while they half carried, half dragged her over the ground. The crunch of feet on gravel changed as she felt herself hoisted up some steps and then through a doorway. She could smell a log fire and feel the warmth of the room on her bare skin. Seconds later, the hood was removed, and she was thrust onto a hard-backed chair in front of a desk. One man pulled her arms behind the chair back and tied them together. The gag in her mouth stopped her from calling out in protest. Her eyes still found it hard to focus, although her hearing was clear and sharp. She also noted the strong aroma of tobacco, not the European kind, but the sort her uncle used to smoke, a type popular in Russia.

'How much of the drug did you give her?' asked voice one. It sounded educated and controlled, with a slight accent that seemed familiar.

'I don't know. I just poured the liquid onto the cloth and held it over her face as you told me to.' Voice two sounded less well-educated and had a distinctive Eastern European edge to it.

'Remove the gag, let her breathe. She'll come to faster and then I can get on with questioning her.'

Anna felt her head pressed forward as hands fumbled with the knot at the back of her head. She kept her chin down, resting it on her chest, figuring the longer she could make them believe she was still unconscious, the more time she would have to think about how to answer their questions when they started. She heard one set of footsteps walk away. The room fell silent except for the ticking of a clock and the crackle of burning logs. She knew at least one person was still in the room with her, as she could still smell the pungent tang of cigarette smoke. She risked opening her eyes, just a crack, to access her immediate location. Her lap was the first thing to come into focus. On either side of the chair, she could see a patterned carpet. She closed her eyes again and listened. Footsteps crossing the room stopped in front of her. A moment later, she was startled by cold water poured over her head.

'Ah, you are finally awake, Miss Moreau. I hope the effects of the ether have worn off?' Anna didn't answer. She just stared at the man in front of her. She didn't see it coming until it was too late. His right hand caught her on the side of her face, almost knocking her off the chair.

'Now that I have your full attention, I will ask you some simple questions. Where is the package that old fool in Paris gave you? The one with the documents and the jewel.'

Anna's tongue licked at the blood running from her lip. She turned the injured side of her face away from the man in front of her and waited for the second blow. When it came, it was far harder than the first one. As his fist hit home, she and the chair toppled over, crashing to the carpet. She cried out when her head hit the floor. Dizziness swirled about her. Then rough hands grabbed at her, lifting her back up into place and a glass of water was thrown in her face.

'Now, now, Miss Moreau, this is only going to get worse. You will tell me where you have hidden the package in the end, so why not save yourself all this discomfort, and tell me now?'

Anna spat a goblet of blood onto the man's shoe, bracing herself for another blow. It didn't come. Instead, the man cleaned the blood from the polished black leather with his handkerchief and stepped toward the fire. He buffed his shoe with the handkerchief one more time and then threw it onto the fire, after which he selected the poker from the fireside companion set and placed it into the flames.

'I don't have the time or the patience to play games with you. Tell me where you have hidden the documents!'

Trembling as she spoke, Anna answered. 'I had considered giving them to you to get you on the condition you left me alone. But now I see what kind of people you are. I'll never tell you where I have hidden them. If I don't live long enough to use the documents and jewel, at least someone else will!'

The lightning-fast slap knocked her from the chair again, only this time, no one picked her up. She felt someone release her from the chair and then force her onto her front. A knee pressed into the small of her back, held her in place. The back of her dress was torn open and the man with the poker crossed toward her. The poker's red glowing tip was held close to her face. Anna screamed as she felt its radiating heat. Eyes wide with fear, she screamed again as the poker was applied to her naked back. The pitch of her scream increasing for a second before being cut short.

*****

The clock chimed nine pm as Jason's eyes began to close. His head lolling to one side whilst he sat in the armchair. He dreamed of Anna. Of their first meeting on the train. That vision of loveliness which had taken his breath away for a moment.

A heavy thud against the front door woke him and made him sit upright. Belle was on her feet first, throwing the front door open. Jason followed. Belle ran up the garden path following the intruder. A shot rang out from the darkness and Belle fell back, a crimson rosette blossoming on her left shoulder. Jason was at her side a second later. In the background, he heard a car racing away.

'Belle, Belle.' Jason lifted her head. Her eyes fluttered open for a moment and then closed. He checked her pulse; at least she was still alive. Using his handkerchief, he pressed it against the wound, then went to fetch a tea towel from the kitchen, using it to tie over her shoulder.

Looking back towards the front door, on the step lay the object which had caused the thud. It was a rock from the garden with a paper attached to it. Ripping off the note, he scanned the message; the meeting was for tomorrow night. He stuffed the note in his pocket and returned to Belle. She was still breathing, but he knew she wouldn't last long. Belle's car was parked alongside the cottage, and he had seen she the key by the front door.

The car started with one crank of the starter handle. Jason placed Belle on the back seat, covered her with a blanket, and then got behind the steering wheel. The gears complained loudly as he selected first gear. Stamping his foot on the accelerator, the car jumped forward.

Once on the road, the car increased speed smoothly up to thirty miles per hour and then struggled as Jason demanded more output from the little engine. Belle lay silent and still on the back seat. Jason adjusted the rear-view mirror so he could keep watch on Belle. He knew Ayr had a hospital and Belle had to be his first priority for the moment before giving his full attention to Anna. As the car struggled at every hill it met, Jason prayed Belle would not bleed to death before they arrived at the hospital. The smell of the overheating engine caught in his nostrils, adding to his worries, so he eased off on the throttle a touch. As he drove, Jason puzzled over Belle. Why had she been so keen to get to the door ahead of him? Why was she at the cottage at all? She hadn't shown any interest in her aunt's cats. In fact, none of them had seen much of the animals in the time they had been staying at the cottage. He hadn't asked Thomas Cook for a housekeeper when booking the cottage; they had insisted that she had come as part of the package. Entering Doonfoot on the outskirts of Ayr, the hospital was only a mile or so away. The streets were empty at this time of night as the car passed the large, newly built houses of the more affluent residents of Ayrshire.

Directing the car into the drive of the Gothic-styled hospital reminded him of visits to fellow pilots from his flying days at Troon. The car skidded to a halt outside the front door of the hospital. A single lamp burned within the porch. Jason squeezed the rubber bulb on the end of the car hooter, alerting the staff that he needed assistance. Turning around in his seat, he checked on Belle in the back. She was still alive, but the tea towel was drenched in blood. By the time he had lifted Belle from the back of the car, the drive in front of the hospital was bathed in bright light. Two hospital orderlies had arrived, whilst two nurses stood in the hospital doorway waiting to receive the untimely newcomer. As the orderlies placed Belle on a stretcher, Jason gave her one last look before returning to the car and driving off with the nurses waving frantically after him from the front of the hospital, their words drowned out by the noise of the car engine.

By the time he got back to the cottage, he was exhausted. He remembered leaving the house lights on in his rush to get Belle to the hospital, but on his return, a visitor had arrived. It was old Mr MacIntyre. Jason found him sitting in an armchair, waiting for him to return. A shotgun lay across his lap. Jason halted in the doorway, one hand still holding onto the handle, taken by surprise at the sight of the old man.

'Shut the door, Laddie, I've only just got the place warmed up,'

Mr MacIntyre propped his shotgun against the wall next to his Martini-Henry rifle. Both guns were still within easy reach.

'Sit yourself down and tell me what's been going on,' demanded the old gardener.

'Why are you here? How did you know Anna had been taken?'

'I didn't. I may be old, but I'm not deaf and I'm not daft. You and the wee lass have been the talk of the district ever since you arrived, and that woman, Belle, is no niece to old

Nell. No one around here has seen her before. When I heard the gunshot, I reckoned you was in trouble, so I came up to see what was going on. I found the door open, the lights left on and blood on the path. I thought it best to stay put till morning. If you dinna come back, I was gonna go to the police. So, which one of the ladies has been shot and where is the other one?'

'I need a drink,' said Jason. 'Will you join me?'

'I wouldn't say no to a wee dram.' Jason poured out two tumblers of single malt and returned to his chair. He removed his service revolver from his pocket before he sat down, placing his gun on a side table. He sank half the glass of whisky before pulling the note from his pocket and reading the instructions fully for the first time.

Bring the documents and the jewel to the abandoned abbey on the way to Maybole at midnight tomorrow.

Wait there until you are contacted.

'That'll be Crossaguel Abbey they're talking about. It's not too far from here. I reckon they are hiding your wee lassie somewhere close by. Do you have what they are after?' said the old gardener.

'No. Anna hid them before we arrived here. I know where they are, but I can't get to them.'

'Um, that's going to make getting her back a little difficult,' said Mr MacIntyre.

'I suspect having the documents and the jewel hidden away is the only thing that is keeping Anna alive. But once the Russians have those, they won't need her anymore. They will kill Anna and destroy the documents, and then no one else will be able to prove their right to the Russian throne.'

'What are you going to do?' asked Mr MacIntyre.

'Go get Anna back, anyway I can.'

'Then, Laddie, we need to get some sleep.' Jason poured himself another tumbler of whisky and proffered the bottle to his companion.

'Not for me Lad and you'd better make that your last, you're gonna need your wits about you tomorrow night.' Jason put the bottle back in the cupboard but took the glass to bed with him.

When Jason got up at first light, Mr MacIntyre was already in the living room. He'd slept in the chair by the fire.

'I'd like to reconnoitre the abbey before we go to the rendezvous tonight. With no package to bargain with, I want to look for a place to surprise the kidnappers from, and find a path to get Anna away as quickly as possible,' said Jason.

'There's no need,' said Mr MacIntyre. 'I know the place like the back of my hand. Sit down and have something to eat, feed your brain and we can work on a plan to get your wee lassie back.' Jason looked at the old man in disbelief.

'Why are you doing this? Why do you want to help me?'

'In my younger days, I was in the Coldstream Guards for a wee while and saw a bit of action. When I left the army, the Marquess, once an officer with the guards, was happy to take me on as his gardener. It gave me time to recover from my wounds. He helped me; I'm helping you. You are helping Anna.'

Jason felt humbled. 'Thank you. I only hope we can get Anna back in one piece. What do you suggest we do?' asked Jason.

'Crossaguel Abbey is a ruin now, but there is a tower next to the main gate. It's the highest point of the abbey still standing. I'll be up there keeping an eye on things. When I let them know they are not going to get everything their own way, be ready to grab your wee lass and run, and ye dunna stop running for hell nor high water. I'll slip away whilst they are trying to figure out where they went wrong.'

Mister MacIntyre's self-confidence put Jason at ease, just as it had done all those years earlier when the gardener had pulled him from the lake. Jason remembered officers during the war who had that same quiet sense of leadership which they passed on to their subordinates. One day, he vowed, he would come back to Maidens and ask his old friend about his time with The Guards.

'Go and give that car a look over; you don't want it to let you down when you're needing it the most. It'll give you something to do while we are waiting. I'm going to have a wee nap. You can make me a cup-o-tea in an hour or two,' instructed Mr MacIntyre.

Four hours later, Mr MacIntyre awoke to see Jason asleep in the chair opposite him. He smiled, picked up his Martini-Henry and went through to the kitchen.

'I'd better give you a bit of a clean and an oiling old girl. We might be going into action again tonight.'

He was just wiping the excess oil from the rifle when Jason walked into the kitchen.

'I'm sorry, I should have woken you earlier.'

'No, Lad, you did exactly what I wanted you to do. Relax and get some more sleep. You'll need it. I want you alert and ready when the time comes to go get Anna.'

Unable to sleep, at Mister MacIntyre's suggestion, Jason packed a couple of bags with food and spare clothes for Anna and himself, along with two thick blankets from his bed and the remains of the bottle of whisky. Then they had made their basic plan of action. However, Mr MacIntyre went on to say that whatever else happened that evening, they would have to improvise their responses to the enemies attack. Jason and the old gardener spent the rest of the afternoon in casual conversation, neither man talking about what was to come

By half-past eleven, they were ready to set off for Crossaguel Abbey.

'One wee dram to keep out the cold,' said Mr MacIntyre, as he removed a bottle of scotch from his bag.'

'Just a small one,' said Jason. As he held his glass in front of him, he made a toast.

'To fallen comrades.' Mister MacIntyre simply nodded as the two men touched glasses.

As they approached the abbey from the south, the ruin was on the right-hand side of the road. Jason eased off on the accelerator.

'No, dunna stop just yet, drive past the entrance. There's a farm track a hundred yards further on. Reverse the car into there.' Jason drove on and turned the car around to reverse it back down the sloping lane to a farm gate twenty yards back from the road.

'We are below the level of the main road now, so anyone driving past won't see our car. Leave the engine running, but turn off the lights,' instructed Mr MacIntyre. Once out of the car, the old man retrieved a storm lamp from the backseat, giving it to Jason.

'Light it, and stand with it at your feet in front of the main gate. Once you have Anna, leave the lamp and bring her back into the abbey, through the grounds, to the car. Then go. I'll make my own way home.'

The two men shook hands. Jason thanked his old friend, but MacIntyre would have none of it, marching off into the night. The last thing Jason heard him say was, 'pah, kids these days.'

Jason walked up the moonlit track to the road and along to the abbey. Standing, as instructed, in front of the main gate. He lit the lamp and placed it on the ground, checked his service revolver was in his coat pocket, then checked the time on his watch and waited. Ten minutes later, he saw the headlights of a large car approaching. As it reached the abbey, it slowed before turning up the drive towards the main gate, its bright lights dazzling Jason. He put his arm up to shield his eyes. The car stopped about halfway along the drive. Its lights dimmed when the engine was switched off. The flare of a cigarette arced through the air from the rear window. Jason could just make out that the car was full, with two people in the front and three in the back. No one moved for a moment, then two of the car's doors opened. The front passenger got out as did two from the back seat, one of whom was Anna. She was being held up by one arm, her head falling forward. She looked drugged and showed no sign of recognising Jason.

'Bring Anna forward so I can see her better.'

The front passenger door opened and a small man got out.

'Where is the package?' shouted the small man.

'I don't have it on me. That would make it too easy for you. However, it is close by. Once I have Anna, I'll tell you where the package is hidden.'

'No, Mr Parva, you will hand it over now or I will shoot you and the girl.'

He pulled a gun from his pocket. In the seconds that Jason spent thinking about what to say next, there was a loud bang from behind and above him. The man with the gun was lifted off his feet and hurled backwards as a heavy bullet from the Martini-Henry rifle passed through him. Jason ducked at the sound, pulling his own gun. He fired in the direction of the car. He heard breaking glass a second before the Martini-Henry fired again. This time the massive rifle bullet took down the man holding onto Anna. She stayed on her feet for a second before falling on top of the dead man at her side.

The car's engine burst into life, its lights dazzling Jason once again. He fired another shot in the car's direction but had no idea if he struck it or not. The car reversed back down the abbey drive. Jason ran towards Anna, firing another shot at the car before it could reach the road. A third shot from the tower went through the car radiator.

Jason grabbed Anna by the arm, dragging her to her feet. She cried out in pain and fell back as Jason changed his grip on her. Desperate to get her away, he picked Anna up and threw her over his shoulder in a fireman's lift. Turning around, he ran back beneath the arch over the main gate and into the abbey grounds. A shot rang out from the car, ricocheting off the stone wall at his side. The compliment was immediately returned with a shot from the tower above, with the sound of shattering glass from the car.

Jason made his way through the grounds towards the lane where he had left the car. Anna moaned each time he stumbled. The pain in his leg was intensifying, but he pushed on. He had no choice. Twice he nearly fell as his feet struck stone blocks sticking out of the earth. In the near blackness, he could only see a few yards ahead of him. He cursed himself for not coming up beforehand to reconnoitre the layout of the ruin. The only bit of security he had was the echo of the powerful Martini-Henry filling the abbey grounds with sound.

Finally, Jason was free of the ruin and making his way over open ground to the track where he had left Belle's car. His pace slowed as the pain in his leg grew worse and, by the time he reached the car, all he could manage was to lay Anna across the bonnet while he opened the back door.

'Anna, Anna, wake up.'

He shook her a little, but got no response. Struggling to lift her again, he only managed to bundle her onto the back seat before closing the door. He limped around to the driver's door and got in, switched on the lights and drove out onto the road.

During their talk, Mr MacIntyre, the old gardener, had told Jason about a friend in Edinburgh who would help them.

Jason sped through the night, pushing the little car to its limits. As he drove into the town of Maybole, his thoughts racing like the engine beneath the bonnet, he prayed the Russians were not following him. But what about Mr MacIntyre? How would he escape? Jason dismissed the thought. The old war veteran was more than capable of looking after himself, especially with that rifle in his hands. However, Jason's mind returned to the task in hand after almost coming off the road on a tight bend. Slowing the car to a steadier pace, he looked in his rear-view-mirror. Anna was showing no sign of recovery or any attempt to steady herself as the car cornered rapidly.

'Anna! Anna; what is wrong? Are you hurt? What they had done to you?' She did not respond.

Jason pressed on, becoming more concerned with every mile with Anna's silence. After passing through another couple of villages, and whilst driving along a deserted road, he caught sight of an isolated cottage set back from the road. Slowing the car, he pulled to a stop next to the house. There were no lights showing from inside, but it was very late now. Getting out of the car, he checked on Anna. She moaned when he touched her. He saw the blood on her face.

'What have they done to you?'

Retrieving Anna from the back of the car, he staggered to the front door of the house with her. Jason banged on the door. It swung open. The smell of damp and cold air greeted him. Stepping inside, he let Anna slump to the floor while he drew a box of matches from his pocket and stuck one. The house had been abandoned. The front door had opened onto a room containing no furniture. There were just bare boards on the floor and painted walls. In the room to his left, he found the kitchen and, deeper inside the house, he found another empty room with plaster missing from the walls. Jason suddenly understood why it was empty. The house was being refurbished. Bringing Anna inside, he lay her on the floor and went to explore further. Some rooms were clean and newly painted, while others were still a mess. After burning his fingertips on a match for a second time, he looked around for a lamp, only finding a box of candles sitting on top of a crate. Setting four lit candles around the room, he returned to fetch Anna. She groaned each time he moved her and it was only as he brought her into the light of the lit room that he learnt why. Her face was the colour of wax and her torn dress revealed the burns on her back. Jason cursed aloud as he laid Anna on the floor face down, making a pillow for her from his coat. From the car, he brought in the things he had prepared earlier in the day and then hid the car around the back of the house, out of sight.

With Anna lying on the floor covered with the blankets, Jason propped himself up in the corner of the room facing the door, his pistol at his side, while he ate a sandwich. He wanted a shot of the whisky to help numb the pain in his leg, but he daren't risk it, he had to stay alert and keep watch. He had let Anna down once. He wasn't about to do it again.

Chapter Thirteen

'Jason, Jason.' His eyes opened, focusing on the door. His hand reached for his gun. The soft voice called his name again.

'Jason.' Anna was awake and calling to him. Crawling across the floor, he sat on the floor beside her and brushed sweat matted hair from her eyes.

'Where are we?' she asked, her voice dry and hoarse.

'Safe, for now. How are you feeling?'

'Terrible. May I have some water?'

Jason got to his feet and limped through to the kitchen. His leg stiff and painful, after sleeping on a hard floor. Morning had broken, and a grey light filled the kitchen coming through a window above the sink. There were no cupboards, just a rectangular white sink, with a single tap over it. In the sink, he found a chipped cup. He washed it as best he could under the cold tap before filling it with water. Returning to Anna, he placed the cup to her lips.

'Where are we?' she asked again after finishing the water.

'I don't know. After I got you away from those men, I just drove through the darkness, unsure where I was going. All I wanted to do was get as far away from them as possible. Mr MacIntyre said we should go to Edinburgh. There is someone there who will help us.'

'Who?'

'A friend of Mr MacIntyre's.'

'Who's house is this?' she asked.

'I don't know. I had to stop somewhere to rest. We're lucky, this house is empty. I've still got my gun. If someone had been living here, I would have forced them to let us stay the night if I had to. From what I've found, someone is in the middle of fixing this place up. Half the rooms are clean and painted, the others still need work doing to them. I expect the owners will be back later today. I just hope we've moved on before they do.'

'Is there anything to eat?'

'Only what I packed yesterday. I have some sandwiches, a pie, some apples, cheese and cold meat.'

'A regular feast then,' Anna smiled for the first time. 'Help me sit up, will you?'

Jason held out his arm for Anna to pull against as she eased herself into a sitting position.

'I've seen your back. I'm sorry. It must be very painful?'

'Yes, but it will heal. They wanted to know where the documents and jewel were hidden. Their leader said he had killed the man who had given them to me, and that the documents and the jewel are more important than I was. They tortured me until I told them that you had taken them away and hidden them. I hoped by telling them a plausible-sounding story they would believe me and that it would buy me enough time until I could escape, but they kept me drugged. How long do you think we can stay here?'

'I'm not sure. The house wasn't locked, so I suppose the owners live close by and come back frequently. I have fresh clothes for you in the bag over there. Change out of that torn dress and we'll be on our way. We can find somewhere else to rest up until you feel a bit better. But first, we eat, then I'll bring the car to the front of the house while you change. There is a cold water tap in the kitchen if you feel like a wash.'

In less than an hour, they were on the road again.

'We are going to get as far away from here as possible; go further north,' said Jason. 'Keep moving; not let them catch up with us. Then we'll turn towards Edinburgh.'

'If you think that is best, but I can't travel far, it's too painful to lay my back against the car seat.'

'I'm sorry, I didn't think. We'll stop for a few days and give those burns a chance to heal.' Jason glanced across to Anna, noticing how pale she had suddenly become.

'Are you alright, do you want me to stop for a minute?'

'No, keep going. I just feel a bit dizzy. It will pass.' He drove on, taking them north until, just as they reached the village of Dalrymple. The car backfired and slowed down.

'No, not now,' complained Jason, as the car slowed to a crawl. The juddering got worse. Jason coaxed the car along the village main street until the car gave up its struggle to survive. With one final bang and a cough of black smoke, the engine stopped. Passers-by stopped to stare at the dead machine and its frustrated occupants.

'Stay in the car. I'll try to find someone who can help,' instructed Jason. After walking along the main street, he found the Kirkton Inn and Hotel. Jason went inside.

'We're not open,' said the man behind the bar. 'You'll have to wait another hour yet.'

'I'm not after a drink. I need help. My car has broken down and I need someone or somewhere to fix it. Is there a garage in the village?'

'Not what you would call a garage, exactly. There's Gordon, the blacksmith, down the way a bit. There's no real call for a garage around here. Those that do have a car take them to Ayr to have them seen to.'

Jason paused as he thought about what to do next. 'Would you happen to have a couple of spare rooms? I have a lady friend, and we'll need somewhere to stay until our car is repaired.'

'Oh, yes, sir. We're not very busy this time of year. How long were you thinking of staying?'

'Just until I can get the car fixed, a few days maybe.'

'Aye, right then, I'll just have a word with the good lady wife and she'll get two rooms fixed up for you straight away.'

'Great. Thank you. That's one problem resolved. I'll get my friend and our luggage.' Fifteen minutes later, Jason and Anna were sitting in her bedroom.

'I'll have to move the car. It can't stay on the main street. I'm going to bring it up to the hotel and around the back, out of sight, just in case anyone comes along the road looking for us.'

Back at the car, Jason cursed it for letting them down. Standing at the roadside, he released the two metal clamps holding the bonnet closed and lifted the cover out of the way. He looked for any obvious reason as to why the car had died on them. There were no loose leads or broken pipes or belts. Turning on the ignition, he went around to the front of the car and cranked the starter handle. After three turns of the handle, and with no sign that the car was going to start, he closed the bonnet and steeled himself for pushing the dead machine out of sight. After struggling with the car for about twenty yards, four boys came along and watched him as he massaged his leg.

'Want a hand, mister?' asked the taller of the lads.

'There's a tanner each for you if you can push the car around the back of the Kirkton Inn.'

The faces of the boys lit up.

'Six-pence-each?' exclaimed the smallest of the four. 'Wow.'

All four lads eagerly got behind the car and started pushing it.

'Wait a minute,' said Jason. I need to steer it.'

Jason got into the driver's seat and the boys got ready to push the car. With the lads eagerly pushing, it was only a matter of minutes before Jason was applying the handbrake in the yard behind the hotel. Jason had found a parking place next to a large chicken run, much to the annoyance of the birds which rushed inside their coop as the car pulled up.

Jason paid the boys their wages and waved them goodbye before returning to Anna. Knocking on her door, he got no reply. He knocked again, then opened it gingerly before peering inside. Anna was asleep on the bed. Creeping up to her, he covered her with the eiderdown and left. He too suddenly felt very tired.

The sound of raised voices woke Jason. His hand slipped up beneath his pillow, ready to retrieve his revolver. As he began to make sense of his surroundings and the distant voices, he relaxed, throwing back the blanket covering him and sitting up. Going to his bedroom door, he looked out towards Anna's room. The voices grew louder with the door open, and he could tell that they were coming from below him. He listened, trying to figure out what was being said. He recognised the voice of the landlord first, the other voice was new to him. The profanities the stranger was using, coupled with his slurred speech, gave Jason the impression the man was very drunk. Standing in the doorway to his room, he continued to listen to the ruckus. As Jason listened, it became clear that the drunk was the hotel chef, and the landlord of the hotel was angry with him for being late on duty as well as being too drunk to do his job. The argument continued with the landlord accusing the cook of stealing two bottles of whisky from behind the bar. From what the landlord was saying to the cook, Jason quickly guessed that there would be nothing to eat tonight in the hotel restaurant. The argument ended with the landlord telling the cook, in no uncertain terms, that he was sacked and was never to return. This was followed by the slamming of a door and then further swearing coming from the yard at the back of the inn.

Jason put the gun in his pocket and went across the hall to Anna's door, and knocked lightly. There was no answer. Opening the door a crack, he looked inside. She was still asleep on the bed, just as he had left her. Closing the door quietly, he returned to his room and put the revolver in his bag. As he lay on his bed thinking, a number of problems were at the forefront of his mind. He was running low on money. How was he going to get the car fixed? How safe was it where they were staying, and how were the Russians able to keep finding their hiding places? He'd only been contemplating the problems for a few minutes when there was a tap on the door.

'Yes,' said Jason, annoyed at the disturbance. The door opened slowly to reveal Anna, looking tired and dishevelled, but smiling.

'I awoke when my door closed. I guessed it was you checking up on me.' Jason swung his feet to the floor and stood up.

'Yes, it was. Come in. How are you feeling?'

'Less tired, but my back is really painful.'

'We could go down to the bar and get a brandy before we eat. That is, if we can get anything to eat.'

'What do you mean?'

'I overheard an argument earlier. I'm surprised it didn't wake you, it did me. It was between the landlord and the cook. It sounded like the cook was drunk and the landlord has fired him.'

'What are we going to do? Do you know if there is anywhere else we can get a meal from tonight?'

'Let's go down and speak to the landlord. We can get a brandy and ask about a menu for this evening. We can also ask him about the whereabouts of a chemist so we can get you some painkillers and cream for your burns.'

They found the landlord wiping down tables in the dining-room.

'Excuse me, we were wondering if we could get a drink and look at tonight's menu?' said Jason.

The landlord stopped what he was doing and wiped his hands on his apron.

'Menu? You'd better come with me.' He led them to the bar. 'What would you like to drink?'

'A large brandy for Miss Moreau, and I'll have a whisky and soda, please.' As the landlord poured out the drinks, he apologised for there being no food available for that evening, or for the foreseeable future as he no longer had a cook.

'I had to get rid of him. He was drinking my profits away. He used to be a good chef; able to cook all manner of things, that is, until his wife left him.'

'What are we to do? Is there anywhere else we can get a meal?' asked Jason.

'I can make you some sandwiches if you like? I have a kitchen full of food, just no one to cook it. As for tonight, when we get busy, I'll no have any time to be preparing food and serve drinks at the same time. My wife will be clearing tables, washing glasses and helping me in here.'

'We also need a chemist so we can buy some painkillers,' said Jason.

'Well, I can help you there. There's no chemist shop in the village, and we no have a doctor either, but there is a village shop that sells everything you'll need. It doubles as a kind of grocer's shop come drug store. Anyone in the village who gets ill or has a medical problem goes to see Granny McTavish. She knows more about doctoring and the like than any of these fancy fellas that have had university schooling. She's just across the way; the shop is on the corner of Church Street.'

'Thank you, we'll do that,' said Jason. He looked at Anna.

'It doesn't seem like we have much choice for now.' They finished their drinks and went in search of the village store.

Granny McTavish's shop was easy to find, being just a few yards down and on the opposite side of the road to the hotel. From the outside, the shop could be easily mistaken for just a house. There were no large windows displaying goods or a large sign for passers-by to take note of its location. It was simply at the end of a row of terraced cottages. All of them were painted white with dark slate roofs. Just a simple wooden placard above the door read Village Shop. It gave no other clue as to what might be inside. As they entered the shop, their senses were assailed by a mixture of smells as the ill-lit interior opened up in front of them. The size of the exterior of the building was deceptive, as once inside, it became apparent that two cottages had been made into one to accommodate the shop and all its stock. One area was devoted to hardware products, another to tinned and packet foods and the third to vegetables. Behind the kitchen table, which doubled as a counter, from floor to ceiling, was a wall of apothecary draws.

Sat next to the table was Granny McTavish, a short, stout, grey-haired lady, wearing wire-rimmed glasses, a tartan shawl around her shoulders, and a black skirt beneath a long white apron which almost reached to the floor. As Jason and Anna approached her, she stood up and eyed them carefully.

'We would like to buy...' said Jason. Only Granny McTavish cut him short.

'You stay there. You lass, come with me.' The old woman turned away towards a curtained door at the rear of the shop. Stopping at the curtain, she beckoned Anna inside.

'Come on. Come with me.' Beyond the curtain, Anna found herself alone with the shopkeeper in a small room. It was just large enough to hold a wooden framed bed covered with a clean sheet and, next to it, a simple straight-backed chair.

'Take your dress off and lay on the bed,' instructed Granny McTavish. Anna hesitated.

'I can see from your posture you have a problem with your back, and the expression on your face tells me you are in pain. Now take off your dress and lay on the bed so I can take a look at it.' Granny McTavish adjusted her spectacles as Anna dropped her dress on the chair and did as she was told.

'Did he do this to you?'

'No, it was someone else. Jason is helping me escape.'

'Wait there. I'll be back in a moment.'

Granny McTavish looked Jason up and down as she came from behind the curtain and climbed the wooden stepladder in front of the apothecary drawers. While on the steps, she opened drawer after drawer, dropping something from within each of them into the large pocket on the front of her apron. Coming back down the steps, she emptied the contents of her apron into a mixing bowl. She added some oil and began to stir the mixture, first one way and then the other. When done, she returned to Anna, mixing bowl in hand.

'I'm going to put this salve on yer back. It'll sting a bit at first, but after a few seconds, the pain will ease. You'll feel a lot happier in yourself when this takes effect. I'm gonna put the rest of it in a jar for you to take home. Put the salve on every day and the burns will heal without troubling you further.'

Anna gave a sharp intake of breath as Granny McTavish spread the salve over her back. After a few seconds, she could feel the remedy easing away her pain. Wiping her hands on a white towel, Granny McTavish instructed Anna to rest a minute before dressing and returning to her man.

Leaving Anna, Granny returned to Jason.

'You'll be needing these and probably one of these.' she placed a wad of rolled-up scraps of cotton fabric on the table along with a thin wooden spatula. 'That'll be ten shillings.'

'What?' gasped Jason, surprised at the price the old woman was demanding.

'Yer wee lassie needed my help. I dinna know what's been going on between ya both, or what kind of trouble yer in. And, I can tell from your voice and manner that a Sasanach like you can afford to pay an old woman her dues.' Jason pulled a ten shilling note from his wallet as Anna came through the curtain.

'Is everything alright?' asked Jason.

'Thank you, Madam McTavish,' said Anna. 'I feel much better already.'

Granny placed the spatula and cotton rags in a brown paper bag and handed it to Jason.

As they left the shop, Anna confessed to Jason that all the pain and stiffness in her back had gone. She held up the jam jar with the salve for Jason to see.

'This is remarkable stuff; she should sell the recipe to a **pharmaceutical company**.'

On the way back to the hotel, Anna made a suggestion to Jason.

'Why don't we ask the landlord if we can cook our own dinner tonight? I am a pretty fair cook.'

'That's a good idea. I'll speak to him as soon as we get in.'

The landlord was nowhere in sight when they arrived back at the hotel, and even a couple of heavy rings on the barbell brought no response. However, as Anna and Jason were about to go upstairs, the landlord appeared from the back of the building wearing a leather apron covered in grime.

'Sorry, can I help you? I've been giving the draymen a hand, there's just been a delivery of beer.'

'Yes,' said Jason. 'Anna has had an idea about dinner tonight. Would you be willing to let us to make our own dinner this evening?'

The landlord scratched his head and thought about it. 'I don't see why not. But, there is one condition. You must make enough for me and the misses as well. If you're prepared to cook for the four of us, you can have free drinks while you're staying at the hotel.'

Anna and Jason agreed immediately.

'We can't keep calling you landlord if we are going to be working together. This is Anna and my name is Jason.'

'You can call me Gordon and the wife's called Maggie. The kitchen is through there. Help yourself. Mind you, it's no but a coal-burning stove, and we dinna have any modern kitchen stuff.'

'That's not a problem. At home on our farm, my mother uses a wood-burning stove to cook on,' Anna reassured him.

Anna got Jason to ignite the range while she went to search through the larder. The shelves were well stocked with a variety of tinned, dried, and fresh produce. A side of bacon hung from a hook in the ceiling. In a cool box, she found a plucked chicken and a large quantity of beef wrapped in paper. She gathered her chosen ingredients and deposited them on the kitchen table.

'I think we will eat well tonight. I have a taste for some home cooking.'

A couple of hours later, Gordon, Maggie, Jason and Anna were sitting in the bar eating chicken sprinkled with lemon and toasted almonds, buttered carrots and sauté potatoes. Gordon had to occasionally leave the table to serve early customers arriving for a drink, and it wasn't long before the pub customers spotted what the four were eating.

'You got a new cook then, Gordon? That looks a bit fancy. What are you eating?'

'Aye, Mack. I've got myself a French cook now,' He pointed his fork at Anna.

'Billy Dalgleish never was any good in the kitchen. It was about time you got rid of that old fraud. He was only interested in the whisky he could get out of you. That does look good. I've a mind to try some of that myself,' said Mack.

'Oh, I'm sorry,' said Anna. 'I only made enough for the four of us, but I've got some Boeuf Bourguignon on the stove. It's supposed to be for tomorrow night, but you could try some of that if you like?'

'What's that?' asked Mack. Anna chuckled to herself.

'I guess you would call it beef stew.'

'Right you are. I'll try some of that then.'

Anna brought Mack a plate of the stew and a couple of thick slices of bread.

'I'm sorry, it could do with cooking a little longer to bring out the full flavour and for the beef to become really tender. I don't have any vegetables left either, but the bread should fill you up.'

Mack dipped the bread in the stew and took a bite.

'Hey, this beef stew is good,' he said, spraying bread crumbs around as he spoke. With Mack telling everyone who came in how good the food was, it wasn't long before more customers were asking for the beef stew and, very soon, it was all gone. After a few complaints that there wasn't enough to go around, Anna promised to make some more for the following evening.

'I think we've had a rather successful day,' Anna confessed to Jason. 'But I'm feeling more than a little tired now. I think I'll go to bed. Goodnight.'

'I'm going to finish my drink first and finish talking to Hamish. He's agreed to collect the car for me. He has a horse that will tow it to his barn where I can have a go at repairing the engine.'

After his chat with Hamish, Jason retired for the evening. He was just about to enter his room when Anna emerged from the bathroom at the end of the corridor. She was barefooted, with wet hair, and she had a large white towel wrapped about her.

'Oh, Jason, I'm pleased you didn't stay down there too long. I need your help. Would you smooth some more of that salve on my back?'

Jason nodded. 'Yes, I'll be right with you.'

'Just one moment. Wait outside the door. I'll call you when I'm ready.' She slipped inside her room and closed the door while Jason waited outside. A couple of minutes later, he heard Anna call his name. Tentatively, he opened the door to see Anna lying face down on the bed. Her back was bare, but she had the bedclothes covering her legs up to her waist.

'The salve is on the table next to the bed,' she informed him. Jason couldn't help but stare for a moment before moving closer.

'I hope your hands are warm,' she said over her shoulder. Jason blew on his hands and rubbed his palms together, unable to take his eyes off the delicate pink form lying on the bed. Picking up the salve, he inserted two fingers into the jar and removed some of the soft, creamy substance. Sitting on the edge of the bed, he leaned over Anna, breathing in the scent of her fresh clean body. His hand shook as he placed his fingers on her back. At first, he avoided the burns that still looked bright and cruel. Then, slowly and gently, he spread the salve over the wounds in a circular motion. He could feel Anna's body responding to his touch as he smoothed the salve across over her skin. She lay with her head turned to one side on the pillow. Her eyes closed and her lips slightly parted as she breathed. A lock of her hair had fallen across her cheek and Jason longed to brush it aside but refrained from doing so. Placing the jar of salve on the bedside table, he stood up and stepped away from the bed.

'All finished. I hope that's done the trick. Good night.'

Anna only just had time to say. 'Thank you.' Before Jason was out of the door.

Back in his own room, Jason lay on his bed, his thoughts dominated by Anna, and his feelings towards her. Sleep eluded him as he struggled with the temptation to confess his growing feelings of affection toward her. But did he have the right to do so? How could he feel this way towards someone who had put their trust in him to keep her safe? He forced himself to think about the car, what might be wrong with it and Hamish bringing the horse to tow it away. A day fixing the car will keep my mind off Anna. He made a mental note of the possible problems with the car before switching off the light and going to sleep.

His dreams were filled with racing through the countryside in the small car. Sometimes his passenger was Celia and other times it was Anna. The dreams came to a head when he was flying again and the enemy plane was being piloted by Celia. The recognition of seeing her face in the Fokker Wolf which shot him down woke him from his nightmare. Throwing back the blankets on the bed, he sat in the dark, rubbing his temples, his heart thumping. He shivered in the cool night air and cursed the war.

After stripping his bed of its damp sheets, he left them in a pile near the door. His wristwatch told him it was five-thirty. He washed and shaved before going down to the kitchen, making bacon and eggs on toast and a pot of tea. As he sat in the bar eating his breakfast, he wondered what it must be like to run a small hotel or pub. It occurred to him that he had no plans for what he was going to do with his life after Anna returned to France. I suppose I could stay at home in Nafferton. I amassed enough money in Africa to do so. He dismissed the thought of buying a pub. No. But I could try farming. That idea had more appeal. However, he quickly dismissed any idea of going back to Kenya. The list of ideas was getting longer, when, to his surprise, Gordon walked into the bar.

'I could smell the bacon and my stomach started rumbling,' he confessed as he sat opposite Jason.

'Would you like me to make you some breakfast?' asked Jason.

'No, thank you, I'll make my own, but I got to thinking last night. I wanted to ask you something, but you went to your bed before I could talk to you. Would the two of you consider staying on a wee while, just until I could get a new cook sorted out? Those meals that your young lassie made had my customers talking all evening. Many of them stayed longer than usual and my takings for the night were the best I've had in a long time.'

'I'd like to help you out, Gordon, but I don't know what our plans for the future are, and I would have to talk it over with Anna first.'

'Aye, I know all that. But I could offer you free lodging while you stay, and it would only be for a few days. I'll soon find another cook, but I bet he won't be as good as Anna.'

'I'll talk it over with Anna. If she agrees, then we'll be happy to help you out. But only until the car is fixed. Then, we must leave.'

'In that case, I can only hope it takes you longer than you think to fix the car. No offence. I'm just thinking about my customers, you understand?'

'Yes, Gordon, I get the picture.'

'There is another thing. I need to apologise to Maggie. I need clean bedding; I had a bit of a bad dream last night. It happens now and again.'

'Dunna worry, Lad, I served my time as well. There are nights when I'm back in the trenches. Maggie will understand. I'll have a word with her.'

'Thanks, I'll go see if Anna is up yet and talk to her about your offer.'

Jason tapped on Anna's door.

'Come in, it's open.'

Anna was dressed and brushing her hair.

'I could smell bacon frying, so I guessed you were up. I don't know how you would manage without a fried breakfast in the morning.'

'It's just one of those English eccentricities. Speaking about food, Gordon has just made us a proposition. His customers were so impressed with your cooking last night that he wants us to stay on with you as cook. It's just for a short time; until he can fill the position permanently, but I said I needed to speak to you first. What do you think?'

'I don't know. It's come as a bit of a surprise. Do you think I could do it? What about us going to Edinburgh?'

'Yes, those were my first thought too. But I need time to get the car fixed and you need time for your back to heal. At least here you can keep the wounds clean and Granny McTavish can make you some more salve if you run out. Gordon has also offered to give us free board until he can get a permanent cook. And, to be honest, I'm also running low on cash until we can get to another bank and withdraw some money. Another point is this. The Soviets are looking for two people on the run and making their way north, not looking for a man and a woman working in a small hotel.'

Anna thought about it for a moment. 'I see. Very well, just for a few days, but I decide what to cook.'

'Great. I'm sure Gordon will be happy with that. Are you're ready to come down? I could do with another cup of tea.'

Chapter Fourteen

Jason, bacon sandwich in hand, waited at the rear of the hotel for Hamish to arrive to tow away the car. He had just finished eating when he heard the heavy footsteps of a horse coming around the corner.

'Good morning, Hamish. Not a bad day, is it?

'Good morning to you, Jason. All ready for me to take the car away?'

'Yes. Once you have the horse hitched up, I'll sit in the car and steer. It's good of you to help me.'

'Ah, well, you see, I have a confession to make. I have an ulterior motive. I reckon that if I see how you fix the problem with your car, that I might be able to do the same to someone else's car. There are more cars on the road since the end of the war, and I think that there is money to be made in fixing them when they go wrong. So I was thinking of getting into this car mending lark before anyone else in these parts got the idea.'

'That's good thinking, but there are lots of things that can go wrong with a car. You won't learn them all just by watching me, Hamish.'

'Aye, that's as may be, but it's a start and I'm sure I can figure out the rest as I go along.' Hamish ran two ropes from the horse's collar to the front bumper of the car.

'Right you are; it's not far to my yard.' As the horse stepped off, the car jerked forward, rocking Jason back in his seat. A few minutes later, they were in the yard at the back of Hamish's farmhouse and pushing the car into a small barn.

'In here, you'll be out of the rain while you're working. I've got a few tools on the bench over there; help yourself to what you need. Are you going to get started now, or come back later?' asked Hamish, eager to get started.

'I was hoping to make a start today if that's alright with you?'

'Yes, good. I was hoping you would say that. Don't start for a minute; I'm just going inside to get Mary to make us a cup of tea while we are working.' Hamish ran into the farmhouse and returned a minute later.

'Right you are. What do we do first?' asked Hamish as he rolled up his shirt sleeves.

'Well, first I was going to check the spark plugs.'

'What do they do?' asked Hamish.

Jason sighed. 'They, you might say, Hamish, keep the heart of the machine beating.' This was going to take far longer than he had expected, thought Jason. Hamish's wife Mary brought them tea and a large plate of cheese and pickle sandwiches for lunch. By mid-afternoon, all Jason had done to his car was check the plugs, the timing and clean the carburettor. Hamish kept interrupting Jason's work, wanting to know what each part of the engine was and how it worked. He was enthralled to learn how the carburettor mixed fuel and air together and then pushed the mixture into the engine to fire the pistons. Fortunately, Jason enjoyed teaching Hamish more than he thought he would and, even though he still hadn't discovered what was preventing the engine from working, he'd had a good day with his trainee mechanic.

'I've had enough for now, Hamish. I'm going back to get cleaned up. May I come back tomorrow to work on the car?'

'Yes. Sure. I'll be waiting for you. Don't you worry, we'll soon find out what is wrong with this little beauty. I'll probably see you in the bar later on for a bit of supper. I'm bringing Mary with me tonight so she can try some of that foreign beef stew your Anna makes.'

Jason smiled at the thought of 'that foreign beef stew.' He thought about the simple home-cooked food most people in these parts were used to and the reaction Anna's cooking was having on them. The new hotel cuisine was the talk of the village.

*****

After breakfast, while Jason was working on the car, Anna began a thorough inventory of the kitchen larder and then, with Maggie's help, the two women cleaned the kitchen from top to bottom.

'It's as good as we'll get it,' said Maggie. 'I dinna think it's been this clean in the past ten years.'

Anna smiled at her while leaning on her mop.

'Well, at least, I'll now be able to find what I'm looking for. The mess your old chef was working in, I'm surprised he could find anything he needed. Look at the time. This has taken us all day, and I haven't even started to prepare food for tonight. I'll have to keep tonight's meal quick and simple.' Maggie followed Anna to the pantry to see which ingredients she would collect.

'May I kill a couple of chickens for the pot?' Anna asked Maggie. 'I'd like to boil them up, make a sauce and serve them with some rice. With any luck, it should be ready by opening time.'

'Yes, by all means. They are a bit of a scrawny lot. Most of them have stopped laying, anyway. I was thinking of getting some younger birds.'

'Right, I'll get the chickens; you put a pan on to boil,' said Anna.

Once the chickens were plucked, cleaned, and put in the pot, the women looked at each other and laughed. They were both splashed with blood and had stray chicken feathers in their hair and stuck to their clothes.

'What a sight we must make,' declared Maggie.

'Let's go get cleaned up and then have a cup of coffee. We can put our feet up while the chickens are boiling,' suggested Anna.

'I'm not so keen on the coffee, I'll stick to my tea, but it'll be nice to have a chat, woman to woman instead of with just him in there, or an occasional hello and what's the weather doing from a guest,' responded Maggie. Ten minutes later, they were sitting in the bar with a hot drink each, wearing clean aprons and free of feathers.

'I wish I could persuade you to stay,' said Maggie. 'I think we could become good friends.'

Anna blushed at the compliment. 'Thank you. I like you too, Maggie, but it can't be. We have to move on soon. I wish we didn't have to, but we don't have a choice.'

'Who are you running away from? Surely things can't be that bad. You're not...you know?' Maggie pointed at her belly.

'No, no, nothing like that. It's complicated – family matters, you might say.'

'You mean parents or another man?'

'Yes, something like that,' lied Anna.

'So that's why you're running away with Jason? I must say, he's a good-looking fella, and well to do if I'm any judge of character. Are you planning on marrying him?'

'What? I, I hadn't thought about it. As I said, things are complicated. What gave you the impression we would get married?'

'Have you not noticed the way he looks at you, lass? When you are not by his side, he's like my Gordon, lost. He has ghosts in his eyes, memories of the war and what went on over there. But when you are with him, his face comes alive. The man's in love with you; if he doesn't know it now, it won't be long before the penny drops.'

'No, he can't be. I, I... come on, those chickens will be nearly ready by now, and I've got the sauce to make and the rice to cook. No, he can't be!'

Anna rushed back to the kitchen, her hands shaking as she collected the ingredients to make a mushroom sauce to go with the chicken.

*****

As Jason entered the hotel, he caught sight of Anna and Maggie sitting in the bar, talking. Leaving them undisturbed, he went upstairs to have a bath before putting on some fresh clothes. When he returned, Anna and Maggie were gone. Gordon was stocking the bar, ready for his evening customers.

'Hello Jason, how's the car coming along?'

'Hello, Gordon. Slowly, very slowly, Hamish is helping me. He wants to know everything there is to know about fixing car engines. He says he wants to set up his own garage.'

'Aye, I expect he will. He's a clever man, is Hamish. Don't misjudge him. You only have to show him how to do something once and he never forgets it.'

'I suppose Anna and Maggie are getting dinner ready for tonight?' asked Jason.

'Yes, they are in the kitchen. They've spent most of the day cleaning it and tidying the larder. Anna said she was going to make something with chicken. The old cook used to make the same things every night, Haggis with Colcannon, and Baggers and Mash with onion gravy. Don't get me wrong, the locals loved it, but it would have been nice to have a change once in a while. He was a good chef before the drink got to him.'

'Well, your customers are certainly getting a change of menu now. Whatever those two are making, it sure does smell good.'

'Would you like to join me in a wee dram before we open?' asked Gordon.

253

'Thank you, I'll have a whisky and soda, if I may?'

'No. No, laddie. I mean, a wee snifter of the good stuff.' Gordon reverently lifted a bottle from the shelf.

'This is a twenty-five-year-old, Glen Scotia, single malt. You don't go spoiling it by adding soda water. I've had to keep this safely hidden away, and I only take a nip now and then. When the mood is on me. You and Anna have done me a good turn, and by the smells coming from the kitchen, I'm going to have some very satisfied customers tonight. So, a wee celebration is in order.'

Jason accepted the glass of whisky, drawing in the scent of the coloured liquid. The aroma reminded him of earthy oak woodlands. The taste was fruitier than he expected. It reminded him of fresh apples and oranges. Then came the after taste with its hint of ginger and vanilla. The whisky left a warm feeling in his mouth and throat, with no sharp burning sensation like the fiery cheaper whiskies from behind the bar.

'That's a fine whisky indeed, Gordon, thank you.' The landlord had no sooner replaced his bottle of scotch in its hiding place when the first two customers arrived.

'Two pints of bitter please, Gordon?'

'Aye, coming right up. Had a busy day, lads?' The two customers went on to elaborate on their working day while Gordon listened. Jason left them to their chat and went through to the kitchen.

'Customers have started arriving,' he announced to Anna and Maggie.

'We're ready for them,' replied Maggie. Anna turned her back on Jason to stir the rice.

'It looks like you two have had a busy day; what's for supper?' asked Jason. Anna didn't reply, leaving it to Maggie to answer Jason.

'It's chicken in a white wine and mushroom sauce served with buttered, boiled rice.'

'I wonder what the locals will think of that?' responded Jason.

Anna spun around on her heel. 'What is wrong with it? What do you want me to do? I've spent all day cleaning this pigsty and now you criticise my cooking. Get out, you don't have to stay and eat it if you don't want to.'

Jason stood, mouth open for a moment. Even Maggie looked shocked at Anna's sudden outburst. Jason returned to the bar, asking Gordon for a whisky and soda before sitting in the corner. It was the first time Anna had turned on him. He was confused. What had he done to upset her?

'What was that all about?' Maggie asked Anna.

'I don't know; yes I do. It's what you said about Jason and me. It took me by surprise. Then, when he came into the kitchen, I didn't know what to do or say to him. I just wanted him to go away. Are you sure he feels that way about me?'

Maggie smiled. 'So, you do have feelings for him, then?'

'I didn't say that. I just didn't know what to say to him, that's all.'

'That's what I mean. If you had no feelings for your man, you would have used kinder words than you did. Whether you like it or not, you were speaking with your heart and not your head. If you're not head over heels in love with him now, you soon will be as soon as you face up to the fact.' Anna was about to respond when Gordon came into the kitchen.

'I've got customers wanting beef stew; is it ready yet?'

'There no beef stew left for tonight, Gordon, it all went last night. It's chicken with rice tonight,' replied Maggie.

'But they are asking for beef stew.'

'Well, they'll just have to have chicken with rice instead,' insisted Maggie.

Gordon retreated to the bar, only to come back a moment later. 'They don't want the chicken. They finished their drinks and left.'

Anna looked at Maggie.

'Is Jason still out there?' asked Anna.

'Yes, he's sitting on his own in the corner of the bar.'

'When your next customers come in, give them a drink and then come and collect Jason's supper. Once people see what he is eating and get a smell of it, with a bit of luck they'll want to try it as well,' said Anna.

Gordon's next two customers were Hamish and Mary, who, seeing Jason on his own, went to sit with him. Gordon did as he was bid. He served them their drinks and then delivered Jason a plate of supper.

'What's that?' asked Hamish.

'Supreme of chicken in a white wine and mushroom sauce with buttered rice,' responded Jason.

'It's all white,' exclaimed Hamish. 'Where's the gravy and the tatters?'

Jason chuckled at Hamish's interpretation of what a good meal needed to have to accompany it.

'Well, I think it smells wonderful,' said Mary. 'Gordon, can I have some supper. I'm starving. Hamish promised me a night out and I'm going to have one.' Tentatively at first, Mary tasted a fork full of rice and then some rice with the white wine sauce.

'Mm, this isn't bad. Next, she tried the chicken coved in the sauce. You know this is very good.' With Hamish watching on Mary tucked into her supper. It wasn't long before she had finished it all and sat back in her chair, pushing her empty plate into the centre of the table.

'That made a nice change from the fry-ups we have most nights,' she said to Hamish.

'You mean you really liked all that white stuff?' asked her husband.

'Aye, you missed a real treat there. I suppose you'll have to make do with sausage and egg when we get home.'

'No fear of that. If you can eat it, so can I.'

Hamish called across to the bar. 'Gordon, let's have another plate of that chicken over here.'

As Hamish ate his supper, more customers arrived. Curiosity soon got the better of them and it wasn't long before they too wanted to sample what Hamish was eating.

To Gordon's surprise, Hamish called over to each new customer and told them about the meal he was eating.

'Hey, you need to try this new supper Gordon is serving. It's even better than the beef stew we had last night. It's got white wine in the sauce. Mind you, it's the kind of meal that only appeals to the more sophisticated diners amongst us,' said Hamish, as he scooped up a fork full of rice.

'Take no notice of Hamish,' said Mary. 'He wouldn't try it when he first saw it. It was only when I had some and told him that he'd have to wait until we got home before he got his supper that he changed his mind about having some. Now he thinks he's a food expert. But I do have to admit that Jason's Anna is a really excellent cook. I bet the new hotel chef, when he arrives, won't be cooking food like this. You'd better try it while you've got the chance.' An hour later, all the food was all gone.

'I've got customers out there that want feeding,' complained Gordon to Anna. 'And I haven't had anything to eat yet.'

'I'm sorry, Gordon, I didn't know how much to make. I'll make more for tomorrow night, I promise. Tell them I'll make something special for tomorrow night to make up for them missing out tonight.' By eight o'clock, Anna and Maggie had closed the kitchen.

'I'm going for a bath and then I'm off to bed,' said Anna.

'I'll see you in the morning. Good night.' Maggie went through to the bar to help Gordon. On seeing Maggie without Anna, Jason went over to speak to her.

'Isn't Anna coming through?' asked Jason.

'No, we've had a long day and she's tired. She said she was going to have a bath and then go to bed.'

Jason went back to Hamish and Mary. 'What are we going to do to the car tomorrow?' asked Hamish.

Jason, distracted for a moment, didn't answer immediately.

'Oh, er, I think I'll check the fuel line. It may have dirt in it, starving the engine of petrol. If there isn't enough fuel getting through to the engine, it will struggle to run.'

'Will that take long? Only I've got some sheep to move to a new pasture tomorrow. The grass is getting a bit thin in the field where they are now.'

'No, not long. The trouble is, if that's not the problem, then I'll have to look for problems inside the engine, and that means there is something seriously wrong with the car. And it will take me a lot longer to fix it. That's if you have the tools for me to do that kind of work.'

After another half an hour of chatting with Hamish and Mary, Jason excused himself and went up to see Anna. The bathroom light was off, so he knocked on her room door. When she opened it, she was wearing her dressing gown and had a towel wrapped around her hair.

'Oh, it's you.' She stepped away from the door, leaving it open.

'I came to see what was wrong; you haven't spoken to me all day except to snap at me in the kitchen.'

Anna sat on the bed and said nothing. Then, looking into her lap, she said.

'I'm sorry. You just caught me at a bad moment. Maggie said something that surprised me and then you came in and...'

'I see. I'll leave you to go to bed.' Jason turned and made for the open door.

'No, wait. I said I was sorry, and I meant it. Please stay. I'd like you to rub some more salve on my back?'

Jason stopped. 'Very well. I'll wait outside until you are ready.'

Once the door was closed, Anna put the salve on the bedside table as she had done the night before. She stripped off her dressing gown and got into bed, just leaving her bare back exposed. 'You can come in now!'

Jason entered and sat on the bed beside her. 'Are you ready?'

Anna closed her eyes as Jason smoothed the salve over her skin, being extra careful as he covered the burns.

Maggie's words about Jason's feelings towards her, danced in Anna's mind as he eased the salve over her skin. Deft, gentle fingers smoothed the cream over her back. She felt herself relaxing at his touch. Alone together, she began to recognise the feelings that had been creeping up on her over the past few days. She felt safe with him around; she enjoyed his company; he'd put her first in most decisions he made and he had asked her for nothing in return. Without realising it before, she recognised now how they had bonded in a way she had never done with the men closer to her age that she had dated in Paris. Jason had always treated her with respect. Maggie was right. She did have feelings for him. Anna's skin tingled as she thought about the possibility of Jason falling in love with her; the feelings growing until she felt stronger sensations building.

'Thank you, Jason, that is enough.' She felt her face burning at the realisation of what was beginning to happen to her. Jason stopped what he was doing and picked up a towel to wipe his hands.

'Thank you, Jason, and I am truly sorry for the way I spoke to you earlier, it won't happen again. Will you forgive me?'

'Already forgotten.' He left her room, closing the door gently behind him.

Anna lay on her bed. A single tear ran down the side of her nose before it dropped onto her pillow.

'What am I going to do now?' she whispered to herself. She couldn't hide it from herself any longer. The more she thought about it, the more she realised it to be true. She had fallen in love with Jason when she had been a child, listening to the way her mother had spoken to her about him. The hero pilot who had suffered so much and not complained, the stories he'd loved to listen to. As a child, she had created a vision of the English pilot in her mind and, on meeting him, Jason had lived up to her expectations in every way. She had always been in love with Jason, she just hadn't fully realised it until now. Somehow, her mother had known and seen it in her. That was why she had encouraged her daughter to seek him out when she would need him most of all. 'Merde, how am I going to face him in the morning?'

Anna awoke early the following morning after a restless night with confusing dreams about Jason. Unable to settle, she dressed and went down to the kitchen. Determined not to run short of meals for this evening, she gathered her ingredients. There was a knock on the back door. When she looked out of the kitchen window, she saw the baker's van. Seconds later, he was in the kitchen.

'I saw the light on, so I thought I'd bring your bread inside.'

'Thank you; would you like some coffee?'

'No, not for me thanks, I've a delivery for Granny McTavish's shop and, if I'm late or the bread's not still warm when I deliver it, she'll give me hell, but thank you for the offer. Bye.'

Anna felt the new loaves, and indeed they were still warm. Breaking off the crust to one loaf, she smothered it with butter and took a bite. It tasted like heaven and reminded her of home when she would sit with her mother at the kitchen table eating fresh bread warm from the farmhouse oven, whilst drinking coffee.

The next person to arrive was the butcher, delivering the shoulders of mutton and steak she had ordered. Finishing her coffee and bread, she set about the mutton, rubbing salt, pepper and a little bit of garlic into the flesh before traying it up ready for roasting. Covering the meat with a cloth, she put it in the larder until the time came for it to go into the oven. Next, she cut the steak into thin strips and placed that next to the mutton. She was just washing her hands when Gordon came in.

'Good morning, Anna. Is there any tea?'

'I'll make you some; would you like breakfast as well?'

'Yes please, I'll need it today. I'm expecting another delivery of beer. Ever since you have been cooking for me, my beer sales have increased. Will you write down your recipes for the new cook when I get one? My customers would be disappointed if they can't get the same food that you have been making for them.'

'I will don't worry. But, if you get a good cook, it will show him how to make them. They are all very common recipes in France.'

As Gordon sat down to his breakfast, first Maggie and then Jason arrived.

'I thought I could smell bacon frying,' said Jason. 'Is there any tea in the pot?'

Anna spun round at the sound of his voice, a beaming smile on her face. Then she saw Maggie. A look of, I told you so, all over her face. Anna turned away embarrassed.

'Would you like one or two eggs with your breakfast?' she asked Jason. 'The tea is in the pot.'

'Two, please.' Jason helped himself to tea and then went to join Gordon in the bar to await his breakfast.

'Sleep well?' Maggie asked Anna.

'Well enough, and you?'

'Oh, yes. It's nice having Gordon to snuggle up to at night.'

'What do you mean by that?'

'Nothing. Have you made it up with Jason yet?'

'Yes. I told him I'd had a long day, and that I was tired. I apologised to him and he was perfectly happy with that.'

'That's nice to hear. What is he doing today?'

'I don't know. I expect he'll be working on the car. We, on the other hand, have lots of vegetables to prepare.'

In the middle of the afternoon, Jason returned to the hotel driving their car. He parked in the yard at the rear, just below the kitchen window. Anna saw him arrive and went to greet him.

'Clever you; what was wrong with it?'

'There was a bit of dirt or rust in the fuel pipe, which was restricting the flow of petrol to the engine. It's running as good as new now, and Hamish has convinced himself that he knows enough about cars to open his own car repair business.'

'Go get cleaned up and I'll make you a cup of tea when you come back down,' said Anna.

Returning to the bar from his bath, Jason found Gordon checking the shelves were fully stocked with bottled beers.

'I shouldn't complain,' said Gordon. 'But we've got so busy on an evening, I now need to bring up extra crates of bottled beer from the cellar. I don't have time to keep running up and down those cellar steps when the bar is full of customers. If it stays this busy, I'll have to get the hotel a barman to help me and a new cook. I'm working all day and evening with hardly a break.'

'Well, I'm sorry to have to tell you that the car is fixed, and it won't be long before Anna and I will be on our way.'

'Oh, I'm sorry to hear that. The new cook can't get here before the weekend. Do you think you could stay until then?'

'I'll speak to Anna, but I don't see why not.'

Anna arrived with tea for the two of them and agreed to stay until Saturday when the new cook arrived from Ayr.

'What's on the menu tonight?' asked Gordon.

'I decided to give your customers a choice. There will be, roast shoulder of mutton with mashed potatoes, carrots, peas and gravy, or Beef Stroganoff,' said Anna.

'The stroganoff is a dish my mother taught me how to cook. Because fillet of beef is so expensive, I've used a cheaper joint of beef. My way is not strictly the correct way to cook it, but it works. I use strips of rump steak cooked in cream, mushrooms and mustard. I've cut the meat into strips, and put it to soak in brandy to help tenderise it. You are supposed to serve Stroganoff with rice, but we had rice last night, so I'm going to serve it with small, crispy roast potatoes.'

'I'll look forward to that,' said Jason. Anna smiled at him, flushed a little red around her cheeks and quickly returned to the kitchen hoping, he hadn't noticed.

When customers began to arrive at the hotel that evening, it was busier than ever. Word was going around the district about the new cook at the Kirkton Inn and the fancy food they were serving.

'I didn't expect this,' said Gordon. 'There are people coming from all over the place to eat here.'

'I see what you mean,' said Jason, as four more people arrived.

'I'll give up my table to make space for them, and help you serve meals.'

An hour later, Jason gave Gordon a message from Anna. All the food was gone again. 'I hope everyone got fed or we're going to have some unhappy customers to deal with.'

'No one else has come in to eat, but tomorrow night, she'll have to make even more. There are so many customers coming for food that I'm just about at my limit. I can hardly keep up with them all. This place wasn't designed as a restaurant, just a place for travellers to get a quick meal and a drink before they moved on,' said Gordon.

'Don't worry, it's nearly closing time. You'll be able to send them home soon.'

'I'm so tired. I'm going to leave most of the clearing up until the morning. I'm just going to lock up and turn in as soon as the last customer has gone. Anna and Maggie have already gone to bed. If you see Anna before you turn in, tell her well done for me, will you?'

'Yes, Gordon, I will. Tomorrow, as I'm not working on the car, I'll give you a hand clearing up. Good night.'

Before Jason reached his bedroom door, he heard voices from Anna's room. He knocked on the door.

'Come in.' Anna and Maggie were sitting on the bed talking.

'I was just about to turn in,' said Jason. 'Gordon asked me to say thank you for him. I've no doubt he'll say it again tomorrow. He said he'll be closing up soon.'

'I'd better be getting to my own bed,' said Maggie 'I'll see you both tomorrow.'

Jason took Maggie's place and sat on the corner of Anna's bed.

'I was just talking about tomorrow night's menu and us leaving on Saturday. You know, in some ways, I wish we could stay here. We could help Gordon and Maggie make a real success of this place,' said Anna.

'Yes, I agree, but we have to leave on Saturday.' Jason turned to go.

'Just a minute; will you rub some salve onto my back?'

'Yes, I'll wait outside while you get ready.'

Jason stood outside in the corridor until he heard Anna call him back. When he returned she was lying as she had done before, in bed, face down, with the covers up to her waist, the salve and a towel on the bedside table. The only light coming from a small lamp on the dressing table by the window. Jason sat beside her and began to massage the salve onto Anna's back. She flinched when he touched her skin, but it wasn't pain that she felt. Her tingling sensations intensified as he gently smoothed the balm into her skin. Anna lay with her eyes closed, her face in silhouette on the pillow. Jason stared at her smooth, unblemished skin and high cheekbones. The way she had her hair tucked behind her ear, her lips slightly parted as she breathed gently beneath the touch of his hands. He swallowed hard and stopped rubbing in the salve.

'I've finished,' said Jason. He got up and wiped his hands on the towel.

Anna opened her eyes. 'Jason. Don't go.' She rolled over onto her back, the sheets slipping lower from her waist. 'I want you to stay.'

It was around four in the morning before Jason returned to his own room.

Chapter Fifteen

'Comrade Petrov, while I was searching for signs of the Tsarina, I overheard something of interest.'

'She is not the Tsarina; she is an escaped criminal of the Soviet Union. The blood of thousands of Russians lay at the feet of her family and all those like her. What have you found out?'

'Sorry, Comrade Colonel. I heard a man speaking of a place called Kirkton. He mentioned a hotel that has a new cook.'

'So, what of it, cooks come and go all the time?'

'This cook is working in a small hotel, preparing French style cuisine for the peasants. What drew my attention to her was that one of her dishes was Beef Stroganoff, an unusual dish for these parts, wouldn't you say, Comrade?'

'Um, the coincidence is interesting, but hardly conclusive evidence of the girl we are looking for. Ever since she came to this country, she has been seen in the company of a man. Why would he let her work as a cook and where is this place, Kirkton?'

'It is a small village north of Dumfries, Comrade Colonel.' Colonel Petrov poured himself a glass of vodka and emptied the glass in one swallow.

'Why would they suddenly turn south when they have been trying so hard to go north?'

'Maybe they think that they can give us the slip, Colonel?'

'Maybe, but why now? The train they boarded in London was heading to Oban. That is still many miles north of here.'

'The girl is hurt. Maybe they need to find a doctor for her? Or maybe she has gone to get the documents?'

'Maybe, maybe, maybe. I must know for sure. Go to this Kirkton place and see what you can find out, Sokolov.' Petrov returned to his bottle.

Sokolov turned and left the room, heading for the car. This was his chance to impress the colonel. Kirkton was a two-hour drive away, and it was already lunchtime.

When Sokolov reached the crossroad in the centre of Kirkton, he was disappointed. The village was far smaller than he had anticipated and there was no inn or hotel in sight, only two churches stood at the heart of the village. He parked the car next to the small triangle of grass and looked around for a hotel. He was sure he had heard the name correctly, Kirkton Hotel, only there was no hotel to be seen. Stopping a woman walking by, he asked about the hotel.

'There is no hotel in this village. You want Dumfries if you want a hotel,' she said and moved on.

Sokolov thanked her and continued his search. 'Colonel Petrov will not be pleased with me if I return with nothing to show for my time,' he muttered to himself. A postman got off his bicycle and leaned it against the wall of a house. Then sifted through his bag in search of a letter to deliver.

'Excuse me. I'm looking for the Kirkton Inn and Hotel?' asked Sokolov.

'There's no hotel here.' He posted his letter and was about to get on his bike when Sokolov stopped him again.

'Is there a hotel of that name anywhere nearby?'

'No.' The postman tried to ride on.

'Wait, please, just one more question. Is there anywhere I can ask about the hotel?'

The postman lifted his hat and scratched his head. 'You could try the main post office in Dumfries. They will know if there is anywhere around here with a hotel of that name.'

'Thank you, sir. I am most grateful for your help.'

On Great King Street in Dumfries, Sokolov found the main post office but, by the time he'd arrived, the place was closing up for the day. One teller was still at her counter finishing up after selling stamps and postal orders to an elderly gent. Sokolov approach her.

'I'm sorry, sir. We are closed now. You can come back tomorrow when the post office will be open at nine o'clock. There will be someone here who could help you him with your enquiry.'

Frustrated by his wasted day, Sokolov went in search of something to eat and a place to stay.

The following morning, Sokolov was at the post office early, waiting for it to open. As soon as the doors were unlocked, he asked the postmaster about the Kirkton Hotel.

'Please, can you help me? I need to find the Kirkton Inn and Hotel.'

'Nowhere around here by that name, sorry. There's a perfectly good hotel just down the road there.' The postmaster pointed down the street.

'No, no. You don't understand. I must find the Kirkton Inn and Hotel. It is very important.'

'Well, as I say, there's nowhere around here by that name and I've been postmaster here for twenty years. Who told you there was a Kirkton Hotel round here?'

'It was not here. I was in Ayr at the time. I found Kirkton on a map and came to find the hotel after it was recommended to me.'

'Ah, you need to try the Ayr post office. If you go there, I expect they will know the place you are looking for.' The postmaster left the questioning foreigner to greet other customers as they entered the post office. Sokolov stood and watched him for a moment, deflated at how much time and effort he had wasted looking for the hotel only to be sent back to where he had started.

By twelve o'clock, he was parking his car outside the main post office in Ayr. Sokolov felt nervous as he stood in front of the sandstone building. If there was no one here to help him, he was at a loss as to how he was going to tell the Colonel about his failure to find Miss Moreau.

'Please, will you help me? I'm looking for the Kirkton Inn and Hotel,' he asked the spectacled man behind the desk.

'Nowhere around here by that name, sorry. There's a good hotel just down the road.'

'No, no. You don't understand. I know there is such a place. I just cannot find it. I don't believe it is in Ayr, but close by, in another town maybe.'

'He must mean the place out at Dalrymple that David McBride has been talking about,' said the clerk from the next desk. 'He said he'd been there. Said how the new cook has transformed the place with all types of foreign cooking. That kind of foreign muck is not to my taste. I like to know what I'm eating.'

'Yes, yes. That sounds like the place. Where is it, please?' demanded Sokolov.

'Dalrymple. Oh, it's about five or six miles away, out towards Hollybush. You leave Ayr on the Castlehill Road and keep going until you see the signs for Dalrymple.'

Half an hour later, Sokolov drove past the front of the Kirkton Inn and Hotel in Dalrymple. Parking his car down the street a short way from the hotel, he watched the building for a few moments, wondering what he should do next. As he waited, the butcher's boy rode up on his bicycle, the basket on the front loaded with red stained paper parcels. The lad turned into the entrance to the hotel yard. Sokolov went to wait on the entrance corner for the boy to return.

'Excuse me!' Sokolov stepped in front of the lad, forcing him to stop. 'I understand they have a new cook here?'

'Yes, sir. She's French and a really good cook. A nice-looking lady, too. Mr Stuart, the butcher, has been in a good mood ever since she started cooking here because his meat sales to the hotel keep increasing. But I hear she'll be moving on soon, now that Jason has repaired his car.'

'Thank you, sonny. You've told me all I need to know.'

Sokolov's car skidded to a halt on the gravel in the drive. Eager to impart the news he had learned to the Colonel. The Russian dashed into the library with the briefest of knocks on the door.

'Forgive me, Comrade Colonel, I have urgent news. I have found the girl. She is working as a cook in a hotel less than ten miles from here.'

Petrov pulled on his cigarette and let the dark blue smoke exit through his nostrils.

'Are you sure, Sokolov?' Doubt played across Sokolov's face.

The colonel recognised his doubt. 'Did you see her?' Petrov went on.

'Not exactly, Comrade. I spoke to a delivery boy.'

'You did what!'

'Comrade Colonel, please. I didn't want to be seen by her. If she had recognised me, she would have escaped before we could get there.'

'You should have stayed hidden and confirmed you have found the correct person, you idiot. Why didn't you just telephone me and say that you had found her? How big is the hotel? What is the layout of the village? Does she ever leave the hotel? Will we have to enter the hotel to get her? Does she have the documents with her?'

'I don't know, Comrade Colonel. I just thought you'd be pleased that I had found her.'

273

'You are a fool, Sokolov. Remind me to have you shot when we return to Mother Russia.'

'Yes, Comrade Colonel.'

'Get out. I need time to think.' Petrov stubbed out the remains of his cigarette and lit another. 'Galkin, telephone the Kirkton Hotel in Dalrymple and book me a table for tonight. Use my English name.'

'But Colonel, the girl will recognise you.'

'No, she won't. During the time we had her here, she was drugged. The only people she saw during her interrogation were Zeleny and Derevo, and they are both dead.'

Colonel Petrov parked his car at the roadside in front of the Kirkton Inn and Hotel. He eyed the building, wondering if the unassuming inn was where his target was hiding. As people entered the premises in twos and threes, he decided to join them.

Everything inside was a lot less formal than he had expected. The hotel was little more than a village pub that offered accommodation and served meals. There were no organised seating arrangements. Customers sat wherever they chose at small pub-style tables and their food was served by the bartender. Standing in the doorway, he asked a man with a handful of drinks if this was the place that served the good food he'd been hearing so much about.

'Aye, it is, and if you want any, you'd better order it quick. They soon run out.'

Petrov made his way to the bar and ordered himself a large vodka and a plate of Hachis Parmentier with buttered carrots and peas. However, before he got the chance to turn around, he felt a tap on the shoulder.

'Dr Stone, what are you doing here?' asked Jason.

Caught off guard, the doctor nearly spilt his drink.

'Ah, Mr Parva, I could ask you the same question?'

'Our car broke down and we needed a place to stay while I repaired it. We got to know the owner of this place and we are now helping out for a day or two.'

'Helping him out?'

'Anna has been doing the cooking until the new chef arrives at the weekend. What brings you here?'

'It seems Anna's cooking is gaining a bit of a reputation. I heard mention of it in Ayr. At the hotel where I am staying. I was so intrigued to hear of a new chef doing so well in a small country hotel that I came to see what all the fuss was about. I certainly didn't expect to see you here,' said the Doctor.

'Come and sit over here. What have you ordered?'

'Hachis Parmentier.'

'Ah, Cheesy Sheppard's Pie is what the locals call it. I've ordered the same. Gordon will bring it over when it's ready.'

Over the following hour, Dr Stone ate his dinner and talked about the holiday he was enjoying touring Scotland, before declaring it was time to leave and return to his own hotel.

'You must say hello to Anna. She will be disappointed if you didn't tell her how much you enjoyed your meal,' said Jason.

'I wish I could, but I don't have the time. Please, apologise to her for me for not staying. Tell her the meal was delicious, and I hope we will meet again soon.' Dr Stone stubbed out his cigarette in the ashtray in the centre of the table, stood up and left, leaving Jason wondering why he wouldn't stay to speak to Anna.

Once the food had run out, the customers began to melt away. Anna came out of the kitchen to join Jason in the near-empty bar. She smiled at him, a long warm smile that lit up her face. It was the same smile she had given him as he left her earlier that morning to return to his own room. She hadn't wanted him to go, but he had insisted for proprieties sake. Jason stood up to greet her and, as they came together, he gave her a kiss on the cheek. She flushed, the colour reddening her cheeks as she sat next to him. At the same time, she caught a knowing look from Maggie, who was watching them both from behind the bar.

'Another successful evening, Chef,' declared Jason.

'Yes, but I'm tired now. It's hard work cooking meals in a hotel kitchen,' her voice dropped to a whisper, 'especially when someone keeps me awake most of the night.'

'Ha, and who started it?'

'Shh,' she said, not wanting their conversation to be overheard.

'Anyway, you'll never guess who came in tonight – Dr Stone. He told me that word of your cooking had reached Ayr, and that he had come to investigate the village hotel with the new chef.' Jason stopped speaking and grew concerned as he watched the expression on Anna's face change from one of pleasure to one of fear.

'What's the matter?'

'That smell. I know that tobacco smell. It's the same type of tobacco my uncle used to smoke. It's Russian tobacco, the same kind I could smell in the house where I was held prisoner.' They both looked at the ashtray in the centre of the table. One half-smoked cigarette lay crumpled in the bottom. Anna got a little closer and sniffed at it before pulling back quickly.

'Who did that belong to?' Jason didn't need to answer; she saw the look of recognition in his eyes.

'We have to go. We have to leave right away.' Anna was on her feet, backing away from the table as though it was about to attack her. Maggie came from behind the bar.

'What's wrong, what's happened?' she took Anna's hand, but Anna pulled it away.

'We have to leave,' but Anna remained frozen to the spot staring at the table, her face white; her body trembling.'

Jason grasped her other hand and led her towards the hall, calling over his shoulder to Maggie, 'I'm sorry we have to go; right now,'

Maggie chased after them. 'What's the matter? What's has happened?'

'It's complicated. We don't have time to explain it all, but Anna is in danger. One of the people who hurt her was in the bar tonight. We have to go before he comes back.'

'I don't understand,' said Maggie. 'Why don't you just go to the police?' Reaching Anna's room, Jason threw open the door, pushing Anna inside and sitting her on the bed.

'We can't...the police are looking for us as well. They think we had something to do with a death on a train, but we didn't. Please, just trust me when I say we have done nothing wrong, but we must go, now, tonight.'

'But where will you go?'

'Somewhere far from here,' said Jason.

'Go to your own room and pack your bags. I will finish packing for Anna. I have an idea.'

As Jason came out of his room, Maggie was leading Anna from hers. Anna carried her own bag and was beginning to recover from her initial shock.

'I have a sister on the Isle of Arran who runs a guest house. Get the ferry to Arran in the morning. I will telephone her to let her know you are coming. I have written her address on a piece of paper and put it in Anna's handbag.'

By the time they had reached the car, Gordon had joined them.

'I'm sorry Gordon, if we ever get the chance, we will explain everything. Good luck with the new cook when he arrives.'

The car started with one turn of the handle and within seconds Jason and Anna were speeding up the Barbiestone Road, heading towards the highlands of Scotland. Within a few minutes, they reached Holybush. Jason turned right onto a better road and accelerated away. As they drove through Drongan, the streets were deserted. He paused at a junction for a moment, working out which way to turn, before turning right. Anna sat silently by his side, her hands clasped tightly together as she stared directly ahead of her. They went through Ochiltree, barely noticing its existence. But as they were leaving the village, a set of large headlights filled his rear-view-mirror, hurting his eyes. He knocked the mirror aside and pushed harder on the accelerator, but their little car was already giving them all it could.

As the car slued around a bend in the road, Anna looked behind her at the light following them. 'There are two sets of lights now!'

Jason readjusted the rear-view mirror to take a look and then knocked it aside again.

'We'll never outrun both of them. I'm going to have to find a place to give them the slip.' They passed a roadside marker showing the village of Cumnock was just ahead.

'Going through the village streets will force them to slow down,' said Jason. 'Our smaller car will have the advantage. I'll try to find a narrow lane to turn down. Hopefully, they won't see us and pass by.' Anna turned to stare out of the rear window again.

'Something is happening to the cars behind us; they are weaving from side to side. I can see flashes of light coming from both of them.' Once again, Jason reset his review mirror. 'They are shooting at us. No, wait, they are shooting at each other.'

'What? Why would they do that?'

'I don't know. Maybe there are more people chasing us than the Russian Secret Police.'

When they entered Cumnock, they seemed to be trapped on the main road. A river ran along one side of the road, shops and houses along the other. Up ahead, the road swept to the right, but at the last minute, Jason spotted a turning to the left, which took a smaller road over the river. Braking hard, he spun the wheel, the tyres screamed as they tried to grip the road. The little car swayed frighteningly from side to side as its springs fought against the sudden deceleration and change of direction. Two wheels hit the kerb bringing the car to a stop for a second before Jason put his foot hard down on the accelerator once again. The car engine coughed and spluttered for a moment and then picked up as they increased speed.

'Have they seen us?' yelled Jason.

'No, not yet,' cried Anna.

When they were across the bridge, Jason stopped and turned off the car's lights. They waited in the darkness as two sets of powerful headlights flash by on the far side of the river. Jason switched on the car's lights and turned right to follow the course of the river once again. The road soon became rough and uneven as they found themselves on a farm track. Sheep grazed in the field to their left, the river was on their right. There was nowhere to turn the car around. They were forced to continue on, but at a much slower pace than they liked. The car bounced from one pothole to the next as Jason forced the car on as fast as he could. Anna braced herself with one hand on the dashboard and the other holding onto the door handle. Suddenly, the car plunged into a deep hole, coming to a metal grinding halt. Steam hissed into the air from the radiator. Jason killed the lights.

'The car is finished. Come on, we'll follow the track on foot,' instructed Jason.

Collecting their rucksacks from the back seat, they left the car. Silence surrounded them; the track, now lined with trees, disappeared into the darkness. As their eyes became accustomed to the dark, they could just see far enough ahead to walk without stumbling. They could hear the trickle of water from the shallow river as the water tumbled over rocks and its pebble bed. An owl hooted close by. The air felt damp and cold. As they followed the track, a scream split the stillness, making them both jump. It took a second or two for them to realise that what they had heard was a train whistle blowing. As they looked ahead into the dark, a slow-moving goods train came into sight on a viaduct over the river. The glow from the engine's firebox illuminated the footplate, showing the driver and fireman.

'Up the bank,' ordered Jason as he grabbed Anna's hand and dragged her towards the train. They scrambled through the undergrowth, tripped over fallen branches and slipped on the muddy surface, but they made it to the top. The train slowly ground to a halt, the wagons clattering into each other as the engine driver applied the brake.

'It's a free ride,' declared Jason as he threw his rucksack into an open-topped wagon. 'Quick as you can.'

Jason helped Anna climb aboard. The empty wagon smelt of coal dust, and they could feel the grit beneath their feet. They sat together holding hands in the dark, their hearts beating as one.

'If they find the car, they'll see the train and they'll figure out where we are,' said Anna.

'I know, but we wouldn't have got far on foot and this train will get us out of the area quicker than looking for some other means of transport. It won't stay here very long. It's probably giving way to a passenger train. As soon as the signals change, we'll be on our way.' As though the train had been listening to Jason, they heard the steam whistle calling. The wagons jolted sharply as the engine began to pull away.

'Where do you think the train is going?' asked Anna.

'I've no idea, just so long as it's far away from here. When we stop, we can make new plans to get us to Edinburgh.'

'Will those men ever stop chasing me?' Anna squeezed Jason's hand.

'Yes, eventually. At some point they'll make a mistake and come to the attention of the police then, they will be the ones on the run.'

'Why do you think the people in the cars following us were shooting at each other?'

'I don't know,' shrugged Jason. 'Maybe there is more than one group of agents chasing you.'

The train shunted through the night, never really picking up any speed, stopping and starting at every signal it met. Jason and Anna huddle together for warmth in the corner of their wagon, sometimes falling asleep before being jolted awake again as the train juddered to a halt. They saw the night grow paler as the first signs of dawn appeared over the rim of the wagon. They watched trees and buildings go by. When it was light enough, each time the train stopped, Jason stood up and looked over the side of the wagon, trying to figure out where they were, but he couldn't tell. The train eventually pulled into a siding and stopped. Jason looked over the side of the wagon and saw the engine being uncouple from the wagons.

'Looks like this is the end of the line.'

They checked the coast was clear before climbing down to the track.

'Where are we?' asked Anna. It didn't take them long to find a sign. It read, 'Ayr Marshalling Yard.'

'Oh no, we're almost back where we started,' bemoaned Anna.

'Yes, but do you remember what Maggie said? In Ayr, we can get the boat to Arran and go stay with Maggie's sister for a while.' Anna's countenance lifted.

'We'll have to get cleaned up first. We look like we've been down a coal mine all night,' declared Anna, brushing bits from her clothes. 'If we can find a public toilet, we can wash the worst of the coal dust off and change our clothes. We'll attract less attention if we are clean.'

'The toilets at Ayr railway station will be open, and we'll be able to get some breakfast from the station buffet,' said Jason.

After a wash and a brush-up, and with a fresh change of clothes, Jason and Anna met at the station buffet. Jason ordered tea and cooked breakfast for them both; even Anna was hungry enough for a fry-up this morning. After a second cup of tea and a stack of toast, Jason suggested they make their way down to the docks to catch the ferry. As they left the buffet and stepped outside, Jason pulled Anna back around the corner into the eatery.

'They're here. In the station. Look.'

Doctor Stone stood between two much taller men dressed in overcoats. It was too late. Whether it was a coincidence or Jason's sudden movement that had attracted Dr Stone, he would never know, but the damage had been done. For a few seconds, the two men glared at one another. Dr Stone pointed at Jason and Anna. A train whistle cried out in pain. Both parties sped off along the station platform. Dr Stone's men slipped their right hands inside their coats; Jason fumbled in his rucksack for his service revolver.

'Up the stairs and across to the other side of the station,' Jason yelled at Anna.

They ran up the steps over the bridge that traversed the tracks to the platform on the far side. As they descended the steps on the far side, passengers from a train which had just departed pushed past them. Thankfully, by the time the passengers reached the top deck of the bridge, they were in time to slow the progress of Dr Stone and his men. Jason and Anna gained headway as they made for the exit. Outside, on Station Road, they ran towards the bridge that crossed the River Ayr, stopping just long enough to look back towards the station. Dr Stone and his men were already on Station Road, pursuing them. The chase continued. Jason and Anna dodged the early morning traffic and ran onto Cragie Road. Anna couldn't keep up, breathless at the fast pace, and Jason could feel his leg weakening. Desperate for somewhere to hide and get their breath back, they headed off down a tree-lined lane, stopping to catch their breath amongst a thicket of trees. Jason sneaked a look toward the head of the lane and spotted Dr Stone with his men. Then the Russians split-up. The two Russian aids crossing the road, while Dr Stone entered the tree-lined lane.

'We've got to go,' said Jason.

'Why don't you just shoot him?' asked Anna.

'Because if I miss him, the other two will join him. That will be three guns against one. Get over that fence; we'll cut through those gardens.'

Dr Stone must have heard them climbing the fence because halfway across the gardens Jason and Anna heard a shout followed by a gunshot. Leaving the garden, they entered a narrow passage that ran along the back of the houses. Their pace increased a little. Another shot rang out, urging them on. Crossing another lane into the cover of more trees, Jason stopped, checked his pistol, and waited.

'We have nothing to lose now,' he said to Anna.

Dr Stone emerged through a garden gate into the narrow passage and waited for his two companions to catch up. Jason pointed his revolver, steadied his hand and then pulled the trigger.

CLICK! The gun failed to fire; desperately, he pulled the trigger again. The gun kicked back hard in his hand. The bullet exploded from the barrel in an ear-shattering bang and cloud of smoke. Jason watched in disbelief as the bullet ricocheted off the gatepost next to the doctor.

Jason cursed. He'd lost his aim in his rush to fire at the doctor. Dr Stone fired in Jason's direction before retreating back through the gate in case Jason fired again. But Jason had taken hold of Anna once again and they were both running through the trees. As they emerged on the far side of the thicket, they were met with the open ground of Ayr Racecourse. There was nowhere else for them to go. All other means of escape were behind them, with Dr Stone and his men.

'Come on, quick,' demanded Jason. The shot I fired at the doctor will make them think twice before they enter these trees. If we can make it to those buildings in the centre of the racecourse, we will have some cover before we need to cross the open ground on the other side.'

The racecourse looked deserted at that time of the morning. 'Why couldn't it have been a race day?' Jason yelled at Anna, as they ran. 'Even at this time of the morning, there would have been lots of people and horses milling about, getting ready for the racing? We could have asked for help or got lost in the crowd.'

As Anna and Jason rounded the first building, Jason pulled Anna to a stop. Painted across the doors of a large hanger were the words 'Ayr Flying Club' and just beyond the building sat two aeroplanes.

'There's our ticket out of here. I can't run anymore,' yelled Jason.

'What?' cried Anna. 'Are you crazy?'

'You're forgetting I'm a pilot. We are going to borrow one of those planes' He pushed Anna towards the first one.

'Put your foot in there and step over into the front seat, then strap yourself in.' Jason helped Anna into the aeroplane. In the rear cockpit, he set the magnetos to the on position, pushed the throttle forward a little, and then went around to the front of the biplane. Giving the propeller a mighty swing, the engine burst into life. After removing the chocks from the wheels, he climbed into the pilot's seat and gunned the engine. Taxiing the aircraft onto the racecourse, he caught sight of Dr Stone and his men running towards them.

'You're too late, Doctor,' Jason yelled over the noise of the engine as he throttled up.

The aeroplane rolled forward. A bullet hole appeared in the small windshield in front of him. Looking behind him, Jason saw the doctor and his men running towards the plane. Jason gave the aeroplane full throttle and let it pick up speed rapidly. There wasn't as much runway as he would have liked, but getting off the ground quickly had been part of his training as an RFC pilot. The wheels lifted off the grass. Jason kept the nose of the plane low, letting the aircraft gain speed as opposed to height. As the edge of the race coursed hurtled toward them, Jason pulled back slightly on the stick. The plane skimmed over the trees at the edge of the racecourse. The aeroplane's speed was increasing rapidly as they passed low over gardens and house rooftops surrounding the racecourse. Happy the engine was running smoothly, he put the aircraft into a gentle left turn and allowed it to gain height more rapidly. To his right, Jason could see the open expanse of the Firth of Clyde and the Isle of Arran. Another turn to the left and he was heading southeast with the racecourse still below him. One final glance at the ground stunned him. The second aeroplane was taxiing to its take-off point. Jason leaned forward and shouted at Anna to look at the racecourse. She looked and then her head swivelled round to look at him, fear etched in her expression.

Chapter Sixteen

'Where are we going?' Anna yelled at Jason.

'Home!' replied Jason, as he put the aircraft onto a south-easterly heading to follow the River Nith through Nith Dale and on to Dumfries. The terrain below him had changed little since his early days as a young Royal Flying Corps pilot and the gunnery school practice he'd been through at Turnberry. All his familiar landmarks were still there, only his aircraft had changed. Climbing up to two thousand feet, he levelled the aircraft. All being well, he estimated they would be home in a little over three hours. Jason scanned the sky around him, looking for the second aeroplane he saw taxiing on the ground after he had taken off. It had to be one of the Russians hoping to follow him.

They were about half an hour into their flight when Jason felt a vibration through the control stick. Instinctively, he looked about him. On his left, and very close behind him, was the second aeroplane from the Ayr Flying Club. The front seat passenger held a gun and was pointing it toward Jason. It had been the poor marksmanship of the shooter, firing from an aeroplane that had caused him to miss his target and put a bullet through Jason's aeroplane rudder instead of its pilot. Jason pulled back on the throttle, and flicked his control stick to the right at the same time pressing down on the right rudder peddle. His aeroplane dropped its right wing and lurched into a controlled spin, losing height rapidly. He heard a long, high-pitched scream from Anna in the front seat, but there had been no time to warn her of his sudden manoeuvre. After two spins, he pulled the aeroplane back up into a tight climb, with the throttle hard forward and the engine roaring at full power. Dr Stone's aeroplane, for he reckoned it could be no other, matched Jason's move, and pulled up behind him not much further back than he had been when Jason first spotted him. As his plane gained height, Jason retrieved his service revolver from his jacket pocket.

Higher up and ahead of him was a pillow of white cloud. Jason planned his next manoeuvre. He would be ready for the doctor this time. Jason's aircraft punched through the cloud, water droplets, cold on his face, and then he emerged from the blanket of white. Unseen from below, he levelled off and pulled the aeroplane into a tight turn, hoping to come in behind the doctor after he emerged from the cloud. If the doctor did not follow him, there was a good chance that Jason could lose him and escape. Jason readied his gun and waited. Only the doctor's aeroplane didn't come out of the cloud. Jason's trap had failed. Jason stuffed his pistol inside his jacket and turned his plane southeast again. At this higher altitude, he could feel the cold intensely. He shuddered, and then saw Anna do the same. He would have to drop to a lower height soon or risk them both freezing to death in the cockpit. He wished there had been a warm flying jacket, helmet, and goggles left in the plane. The only clothing they both had to protect them from the wind and the cold was the hiking gear they were wearing. After ten minutes of level flight, he let the aircraft descend back to two thousand feet through a break in the clouds. Up ahead, a large town came into view and beyond it was a wide expanse of water, before becoming land again. From his training days, he knew the town to be Dumfries and the water to be the Solway estuary, and the hills in the distance to be Cumbria.

'We'll soon be over Carlisle,' Jason yelled into the speaking tube. 'Then I can turn left and follow the road that runs alongside Hadrian's Wall. It will take us all the way to Newcastle.' He plotted the route in his head, planning to follow major landmarks back to Nafferton.

The main panel in the windshield shattered, covering Jason in broken glass. He turned his head to see Dr Stone's aeroplane had caught up with him once again, only this time it was much closer than before. Jason put his aircraft into a dive. It was time to see how good a pilot Dr Stone really was. The ground was coming up fast. Jason could see Anna's hands gripping the front edge of her open cockpit as she pushed herself back against her seat. The roar of the engine increased, and then he pulled back on the stick. The aeroplane climbed rapidly, turning on its back. Jason was going to perform to loop the aeroplane. All the land disappeared from his view. All he could see was the bright blue of the heavens above him. He heard Anna scream as she was pushed back into her seat with the force of gravity. Then, moments later, their seat harnesses dug into their shoulders as the aeroplane inverted at the top of the loop and gravity tried to pull them out of their seats. Before the aircraft could dive once again, Jason nudged the control stick to the right. The aeroplane righted itself; he was now pointing back towards Aye. He kicked in lots of left rudder and eased the stick to the right in a very tight sixty-degree turn. Jason hoped that if he had timed his move correctly, he would come out of his turn to find himself on the tail of the doctor's aircraft. Craning his neck to look for the second aeroplane coming to the top of its loop, he spotted the doctor. The Doctor's aircraft looked unsteady as it rolled and came upright as Jason's had done. The doctor had made a much poorer job of the advanced aircraft manoeuvre.

The doctor's aircraft slowed rapidly as he struggled to bring it under control once again. This was working out better than Jason had hoped, he would not only be able to get much closer to the Doctor, but he could also cut across him if he needed to. Jason felt inside his jacket for his service revolver. Resting his aiming hand on top of the fuselage in front of him, he took aim at the Doctor. Jason waited. The closer he got, the better the chance of a clean kill with the first shot. Jason was closing fast on his enemy. He eased back the hammer on the gun. At this range, he couldn't miss the doctor, who hadn't noticed him approaching from a higher altitude, behind and from the side. Suddenly, Jason's aircraft bounced as it hit turbulence. His hand, holding the gun, slid sideways and struck the broken frame of his windshield. The pain caused him to release his grip on the pistol and he watched it, as if in slow motion, as it slid across the top of the fuselage and fell out of reach and out of sight to the Scottish boarders below. The Doctor's aeroplane loomed up quickly in his vision, Jason turned his aeroplane left to avoid a collision, but one wheel of Jason's undercarriage struck the Doctor's plane, ripping away the top portion of its rudder.

Jason continued his left turn. Wanting to see how much damage he had done to the Doctor's aeroplane. On completing his turn, Jason got a good view of the doctor's plane. The damage Jason's undercarriage had done to the Doctor's rudder was very evident. The enemy aircraft was in a shallow descent, yawing from side to side as the Doctor struggled to maintain control. Dr Stone's aeroplane was in no condition to follow him now. In fact, it would test the doctor's flying ability to the limit when it came time to land the stricken aircraft.

Jason turned his aircraft back towards England. Reaching forward, he tapped Anna on the shoulder; she turned her head to face him.

'Are you alright?' he shouted at her, but he got no response. She looked pale, wide-eyed, and very, very frightened. 'It's all over now,' he tried to reassure her. He smiled at her, but she didn't return it. She turned back and hunkered down as low as possible in her seat. There was nothing more he could do to help her for the next couple of hours except fly the plane as smoothly as possible. The one urgent question nagged at him. How much damage had he done to his undercarriage in the collision?

The next two hours passed uneventfully, his waypoints easily spotted from the air. After Carlisle, they turned east to follow the features of Hadrian's Wall. They were intermittent at first, but soon the remains of Roman forts were visible and the much more modern road running alongside the wall to Newcastle was easier to spot from the air. They were only about halfway across the country when they saw the black smoke of Newcastle hanging like a cloud of doom above the city. Beyond it and to each side, the sun reflected off the North Sea. From two thousand feet and still thirty miles away, the black smoke hanging over the city gave it the impression of a city on fire, only the smoke came from the fires of industry, not war or disaster.

As the coastline got closer, Jason turned the aeroplane south over the industrial north eastern landscape. Slowly, the terrain below changed from towns devoted to heavy industry to that of green moorland. The open landscape of the Yorkshire Moors loomed up before them, a marked contrast to the industrial scarred land they were leaving behind. Sheep farm dotted the uplands of the Yorkshire Moors. The white fleecy animals were easy to pick out on the hillsides as they roamed free to graze where ever the fancy took them.

Next, the skeleton of Whitby Abbey stood proudly defiant on the cliff top above the town. The Benedictine monks were long gone. The ruined abbey was now more famous for its association with Bram Stoker and his story of Dracula.

Jason flew closer to the abbey to give Anna a better look at the ruin. He saw fishing boats moored in the harbour, and people looking up at the aeroplane. The sight of the white-painted buildings along the harbour brought back memories of childhood visits with his parents before the war. The wind was coming in off the North Sea. Jason could feel the effects of the turbulence caused by the wind striking the cliffs and then being forced upward, upsetting the air that he was flying through. Turning inland, the air smoothed out. They passed by Scarborough and Flamborough Head. Bridlington was just up ahead, Jason's last turning point, before heading southwest to Nafferton.

After a few minutes on his new heading, he spotted All Saints'' Church as it stood proud on its raised ground overlooking Nafferton Mere. The sight of the church spire, a welcome home beacon to the fleeing flyers.

Jason circled the village. He could see his home close to the church and behind his house, an open field with sheep grazing in it. The rest of the fields around the village were full of crops. If he was going to stand any chance of landing the De Havilland Moth successfully, it was going to have to be in the field with the sheep in it. After one more circuit of the village, Jason made a low pass over the field. The sheep scattered in all directions, but most ran to the far end of the field and pressed together into a corner. Circling the village once again, he could see people coming out of their houses to see what was happening. As Jason lined the plane up with the field, he could see the other stray sheep had gone to join the main flock, still pressed into the furthest corner away from the scary monster in the sky.

Jason prayed. He had to land. He was almost out of fuel. Only, he didn't know how much damage had been done to his undercarriage when he hit Dr Stone's plane. Bringing his biplane in from the north, he crossed the Driffield road as low as he dare, skimming the hedge that bordered the sheep field. He let his airspeed bleed away by holding the nose of the plane up as long as possible. The slower he was travelling when his wheels touched down, the more chance they had of walking away from a crash. It seemed to take forever before the wheels touched the ground. The undercarriage didn't collapse, but he was going to run out of field before the aeroplane could stop. He killed the engine and shouted at Anna.

'Brace yourself!'

The aeroplane came to a shuddering halt as it buried its nose in the hedge at the far end of the field. Sheep scattered in all directions, running and jumping as though the hounds of hell were chasing them. Jason unfastened his seat belts and jumped out. Anna hadn't moved. He put his foot in the stirrup step beside Anna's cockpit and hoisted himself up to her.

'Are you alright?' He began to unfasten her seat belts. She said nothing. She just held up her arms for him to help her out of her seat. He could feel her whole body shaking. She struggled to stand, so he dragged her from the cockpit. Once on the ground, she dropped to her knees, tears running freely over her cheeks.

'Never again, never again,' she sobbed.

Jason guided her across the field to a gate. By the time they had reached it, a crowd from the Blue Bell Inn had gathered in the lane to see who had been in the flying machine. Police Constable Lewis was at their head.

'Well, I never. I didn't reckon on it being you in that thing, Mister Parva.'

'What you going to do about my sheep, look there's two dead over there, died of shock most like, and I'll bet there'll be more before long,' complained a man wearing a cloth cap and overalls.

'Don't worry, Mister Coverton. I will make sure you are recompensed for your dead sheep,' said Jason.

'And what about my hedge?' I won't be able to use my field with an aeroplane stuck in my hedge,' continued Mister Coverton.

'I'll see to it that your hedge is repaired as well.'

'Alright, alright, stand back. Let Mr Parva and his lady friend through. I'm sorry, Mr Parva, but I'm going to have to telephone my sergeant in Driffield. I've never had to deal with no aeroplane before. I don't quite know what to do about it,' said the constable.

'That's quite alright. I will be at home if you need to find me. Now, if you would all let us through, I would like to take my Friend home. She's had rather a long day.' The crowd followed Anna and Jason up the lane, only stopping when they entered the grounds of Parva Hall.

Mr and Mrs Dendridge were at the front door waiting for them to arrive. As Jason and Anna approached the house, the servants rushed forward to assist them.

'Mrs Dendridge, would you see to Miss Moreau? She's had a bit of a traumatic time this morning, and please, send for

Doctor Finch. Ask him if he would kindly come over as soon as possible to have a look at her.'

'Mr Dendridge, I would like you to speak to Mr Coverton. Get some men and have the aeroplane removed from his hedge. They can leave it in the field for now. Then I'd like you to assess the damage to the hedge and arrange for it to be repaired.'

'What about the aeroplane, sir?'

'Leave that for now. I will inspect it later. If anything is broken on the aeroplane, I will need to get it repaired before I return it.'

Jason entered the library, throwing his jacket over a chair. He poured himself a whisky and soda, then slumped into an armchair.

Jason's mind raced through what was likely to happen next.

The Driffield police should arrive within the next hour. I'll tell them I borrowed the plane and crash-landed with engine trouble. In the meantime, I'll write a letter to the Chief Constable explaining who Anna is and ask for his help to resolve matters in Ayr. It's time to settle this matter once and for all. I should have insisted on doing that right from the start.

A knock on the door, followed by a slight cough, made Jason open his eyes. Doctor Finch and Mrs Dendridge entered the library.

'Begging your pardon, sir, Doctor Finch has finished with Miss Moreau.' Jason rubbed the sleep from his eyes.

'I'm sorry, Doctor, please, sit down. Would you like some tea?'

'No, thank you.'

'I would like some tea, please, Mrs Dendridge.' The housekeeper left the men alone.

'Now then, Doctor, how is Miss Moreau?'

'She is exhausted and in shock. She wouldn't tell me how she got the burns on her back, but they are healing nicely, though they will obviously leave scars. I suggest she stay in bed for a week or so to recuperate, after which, she will be as right as rain. She's had a sedative to help her sleep. I will return tomorrow to see her again. It will be easier to assess her mental state after she has had some rest.'

Jason looked at the clock. More than an hour had passed since he had arrived home.

'I will ask Mrs Dendridge to assist you if you wish, as I may not be here tomorrow. I am expecting a visit from the police.'

'Surely the police wouldn't arrest you for landing an aeroplane in Mr Coverton's field?'

'Probably not, Doctor, but it's rather more complicated than that. For a start, the aeroplane is not mine. It's a long story better saved for another day.'

'Then I'll bid you good day and hope the police are sympathetic to your story. I'll look forward to hearing the story at dinner some time.'

'Yes, it would make a good after dinner tale, but you may have to wait a few years before you hear it from my lips if the police decide to arrest me.' The doctor looked at Jason, somewhat surprised by his statement but didn't follow it up.

'Goodbye, Jason. I hope everything works out for the best.'

Jason waited all afternoon for the police to arrive. Mrs Dendridge brought tea and cake into the library at four-thirty.

What time would you like dinner, sir?' Jason looked at the clock on the mantle.

'Would six suit? What are we having?' said Jason.

'Meat pie, sir. I didn't know you were coming home or if you would be staying.'

'Yes, I'm sorry, Mrs Dendridge. I've had rather a lot to think about. One of your meat pies sounds wonderful.'

By ten o'clock that evening, there was still no sign of the police. As the clock finished its chimes, Jason rose and stretched.

'Time for bed,' he told the glowing embers in the hearth. On the way to his room, he looked in on Anna and found her sleeping soundly.

As he lay in his own bed, he heard All Saints'' church strike the half hour. An owl hooted from the trees, which ran alongside the graveyard. The familiar sounds were comforting and reassuring. Just before closing his eyes, his last thoughts were of the local police.

The plane crash can't be very important to them. Tomorrow, when I'm not so tired, I'll have time to prepare for the police interview. Tiredness overwhelmed him. He didn't hear the church clock strike the third quarter hour.

'It's a nice day, sir.' Mrs Dendridge placed a cup of tea on the bedside table and went to open the curtains. 'Miss Moreau is awake and looking a lot better this morning. Shall I start breakfast?'

'Give me half an hour please, Mrs Dendridge.' Jason drank his tea before running a bath, all the while trying to decide what he would tell the police when they arrived. It would be best to talk to Anna first. Get their story straight. But he'd made his mind up on one matter. The police needed to see Anna's documents and to recognise Anna's status as Empress of Russia, even if the Soviets refused to do so. He also had to telephone the Ayr Flying Club and give them a generous offer of compensation along with a profound apology for taking their aeroplane without permission.

With one of Mrs Dendridge's breakfasts inside him, apart from a little stiffness in his leg, he felt ready to tackle the world. First, Jason picked up the telephone and called his solicitor's office, Letwing, Letwing, and Letterman. Mr Letwing would help him handle the police. The call was taken by Mr Letwing's secretary, who promised to pass on Jason's message. Satisfied with his plan of action for the day, he followed the call with a visit to Anna's room. Jason knocked on the door and waited. When he went in, Anna was sitting up in bed reading a magazine, coffee on the bedside table. She'd already brushed her hair.

'I hoped you would come in to see me.'

She patted the bed, indicating for him to sit next to her. He hesitated and looked at the door.

She gave a little laugh. 'Frightened, Mrs Dendridge is watching through the keyhole?' Jason blushed and sat down.

She took his hand and squeezed it gently with her right hand, running her left hand over the back of his.

'I've always known you were a pilot,' said Anna. 'But I never imagined that flying was anything like what happened yesterday. I think I understand a little of the fear you must have gone through every day. There is something else you need to know.' She paused before continuing. Looking into his eyes, she continued. 'I love you. I'm sorry, I shouldn't have just come out with it like this, but yesterday I thought I was going to die without being able to tell you how I felt. I have always loved you. I fell in love with you as my mother told me stories about you. I just didn't know it until that last night in the hotel. Please, don't be angry with me. I will leave if you are. I just wanted you to know that night was special; my first time.' She looked down at his hand held in hers and waited for his response.

'I've dreamed you might say something like this. I felt there was something special between us from the first time I saw you on the train. Then, when I found out it was you who was asking for my help, it felt like destiny had brought us together. I only hope that I am allowed to return your love. I expected the police to arrive yesterday, so they must turn up today. Once they realise we are the people they have been looking for, I, we, may be arrested. It could be years before we are together again, and that is if I am not convicted of murder for the death of the man on the train and the shootings in Scotland. You may even be deported. I have asked for my solicitor to call round to advise us on what to do and say. But, however, things turn out, remember this. I love you too.'

Jason put his arms around Anna. They hugged and kissed for a moment before parting.

'I must prepare for my solicitor and the arrival of the police. Rest now, they may insist on speaking to you.' Jason stood up, gave Anna's hand a gentle squeeze and left the room.

Downstairs in the library, Jason waited. The clock sitting on the mantle struck ten, as did the church clock. He checked the time with his wristwatch. They all agreed. He pushed the call button on the wall to summon Mrs Dendridge.

'Yes, sir. Would you like me to bring you some tea?'

'No, thank you. Have any messages arrived? I was expecting a visit from Mister Letwing first thing this morning.'

'No, sir, no messages and no telephone calls.'

'Is something wrong?' asked Anna as she entered the room. 'I couldn't help but overhear what you were saying.'

'I thought the doctor ordered you to stay in bed for a week, to rest and recuperate,' said Jason.

'If you think I am going to be arrested wearing a borrowed nightdress, no offence, Mrs Dendridge, then you are sadly mistaken. When are they supposed to be coming?'

'I thought the police would have arrived by now. I telephoned my solicitor this morning, and he hasn't turned up either. Something is not right. I was just asking Mrs Dendridge if there had been any messages when you came in. I'm going to telephone my solicitor again, find out what is holding him up.'

Anna and Mrs Dendridge waited as Jason made his phone call to Mr Letwing.

303

'Oh, hello, it's Mr Parva calling, please may I speak to Mr Letwing senior? When will he be available? What about his son? Well, how about Mr Letterman? What do you mean, they are all unavailable? But when I telephoned earlier you said he would come to see me this morning.' Jason held the telephone earpiece away from his head.

'Mr Letwing's secretary hung up on me. I don't understand what is happening. That firm has been our family solicitors for as long as I can remember.' A knock at the front door sent Mrs Dendridge scurrying to answer it.

'That's probably the police now,' said Jason. Mrs Dendridge returned with the vicar.

'I'll go make some tea,' said the servant.

'Good morning, Jason. I do hope I'm not disturbing you. It's just that someone has broken into the church.'

Jason, puzzled by the vicar's remark, wondered what the vicar expected him to do about it.

'Have you called the police?' asked Jason.

'Oh, yes, Police Constable Lewis is there now, but he can't get in.'

'You mean someone has broken into the church and then locked himself inside? Have you spoken to him to find out why?'

'I tried. So has Constable Lewis, but there was no response.' The vicar led Jason to the window to look across to the church. A second latter, a bullet came through the glass, spinning the vicar around and lifting him off his feet, causing him to fall in a crumpled heap on the floor. Anna screamed.

Jason jumped away from the window, taking hold of Anna and dragging her to the floor.

'How have they found us so soon?' whispered Jason.

'What do we do now?' asked Anna, her throat dry with fear. 'Is he dead?'

Jason looked across to where the vicar lay. He wasn't moving, and was still in plain sight of anyone looking through the window.

Chapter Seventeen

'I have shotguns in the gun-room. Do you know how to use one?'

'Yes. I was brought up on a farm, remember? But I've never shot at another person.'

'I'll get them. We just have to defend ourselves until the police arrive.'

The curtains twitched as another bullet came through the window, shattering a vase on the table close to where Jason and Anna stood. They pressed further into the corner of the room. A shot rang out followed by the sound of breaking glass from the room next door.

'They are shooting at different windows to get us to panic and run,' whispered Jason.

'The shooter must be the person who has locked himself in the church.'

'Can you get to the vicar?' asked Anna.

'I don't know, I'll try.'

'Be careful.'

Jason crawled around the table to the other side of the room to get a look at the vicar. He lay with his eyes wide open and unblinking. His wire-rim spectacles lay askew across his face. Jason felt for a pulse in the vicar's neck that he knew wouldn't be there, but he had to know for sure. Looking back at Anna, he shook his head. Unexpectedly, Mrs Dendridge appeared in the doorway. She looked alarmed and confused. First, she saw Anna standing in the corner and then spotted Jason with the vicar. Lifting her apron to her mouth she stifled a scream before running from the room.

'Mrs Dendridge!' Jason called after her, but she was gone.

The telephone was just above Jason's head on a side table. He reached up and brought it down to floor level. Lifting the earpiece from its cradle, he dialled nine-nine-nine, but stopped to tap the cradle.

'The telephone has stopped working,' Jason called to Anna.

A bullet hit the telephone stand, knocking the small table onto its side. Jason dropped the phone and shuffled back to Anna as another bullet entered the floor where he had just been laying.

'We must get to the gun-room. If we don't shoot back, the next thing they'll try is to get into the house.'

Jason and Anna crawled through the door into the hall before standing up.

'It's at the back of the house, next to the kitchen.'

'If all this shooting doesn't bring the police then nothing will. We just have to hold out until they arrive.'

307

Jason opened the gun cabinet and handed Anna a gun, selecting another for himself. From a drawer, he removed two boxes of cartridges, giving one box to Anna.

'I'll go back to the library. You go to the lounge. Stay close to the wall and make your way to the window. Wait for me to fire first, aim up at the church bell tower. Fire both barrels separately, waiting three seconds between shots. I want them to know there are at least two armed people in here waiting for them. It will slow them down and make them think twice before they try to rush us. Meet me in the hall after your second shot.'

'Why not keep shooting at the man in the church?'

'Because during the war, this kind of tactic was used to keep small pockets of the enemy pinned down until reinforcements arrived. The sniper on the tower is doing the same job. He keeps us busy on this side of the house whilst someone else breaks in on the far side of the house and takes us by surprise. The most likely places they'll try to get in are through the kitchen, dining room or the front door. After we meet up in the hall, I want you to ensure the front door is locked. I'll check the kitchen door and find Mrs Dendridge. When you've done that, stay in the hall where I can find you. I don't want to hear a noise in a room and shoot you thinking you are someone else.'

*****

Two black cars raced down Middle Street in Nafferton. Pulling to a stop in front of the horse-wash at Nafferton Mere. Chief Inspector Goodman jumped out of the leading car before the driver could slam on the handbrake. He found Constable

Lewis sheltering behind the wall, which ran down to the water's edge.

'What's the situation Constable?'

'As far as I can tell, sir, there is one man on top of the church's bell tower and I've seen two more crossing the churchyard going towards the house. I tried to telephone Mr Parva just before you arrived, but the line is down.'

'Very good, Constable, what I want you to do now is telephone Driffield police station; tell the Inspector on duty that Chief Inspector Goodman of the Special Branch wants four armed marksmen here as soon as possible. Then come back here.'

'Right away, sir.'

Inspector Goodman turned to his four fellow Special Branch officers.

'Jack, Bill, you two go up towards the house through the churchyard and see if you can spot the two men that are heading towards the house from that direction. I'm going up that road.' He pointed across to Rectory Lane. 'It leads up to the Parva house. I want to see if I can get a better picture of what is going on from there.' 'Tom, George, you two go up Westgate over there and work your way around to the west side of the house from that direction. I want to know how many men are trying to get into the house and their locations before we act. We all meet back here when we are done, and *be careful* these men know what they are doing.'

Two shots rang out from beyond the church, attracting their attention.

'Alright, check your weapons and off you go. Good luck.'

Two more shots rang out from the far side of the house.

*****

'Mrs Dendridge, Mrs Dendridge, where are you?' The pantry door slowly creaked open.

'Oh, it's you, Mr Parva. I thought someone was coming to kill me.'

'Don't worry, Mrs Dendridge, it's not you who they want. I've just come to check that the back door is locked.'

'Oh, it's locked alright, and bolted and I have shoved a chair underneath the door handle to brace it.'

'Good for you, Mrs Dendridge. I don't suppose you shoot, do you?'

'Oh my goodness, no. It's my Len you need. He was a soldier in the Boar War.'

'Thank you, Mrs Dendridge. I suggest you return to the pantry now and stay there until this is over.'

Jason returned to the hall to find Anna pointing her shotgun at the front door.

'Has someone tried to get in?'

'No. I was just getting ready to shoot the first person who tried.' Jason smiled at Anna's pluck.

'Let's go into the dining room and find out what is happening on that side of the house.'

Anna followed Jason from the hall.

'Stay close to the wall and work your way around to the window. I'll go this way. You go that way around the room'

Once they had made it to either side of the windows, they risked a tentative look outside. Jason saw no one as he scanned toward the front of the house. From Anna's position, she was looking towards the back of the house across the lawn.

'I can see Mr Dendridge... what is he doing... he's got a spade in his hands and heading towards some trees. He's seen something; he's holding the spade above his head. Oh no, it's Dr Stone, and he's got a gun.'

Jason stepped in front of the window, pushing the barrel of his shotgun through the glass. Before he could fire, he heard the shot from Dr Stone's gun a split second before he pulled his own trigger. Anna turned away from the window as Mr Dendridge fell to the grass. Dr Stone was too far away from the house to get an accurate shot. It would have been a million-to-one chance of Jason's shot being good enough to kill or wound Dr Stone. The best Jason could have hoped to do was to warn Mr Dendridge away, but it was too late now. Jason fired a frustrating shot from the house. The doctor retreated behind an old oak for cover.

'Poor Mr Dendridge,' exclaimed Anna.

The sound of more shots and breaking glass from the library side of the house drew their attention away from the window. They looked at each other.

'I have to go to the library. We can't cover both sides of the house by staying together,' said Jason.

'I know. You go, I'll stay here. I love you.' Jason kissed her on the lips.

'I love you too.'

Jason reached the library window just in time to see someone climb over the churchyard wall and into the garden. Jason let him run towards the window before firing both barrels through the glass. The man with a pistol in his hand fell back, showered in broken glass, a large bloodstain on his chest. A second later, a bullet came through the window from the direction of the church tower, but Jason had moved away from the window. The sound of a shotgun blast from the dining-room sent Jason hurrying back to Anna.

*****

Back behind the horse-wash wall at the top of Coppergate, Inspector Goodman received a report from each of his officers. As they were speaking, another police car drew up behind the others and four men with rifles climbed out. Two immediately took position behind the car with their rifles trained on All Saints'' Church. The second two, one a sergeant, joined Inspector Goodman and his men. They heard two more shots from the direction of the house. The marksmen instinctively ducked down at the sound.

'I'm Sergeant Williams, sir. My men are all veterans and highly trained. Where do you want us?'

'I don't know yet. All we know for sure is that there is one man on top of the church tower and at least two others making their way toward the house. Several shots have been fired already. I've seen one man go down in the garden on the far side of the house. It was a member of the staff, I think from the look of him. What we need is some kind of advantage over the man on the church tower. He must have seen us by now, but from up there he can prevent my men from getting close to the house.'

As if to prove the Inspector's point, two shots in quick succession rang out from the church tower, the bullets striking the police car close to where the police marksmen were standing.

'There's the Malting House, sir,' interrupted Constable Lewis. He pointed across the water of Nafferton Mere towards the building on the far side. It's five stories high. Though it's on lower ground than that of the church, the roof of the Malting House must be about the same height as the church tower.

'Very good, Constable.' 'Sergeant; send your two best marksmen up onto the top of the Malting House and shoot at the man on top of the church tower. I don't want him killed. I just want him to understand he has no choice but to surrender and come down. But I want him distracted so my men can deal with those Russian agents who are trying to get into the house.'

'Yes inspector, but you are asking a lot of my men. From that distance, I can't guarantee a stray shot or ricochet wouldn't kill the man on the tower.'

'I have every confidence in you and your men, Sergeant. Do the best that you can, but I want him alive.'

*****

Anna looked up in alarm while reloading her shotgun. She turned to face the door as it crashed against the wall. She relaxed when she saw it was Jason.

'I heard the shot and came to help.'

'I'm fine. Doctor Stone tried crossing the lawn towards the windows. I'm afraid I fired too soon; all I did was send him running for cover.'

'That's good enough. Someone must have called the police by now; we just have to hold out a little longer. I managed to bag one of Dr Stone's men on my side of the house, but I can't get a clear shot at the man on the church tower with one of these,' he indicated to his own shotgun.

'You had better go back; I don't want anyone sneaking up to the house while you are in here with me,' suggested Anna.

Jason made it back to the library window just in time to see someone climb over the churchyard wall. He pointed his shotgun through the remnants of the library window and fired. His target fell back against the churchyard wall, clutching his shoulder. However, he staggered to his feet, toppling back over the wall again before Jason could reload.

With one hand holding an empty gun and his other hand in his jacket pocket to find more cartridges, Jason saw a shadow move in front of the window. He looked up as a flash lit the remains of glass in the window. At the same time, a stab of pain ripped through his side. He dropped his shotgun as he fell against an armchair and then to the floor. The last thing he heard was the sound of another shot from behind him and more breaking glass.

*****

Sergeant Williams drove two of his men around to the malting house. All the men who worked there were out in the yard as he drove in. Excitement rose amongst the workers as armed officers got out of the police car.

'Who's in charge here?' asked Sergeant Williams.

'That'll be me. I'm the manager. What's going on? Have the Germans attacked again?'

'What's your name?' asked the sergeant.

'Harold Moor, what's yours?'

'Sergeant Williams.' I need to get my men onto your roof. How do we get up there?'

'Wait a minute, you can't just come in here and take over the place. I need to speak to the owner and find out what he thinks about it,' protested the manager.

'Constable, arrest this man for obstruction of a police officer. Handcuff him and put him in the car.'

'Hey up, you can't do that,' protested the manager, taking a step backwards.

'The stairs to the top floor are just inside the door over yonder. They will take you up to the top floor. The hoist tower is at the back and sticks out over the water. It's in there that you'll find the door through to the roof.'

'Leave him for now, Constable. Come on, Mr Moor, you can show us the way.'

Sergeant Williams took the manager by the arm and led him towards the open door of the malt house. The marksmen followed, and the workers brought up the rear, some laughing and joking about how quickly Mr Moor had changed his tune when faced with arrest.

Sergeant Williams ushered Mr Moor ahead of him as they climbed the wooden stairs to the hoist tower. By the time they reached the top floor, Mr Moor was out of breath and would go no further. He pointed to the place where the hoist was located.

'The floor in the hoist room only opens upwards. It's quite safe to stand on it. In the wall, you'll see the door that will let you onto the roof.'

'Thank you, Mr Moor, we will take it from here. You can go make your telephone call to the owner now.'

Sergeant Williams and his men scrambled out onto the roof to find the view over the top of the hoist tower gave them a perfect line of fire towards All Saints' Church Tower. The marksmen adjusted their telescopic sights to focus on the bell tower.

'We are ready, Sergeant,' said one of the marksmen.

'Right, take a couple of shots each at the brickwork where you think the shooter is hiding. Let him know he's got company.'

The two constables fired two shots each. The bullets were carefully aimed to ricochet off the top of the church parapet.

*****

Inside the house, Jason awoke to hear distant shooting and wondered who was firing at whom?

'Everything all right?' He shouted through to Anna then, regretted his exertion as pain stabbed through his body. He put a hand to his side and felt his own warm, sticky blood coming from a wound where a bullet had creased him.

'Yes, all quiet on this side,' came the reply. 'Wait a minute, there is a movement in the trees.' Jason rolled onto his side to see a man laying half in, and half out of the library window.

'Looks like the cavalry has finally arrived,' he said to himself. He propped himself up on the body that had fallen through the library window to take a quick look across to the church. There was no sign of movement. He rolled away, nursing his wound. By using a chair for support, he got to his feet, and by using the empty shotgun as a walking stick, he staggered through to Anna.

*****

All the Special Branch officers returned except one.

'Where's Jack?' snapped Inspector Goodman.

'He went to get a closer look at the house, but he didn't return. I was busy at the other end of the house. I saw one of Petrov's men standing at a window. He raised his gun and fired into the house just before I was able to shoot him. I'm sorry, sir, I didn't go to investigate who he had been shooting at because of the sniper on the church roof,' answered Bill.

'Right, you come with me.' The Inspector pointed at Tom 'We are going up Rectory Lane.' 'Bill, you take George back to the house from the church side. Find Jack. Then go back to the window where you shot the Russian. The police marksmen will keep the sniper's head down, and the two constables I sent to break into the church should be just about through the door by now, so you shouldn't have any trouble from the sniper. Right, let's get started.'

*****

'Anna.' was the only word Jason managed to say when he entered the dining room.

'Jason!' She dropped her shotgun and rushed towards him as he slid down the wall, leaving a large smear of blood on the wall. Kneeling by his side, she wondered what she should do to stop the bleeding. Desperately, she pulled his shirt open to get her first sight of the wound. She put her hand over it, but the blood ran between her fingers.

'I'll be back in a minute,' she told him, then brushed the hair from Jason's face, leaving a blood smear across his forehead.

'Mrs Dendridge, Mrs Dendridge!' called Anna, as she ran into the kitchen. The pantry door creaked open.

'Is it over?' asked the housekeeper, before she caught sight of the blood on Anna's hands and clothing.

'Are you hurt, my dear? Then came the realisation that it wasn't Anna who needed the help.

'Where is he? Is he?'

'No, but he's been shot. I need towels and bandages to stop the bleeding.'

'There's a first aid box in the cupboard in the gunroom. Take these tea towels and fold them into pads to put over the wound. I'll be with you in a minute, instructed Mrs Dendridge.'

*****

The Inspector led Tom up Rectory Lane. They were protected from the church by a tall brick wall that ran the length of the rectory garden.

'We have plenty of cover from this side until we reach the end of the lane. Then it turns towards the house with a few trees at the entrance to the drive. Once we reach the drive, you go right, I'll go left. If you see Colonel Petrov, come and find me. If you come across one of his men, try to arrest him, but shoot if you have to. Don't take chances. I may have lost one man already today; I don't want to lose anymore.'

'Yes, sir.'

The two men split up, Inspector Goodman working his way along the inside of the boundary wall, watching and listening for movement in the shrubbery. Through a gap in the foliage, he spotted the body of the gardener on the lawn. It wasn't moving, so he continued on. The sound of a snapping twig alerted the inspector, making him freeze. He wasn't alone. Crouching down, he made himself as small as possible and leaned into a rhododendron bush for extra cover. There came the sound of another breaking twig, only closer this time. The Inspector held his breath, his senses alert to everything around him. Someone was close, very close, but where was he? The Inspector released his breath slowly, his lungs aching for more oxygen. He fought against the urge to gulp in air. The sound of more movement to his left made him turn his head. He could see feet slowly passing the bush where he was hiding. It was now or never. The Inspector leapt up and over the rhododendron bush onto the person on the far side. After a brief struggle, the Inspector had the better of his smaller adversary.

'Colonel Petrov, I get to meet you at last. I am looking forward to interviewing you.'

'I will tell you nothing, Inspector.'

'Now, now, Colonel, let's not be hasty. I have a proposition to put to you.' Colonel Petrov looked up doubtfully at Chief Inspector Goodman.

'Yes, it is quite true. But it will have to wait until I get you back to the station.'

Tom emerged through the shrubbery, his pistol in his hand.

'Need any help, sir?'

'You can cuff this one, but take great care of him. This is Colonel Petrov of the Russian Secret Police. I want to talk to him later. Get him back to the car and stay with him. No one is allowed near him or to speak to him. I want to stay here. I need to get into the house as soon as possible.' After working his way through the bushes, Inspector Goodman called out to the house.

'Mr Parva, this is the police. May I come towards the house?'

*****

Anna helped Mrs Dendridge tie bandages around Jason. He was awake now, but looking very pale.

'The bullet has gone right through,' said Anna. 'The best we can do is to try to stop the bleeding. I hope help arrives soon.'

'Fancy Mr Parva going through that awful war and the wilds of Africa to come home to this. What is the world coming to?' Anna was about to tell Mrs Dendridge about her husband when she heard a shout from outside.

'Mr Parva, this is the police. May I come towards the house?'

Anna and the housekeeper looked at each other.

'I'll go see,' said Anna. She peeked through the dining-room window to see, standing a few feet from the body of Mr Dendridge, a man with his hands in the air.

'My name is Detective Chief Inspector Goodman, from Special Branch. I have captured Doctor Stone and my men have the house surrounded. Are you all right, Mr Parva? May I come towards the house?'

The Inspector walked slowly towards the house. As he did so, uniformed Police Constable Lewis ran to his side.

'It's me, Mr Parva, Constable Lewis. It's alright you can come out now.'

'Thank you, Constable, that is very brave of you,' said the Inspector.

At the sight of the police constable's uniform, Anna dropped her shotgun and shouted through the shattered window.

'Jason has been shot. He needs a doctor.'

'Constable, go fetch a doctor, on the double.' The Inspector dropped his hands and withdrew a whistle from his pocket, giving it a long blow before running towards the house.

*****

At the sound of the whistle, Special Branch officers Bill and George called up to the sniper on the Church bell tower to tell him it was over and that he should come down.

Inside the church, the police officers had broken into the office and were waiting at the bottom of the stairs to the church tower. Through the open door, the police officers saw a rifle come clattering down the stone steps. The rifle was slowly followed by the last of the Russian Secret Police officers.

'I am unarmed. I surrender.'

Chapter Eighteen

The interview room of Driffield Police Station had no windows. In the centre of the small, unheated room was a rough unpolished table with two equally plain chairs on either side of it. The floor was unpolished floorboards, and the walls were covered in green glazed tiles from floor to ceiling. A single light bulb hung from a flex above the table, protected by a wire cage. Colonel Petrov sat handcuffed at the table, smoking a cigarette. He was dressed in a prison khaki suit adorned with thick, black arrows. Two police officers stood silently by the room's door. The Colonel shivered in the unheated room. Petrov drew deeply on his cigarette hoping to extract some warmth from it while he waited for Inspector Goodman and his interrogation to begin. He had no idea if it was day or night. The cell in which he had been held had no window and the cell light was never switched off. He could only guess at the number of days he'd been kept at the station. The Russian colonel stubbed out his cigarette on the tabletop, the scorch mark joining many others, each one a reminder of previous occupants of his seat. He looked around the room, trying to find something of interest to focus his mind on instead of this long silent wait for the Inspector to arrive. As he scanned the unadorned room, there was nothing to distract his mind. It reminded him of the cells in Russian prisons, so he began to count the tiles on the wall in front of him. The more he concentrated on the tiles, the harder his eyes found it to focus on the bland surface. He lost track of the tiles he had counted before completing the first row. He rubbed his eyes and started again. He was almost finished when the door opened and the Inspector walked in. He cursed the Inspector under his breath. Another few seconds and he would have finished counting.

'What is this deal you promised me?'

Inspector Goodman stopped halfway to the table and looked up from his file of papers.

'Deal, did I promise you a deal? Ah, yes, I remember. I would have said anything to get you to give up without a struggle.' The Inspector smiled at him and continued to his seat at the table.

'Then I shall tell you nothing.'

'Um, that's fine, less paperwork for me to deal with. I have to type up everything you say. All I have to do now is just fill in a couple of forms to say you will not cooperate, and then I can get you transferred to London for execution as a foreign enemy of the state, who has murdered a British subject. You know, I owe you some thanks, Colonel. Capturing you is going to be quite a feather in my cap. I've never caught a high-ranking Russian spy before. I may even get a promotion out of this. Yes, I think it would be better if you don't say anything.

The less you say, the simpler it stays and the quicker you are dealt with. Are you absolutely sure you wouldn't like to cooperate? You see, I have a car waiting for me outside, to take me back to London so I can hand in my report on you. This will be the last time we speak. You know there will be no trial. It would be a waste of time and taxpayer's money. Your death won't even be reported in the newspapers – top secret and all that. We hang spies. I believe your people shoot them. Is that correct?'

The Inspector closed his file and waited a moment, giving the Colonel a pleasant smile before getting up from the table.

'Goodbye, Colonel.' The Inspector tucked his file of papers under his arm and headed for the door.

'Wait! I will cooperate. But, I want a deal.'

'Deal, deal, deal. What is all this about a deal? I don't need a deal. The Tsarina is safe. I have you in prison. Your men are either dead or captured. What more could you possibly offer me? No, Colonel. Let's keep it simple. Oh, by the way. Do you have any family you would like me to notify after your execution?'

'There are more people in my network, here in England,' responded Petrov.

'Who? Where? I will have to verify your story before I can make any promises. You do understand. After all, I wouldn't want to put my promotion in jeopardy.'

'They are small fish. Your own people, students and idealists who play at being communists, but who have no idea what the Soviet Union is really about. They are simply soldiers in a war against the oppression of the people by the greedy industrialists.'

'You mean they are expendable?' The Colonel shrugged his shoulders.

'Well, give me their names and addresses. If they prove to be correct, I'll see what I can do for you,' said Inspector Goodman. 'However, if you want a guarantee to save your neck I'll need the name of your boss.'

Two days later, Inspector Goodman found himself back in Driffield Police Station.

'How is our prisoner coming along, Sergeant?'

'Very well, sir. We've been doing as you asked, waking him up every four hours, taking him the same meal each time. He sees no one, and no one speaks to him. He's stopped complaining and banging on the door now. He just eats his food and sits on his bed. When we turn the light off he lies down and goes to sleep. When we turn it on he wakes up and sits on his bed. He's turning into one of those automatons you see at the fairground; you put a penny in and it performs for you. We have also stopped his cigarette ration as you instructed.'

'Thank you, Sergeant. I will see him now.'

The Inspector was waiting in the interview room when Colonel Petrov was brought in.

'Ah, Colonel, how nice to see you again; please, sit down, would you like a cigarette?' The Inspector lit one for him and handed it over. The Colonel snatched it from his hand and drew deeply on it, letting the smoke drift from his lungs as he sighed.

'We rounded up the people at the addresses you gave us. You were right, all no-hopers, the lot of them, but it does tidy things up and, if there is one thing His Majesty's Government really likes, it is things tidied up. We are keeping a close eye on General Asimov, thank you. Now, it took a lot of effort on your behalf, but I managed to get my superiors to agree to a deal for you. It's a very simple one. You give us the names of all the members of your network here in Britain, and we will hand you over to the French. They will claim the credit for your capture, and exchange you for some of their people in Russian prisons.'

'I have already given you the names of all the people in my network here in England.'

'Yes, but my bosses think there might be one or two more senior ones hidden away somewhere. So they said I have to ask you for them or there is no deal.'

The Colonel looked into the Inspector's face. The Inspector smiled back. 'If you wouldn't mind, that is. After all, they are soldiers, casualties of war, as you like to say. They will become heroes of the great revolution. Their names will be celebrated in the history books of the Motherland. All martyrs for the cause. Would you like some tea? Constable, go ask the sergeant to make the Colonel some tea.'

'Russian tea, please,' added the Colonel.

One of the constables by the door looked at his partner, hesitated a moment, and then left the room.

'Now then, where were we? Oh yes, you were giving me the names of those other friends of yours.' The Inspector licked the tip of his pencil as Colonel Petrov recited more names.

'Thank you, Colonel; my superiors will be very pleased with you. We will be able to clean out this little nest of vipers, and you will go into the hands of the French once we've arrested this lot. When the French send you home, you will be able to claim you knew nothing about our purge of Russian agents because you were in a French jail. The French Ambassador in Moscow will inform the Kremlin of their exchange plan. When you get home, they will probably give you a medal.'

'How do I know I can trust you, Inspector?'

'You don't. But if we execute you, your government will execute some of our agents who are in prison in Russia. If we give you to the French and something goes amiss, your friends' back home will take it out on the French, not the British. So you see, it is in our interest to send you home.'

*****

'The doctor said you will be able to come home in a day or two,' said Anna.

'How are things back there?' asked Jason.

'Fine. With the help and advice of some of the villagers, I have men making repairs to the house. Mrs Dendridge has gone to stay with her sister in Bridlington, now that her husband's funeral is over. We held the wake at the house. I hope you don't mind?'

'No, not at all. I'm pleased you did, for Mrs Dendridge's sake. What do you intend to do now the Russians have been arrested?' asked Jason.

'I don't know. Inspector Goodman wants me to stay in Nafferton until he finalises some things he has to do, and then he wants us to go down to Scotland Yard in London. He has a few questions of his own to ask us, but he says they can wait until you are well enough to travel.'

'Have you thought about the future?' asked Jason.

'Yes, of course, all the time.'

'Well?'

'Well, what? I don't precisely know what I will do; it depends on lots of things,' said Anna.

'Such as... if you will marry me or not?' said Jason.

'No! Yes! I don't know... Yes. Do you mean it?' stammered Anna.

'I'm sorry. I'm not in any state to get out of bed and go down on one knee to ask you properly, but will you marry me?'

'Yes, you know I will.'

Chapter Nineteen

'Congratulations, I hear you two were married last week,' said Chief Inspector Goodman as Jason and Anna sat down in front of his desk.

'Thank you, Inspector,' answered Jason, as he held hands with his new wife.

'Are you recovering well from your wounds?'

'Yes, I was lucky. The bullet broke a rib before passing right through my body, missing everything of importance,' replied Jason.

'I asked you here for two reasons. One to apologise for the ordeal you had to go through being chased across the country the way you were. You see, we knew the Russians had agents working in Britain, we just couldn't find them. Then we got wind of the assassinations in France and what they were about. So when Miss Moreau, sorry Mrs Parva, came to Britain, it gave us the ideal opportunity to flush the Russians out. And, secondly, to discover what her plans are for the future. After all, you are a person of significant political importance.'

Anna and Jason just looked at each other for a few moments before Anna answered the Inspector.

'Yes Inspector, that may be true, but I don't foresee a time when I will ever be able to lay claim to my inheritance. I, we plan to forget about it and live as normal a life as possible.'

'That sounds very sensible, though there is one thing I would like to ask. I don't understand why, when you left France, you didn't just stay in London. That created a panic at Scotland Yard and the Foreign Office,' said the Inspector.

'I was on the run Inspector. I didn't know you were watching me.'

'Yes, maybe we should have been more open with our plans. I have to admit, when you were on the train and you got Constable Potter to leave that note for Mr Parva, you had us wondering what was going on and who Mr Parva was. We guessed you trusted him or else you wouldn't have sent him the note. It took a couple of days before we tracked down his war record and discovered who he was. But what was it that made you get off the train?'

'I was being followed by three heavy-set men. They were on the train.'

'Those three heavies, as you call them, are white Russians, loyal to the Romanov Family and were sent by expatriates to protect you. In England, they weren't officially working with the British police and had been told not to interfere in what we were doing. Only, the Foreign Office said to allow them to help out. It was they who followed you to Wales and later spotted your car in the garage near Wrexham. What we didn't know at the time was that the assassins were following your guardian angels.'

'That would be Doctor Stone?' said Jason.

'Yes, the little man going by the name of Doctor Martin Stone. His real name is Colonel Maxim Petrov. He is head of his department at the Russian Secret Police. It was he we wanted to capture. We just didn't know his cover identity until he tried to kill you both. He didn't need to try to find you. He left that to the friendly Russians who were protecting you. All he had to do was follow the White Russians, and they led him straight to you. As soon as the colonel knew where you were, he could choose his own time and place to complete his mission.'

'How did you manage to track us? It seemed as though, no matter where we went, you were only a day or so behind us,' asked Jason.

'That was the simple part. I had a man stationed at your bank. Each time you telephoned to arrange for more funds to be transferred to a local bank branch where you were located, we found out where you were. It was the same with Thomas Cook's. Then I simply arranged for my men, with the aid of the local police, to find you,' said the Inspector. 'Special Branch had you under observation by using an elderly couple who used to work for us. With them being a retired couple, most people ignore them. They became invisible, so to speak. They could hide in plain sight and report back what they learned. When you paid for a week's stay at the hotel in Chester but seemed to be very light on luggage, they became suspicious and informed the local police, asking them to search all hotels, guest houses and ticket offices to try to work out what your next move was going to be. Once we knew that you were using Thomas Cook to book ahead, we had them inform us each time you made a booking. It helped us to influence where you stayed.'

'Who were the couple on the boat?' asked Anna.

'We have no idea who Felicity and Barry are. But we found two bodies by the roadside fitting the description you gave us of them. They'd been shot. At first, I thought you may have done it but, after the bodies had been examined we found that the bullets that had killed them came from a smaller calibre weapon than a British service revolver. So I attributed the killing to Colonel Petrov. We are still trying to discover the identity of the dead couple; hopefully someone will put in a missing person's report that fits the description of one of them.'

'Could that have been our fault for asking them aboard our boat?' asked Anna.

'I doubt it. I suspect we will find out that they were communist sympathisers and believed they were helping the cause,' said the Inspector.

'In a twisted sort of way, I hope they were involved in tracking us down. I would hate to think two innocent people died because of a mistake on my part,' said Anna. 'After all, it was me who invited them aboard our boat.'

'I suspect they may have been university students indoctrinated by communist thinking. From what you have told me about them, they don't sound like they come from abroad. When you disappeared after the boat explosion, you gave us a real scare. I had to put out a warning to every police station in the country to keep a lookout for two strangers fitting your descriptions. It was only sheer luck that a keen-eyed new recruit, wanting to impress his sergeant, spotted you getting off the bus in Carlisle. He followed you to the hotel. We monitored your phone call from the hotel to Thomas Cook, and arranged our own cottage for you, with one of our own operatives as your housekeeper.'

'That was Belle!' said Jason.

'Yes, Sergeant Summers is one of our most experienced female officers and dedicated to her work.'

'How did Colonel Petrov discover we were staying in Maidens?' asked Anna.

'That was our fault,' confessed the Inspector. 'Belle phoned me to ask for your luggage to be collected from the hotel. I arranged, through the local police station, for two police officers to collect it and ensure it was put on the next train to Ayr. It was they who put the labels on the luggage. I can only assume the Colonel or one of his men was watching and read the labels. Once I saw the labels on your luggage, I removed them. But I was too late.'

'What about the newspaper headlines about us? After seeing them, I was expected people to point us out to the police,' asked Anna.

'Oh that. I'm sorry. That was a simple subterfuge to keep you out of sight. Because Jason collected a newspaper each morning from the local shop, it was easy for us to put our own version of the paper there for you to buy. The local police inspector went to the shop and explained to the shopkeeper that you were undercover police officers on a secret mission and the newspaper was how we communicated with you. The shopkeeper was told to give you our copy of the newspaper and, in return for her help and silence, she would receive a citation and medal for helping her country. No doubt she'll be the toast of the village for years to come.'

'How is Belle?' asked Jason.

'You saved her life that night. The doctor said a few more minutes and she would have bled to death. They had no idea who she was, but as it was a gunshot wound, they called in the local police, who later called my lot in. She didn't regain consciousness for about forty-eight hours. By the time we got to know what was happening and got to the house, you were gone.'

'What will happen to Mister MacIntyre?' asked Jason.

'Yes. He gave us something to think about. You can't just go around shooting people you don't like, even if they are enemies of the state. I went to see him and read him the riot act. I threatened to lock him up and throw away the key, or worse. Then I handed him a letter of thanks from the Foreign Secretary commending him for saving the life of a relative of the King. But I did take his rifle off him; after all, he didn't have a licence for it.'

'I got the impression that he and that rifle had had a long history together,' said Jason.

'Maybe so, but after Belle had been shot, and we'd lost track of you both again, our friendly Russians complained to the King saying that we had made a mess of the investigation. So the Foreign Office gave their agents details of everyone who was on the train that day. They started their own investigation. Once they realised Doctor Stone was Colonel Petrov they kept an eye on him, but they didn't trust us with the information. As it turned out, it was Anna's supporters who followed Petrov from the Kirkton Hotel when the Colonel was chasing you in the car. They are the ones who were involved in the shoot-out during the car chase. Thankfully, no one was hurt, but it was enough for me to have them arrested and keep them out of my way until we captured the Colonel.'

Once you had stolen the aeroplane from Ayr, we were back in control of the investigation. It also helped when Petrov stole the second aircraft. Two aeroplanes flying together are a rare sight in the skies over Britain, so by getting all the local police stations in the area to keep a look-out for you we soon got your direction of travel, and from that, we could estimate where you were heading. However, it took us longer than we thought to catch up with you.'

'I take it that it was you who stopped my solicitor from visiting my house?' asked Jason.

'Yes. I didn't want innocents turning up on your doorstep and complicating matters further. Unfortunately, the vicar didn't get the message in time,' said the Inspector.

'What will happen to Dr Stone?' asked Jason.

'He will be returned to Russia. He's too important to both sides to keep in prison for very long.'

'Is that the same for the man in the church tower?' asked Anna.

'No, as a low-ranking agent, he will stay with us for a while. After a year or two in prison, we'll help him make an escape, and then return him to Russia, but not before we have turned him into a double agent.'

'So, am I safe now? That is what I really want to know?' asked Anna.

'Yes, I think so. You have changed your name. We have also sent out a few clues about you returning to a remote part of France, under an assumed name, and I have released a fake story to the press about this whole incident. Yes, as long as you don't go around advertising the fact you have a legitimate claim to being the Empress of all Russia, I think you will be fine. But I must ask you, what happened to the documents and the jewel?'

'I no longer have them, Inspector, and I would like to leave it at that, if I may.'

'Yes, it would probably be for the best if it stayed that way, Mrs Parva.'

The telephone interrupted their conversation.

'Hello...Yes...I'll be there in a minute.' The Inspector replaced the handset.

'I'm sorry, I have to go. The minister wants my opinion on the latest developments in Germany. It seems the Austrian banking system has collapsed, and the Germans have stopped all war reparation payments to the allies. The German Ambassador has arrived and wants to talk to the Prime Minister. I hope you will both be very happy, and if you need me, you know where to find me.'

*****

On her sixtieth birthday, Anna drove the short distance into Driffield to keep an appointment she had made with her solicitors, Letwing, Letwing, and Letterman in Exchange Street.

'Mr Letwing, the time has come for me to write my will but, first of all, I have some information I must divulge to you and you alone. Do I have your word that what I am about to tell you will go no further?'

Mr Letwing sat back in his leather chair, looking at Anna Parva very intently.

'Mrs Parva, Anna. I have been your solicitor ever since my father died and left the firm to me. I have been your friend for longer than that. Anything you say will not go beyond these four walls unless you direct me to allow it to happen. Now, what could be so serious that in divulging your secret it would worry you so much as to question our friendship and my professional integrity in this way?'

'I'm sorry, Andrew, but in a moment you will understand.' Anna went on to explain all about how she was the heir to the Russian throne and empire. As she explained the story of her inheritance and how she really met Jason, Andrew Letwing's jaw dropped; the look of astonishment on his face worthy of a photograph. When Anna had finished her telling of her premarital years, they both sat in silence for a few moments while Andrew gathered his thoughts.

'I can now see how this inheritance will complicate any normal writing of a will,' confessed the solicitor.

'Yes, and there is one more bit of information I need to inform you about. I placed the documents and the diamond-encrusted Firebird jewel in a bank vault in Hinckley, Leicestershire. After my death, you will arrange for them to be collected so they can be passed to my son. You must ensure that the package is not opened and is protected by the most stringent secrecy and security. Once my son has been made aware of his Russian heritage, it must be down to him as to what he does with it, except for one proviso. The documents and Jewel must be kept safe until he or his descendants are of an age to take responsibility for them, and when the time is right, for the Romanovs to return to Russia.'

Now you can buy any of these books direct from the publisher.

Also by Steven Turner-Bone

Friends and Enemies

The Enemy Within

Farewell to a friend

In need of a Friend

The Firebird Inheritance

Also

Under the name S C Southcoat

Invitation to a Murder

The Five-Pound Murders

Facebook: Steven Turner-Bone

or

Email: steventurnerbone@aol.com

Prices and availability subject to change without notice.